D1826072

SAM CRESCENT

EVERNIGHT PUBLISHING ®

www.evernightpublishing.com

SAM CRESCENT

DEDICATION

Wow, I cannot believe I'm writing this. As always, I have got to say a big thank you to Evernight Publishing and Karyn White. They are amazing and have given so many of my books a home, and even this duet. You help to make my dream come true, and I just adore working with you guys.

Now, I also have to say a big shout out to the following peeps, Stacey Espino, Nathasha Knight, Celia Aaron, Alta Hensley, and Sam Mariano. If you guys have not given their books a try, please do. They are amazingly talented women, fantastic authors, and so supportive.

And of course, to my readers. You guys rock my world, and I really hope you enjoy Draven and Harper's journey. It was an intense one for me, but I loved every second of it.

SAM CRESCENT

THE INITIATION

Darkness Within Duet, 1

Sam Crescemt

Copyright © 2019

Prologue

Harper Miller stared out of her bedroom window just like she had for many years, in a different house, a different room. A house that was once her home but not anymore. The night was dark, but then it had always called to her. The only light cast was by the moon, and that was because of a power outage in the town of Stonewall, a once-promising town for tourism, real estate, and beauty. In recent years, that had changed. The town was no longer a place for promise but a death sentence.

There were crooks, criminals, and abuse at every corner. Harper knew her father was a lawyer. He'd helped many of the men in this town get away with murder and fraud.

Pressing her face against the window, she saw them. The four men waiting for her. They were not boys. True, they all went to high school, but the small group of four were anything but boys. She didn't know what had changed in them, but they were deadly.

Not too long ago that danger would have scared her. She'd try to run, to hide away from what they were, but now, there was no hiding. She yearned for the peace that came over her because being around them meant she was still alive.

She'd heard other students refer to them as being fearless, deadly, dangerous. No one was allowed to join their little gang. It was just the four of them, until tonight.

They waited by the tree in the front yard. They were dressed in black, each of them staring up at her bedroom window as they had been doing for the past nine months.

Nine months of planning.

Of preparing.

Of getting ready for this moment.

She already had the ink on her back declaring herself theirs. That had been an experience she had no interest in repeating.

Harper had no doubt that the rumors at school would run wild. That was all people cared about. Their image. Bringing others down. Making others feel small so they could rise up. She hated it. Hated the world. Hated her family. Hated everything that she could think of. Anything that got in her way. Men, women, kids. None of them were of any importance to her.

Not anymore.

A year ago, she'd have said differently.

A year ago, she wouldn't have looked down at her front lawn at the four men waiting for her and eagerly awaited what was coming to her.

No.

She'd have still been going through the motions, still in pain, but she'd have been a good girl, always doing the right thing.

Only, doing the right thing stopped having any meaning to her.

All it did was make her so angry, so pissed off, and she hated the world around her.

Pulling her hair up into a tight ponytail, she opened her window and climbed out to what awaited her.

Draven Barries.

Axel Cook.

Buck Perry.

Jett Henry.

They were her salvation.

Her fight for survival.

They would belong to her just as she did to them.

It wasn't supposed to be like this, but she had no choice. They were the only ones to understand, to get her, to know her.

There was no turning back.

The initiation had begun months ago.

Chapter One

One year ago

"I don't want you causing trouble," her father, Ian Miller, said as he pulled up outside of his mansion.

Harper stared up at the large, pristine-looking house that fit in on the streets of Stonewall. One look and instantly she knew she was in the wealthy side of town. The nice side. The place everyone wanted to be and those that were there were happy to make others feel small.

She held her bag in her fist.

Of course, there would only be the best for his new wife, the twenty-something blonde he'd left her mother for years ago.

"I've never caused trouble," she said.

She hadn't.

Anyone who spoke of Harper Miller always talked about her being a good girl. A nice girl. The kind of person who was nice to everyone, sweet, kind, generous. Her mother had taught her to be nice.

"There's enough badness in the world, Harper. The least you can do is be a reason for someone to smile."

She adored her mother. Even after the divorce, her mother found a reason to keep on smiling.

That had all been a lie.

She stared out of the window as she recalled the tub, soaked with her mother's blood, the water spilling over the edge.

For a few seconds once she saw her mother's dead body, she didn't react. There was no fear. No pain. Just … shock.

She couldn't register what she'd seen, what was right there in front of her.

None of it made sense.

Then reality set in.

Her mother had slit her wrists in the bathtub while Harper had been at school.

Harper didn't know if she did it first thing in the morning, the moment she left, or just before she arrived. She hadn't taken too long to get home. She never did.

Unlike her father, Catherine Miller had been poor, and the divorce had kept her poor.

Up until this moment, Harper had lived with her mother, opting to stay on the wrong side of the tracks rather than go up in the world.

Her father's new wife had already had a baby, and they were a perfectly happy family. With her raven hair, Harper wouldn't fit in. She had her mother's hair, her mother's blue eyes, and she hated her father.

"Yes, of course. Sorry. I guess we should grab your stuff."

By stuff, he meant the few bags of clothing he'd allowed her to take.

"I'll get Hannah to take you shopping. She loves to shop, and there's no expense. You can buy what you want."

She wanted her mother's old furniture, but she wasn't allowed that. He'd tossed it aside as if it was nothing.

Pulling the bag onto her shoulder, she climbed out of the car, staring up at the house.

This was her life for the next year until she went to college, if she even got into one. Hannah appeared in the doorway. The perfect little blonde wife.

"It's so good to see you, Harper. So happy to have you here."

Before she could stop her, Hannah had her arms wrapped around her. Staying still, Harper counted to ten, then to twenty.

Could it get any more awkward?

Finally, her stepmother let her go.

She couldn't even believe she called her a stepmother. The woman that ruined her parents' marriage didn't deserve to be anything.

Staring at her, Harper didn't let her feelings show. She waited as Hannah grabbed her hand, and either ignored the blatant lack of response or didn't care.

"We've got you the perfect room. You're going to love it."

She was dragged up two flights of stairs. The house they lived in was way too big for three people. Four now if she counted herself.

She had to count herself.

There was nowhere else for her to go, and when she suggested a rented apartment so she didn't impose on his life, her father refused.

Hannah opened the door at the end of the long corridor.

Pink. Everywhere. Also teddy bears with unicorns and other shit.

Hannah breathed in and laughed. "Don't you just love it? I think this is so amazing. So pretty. So beautiful. You're going to love it." She ran toward the window. "Look, you get to see the entire street, and also a side window as well."

Harper stood perfectly still. Hannah's laughter irritated her.

"She loves it," Ian said, dropping her bags on the floor. "You'll be taking her shopping tomorrow. I've got to meet a client. You understand."

"Of course. Of course. You've got all your work that is so important to you." Hannah rushed to his side.

Harper didn't turn as the sound of their kissing filled the air.

Dropping her bag to the floor, she walked over to two of the doors. Opening one, she saw the en-suite bathroom.

Again, so much pink.

Finding the closet, she ignored the two people who were now her parents and started to unpack her clothes.

They stood out against the silk of the sheets. Silk wasn't something she was used to. The grandeur of this house glared at her, reminding her once again of everything her mother never had.

"So, what do you think?" Ian asked.

She glanced over at him. His arm was wrapped around Hannah.

"It's fine."

She hated it, but it didn't matter what she said. They didn't care.

"It'll grow on you, sweetie. Believe me, at your age, I was mad for pink anything. I know what it is you're going through, and there's no shame in loving a bit of pink."

"Your mother slit her wrists in the bath as well?" she asked.

Any color in Hannah's face drained away as she simply stared at the woman.

The homewrecking whore.

The woman that had something her own mother didn't have.

She tilted her head to the side. "You want to compare notes."

"Sweetie, go and make dinner. I bet Harper is hungry."

Hannah didn't argue and made the escape quickly.

"I don't want you bringing that incident up, do

you understand?"

Harper stayed silent as she waited for whatever he had to say.

Be silent. Keep it secret. Don't say anything. Pretend it didn't happen.

"I want you to have fun tomorrow."

"I don't want to go shopping."

"Stop being difficult, Harper. Seriously, enough."

She watched him turn on his heel and walk away. Sitting on the edge of the bed in the large room, she felt like a stranger. She didn't belong here.

Harper Miller was part of his old life, not the new one.

At eighteen years old, she'd seen the heartache her mother had to go through. Ian didn't move towns.

No, her father decided to stay in the same town, moving to the good part of it, the wealthy part. When she went shopping with her mother, they'd see him with his new trophy wife.

Looking back, Harper should have known her mother wasn't happy, that she was finding it hard to cope, but she didn't see it in time.

Standing up, she filled her closet with the few pairs of jeans and shirts she'd kept. Within twenty minutes, her life was neatly packed away in the closet. There was nowhere else for to her to go. This house, her father, Hannah, were all part of her life. She didn't have the means to take care of herself. No house, no job, nothing. She depended on him, and she hated knowing that she did.

She sat on the edge of the bed, fingers locked together, staring at … nothing.

The empty void had come to her when the ambulance came to take her mother away, as she sat in the hospital for three hours waiting for her father to arrive, to take her home.

She moved toward the window and stared out toward the sterile street. Not a piece of trash in sight, nor any loud neighbors.

Just silence.

This life, she already hated.

Nothing made sense to her.

"Harper, dinner."

She looked toward the door and frowned. That wasn't her mother.

Gritting her teeth, she wanted nothing more than to climb out of her window and run. To rebel. To not conform.

Instead, she walked quietly to the bedroom door, closed it behind her, and headed downstairs to her new family. Slowly, step by step, she walked downstairs, coming to a stop near the entrance to the dining room.

She'd visited her father twice since he left.

"These potatoes are stunning," he said. "You make them so creamy."

"I fill everything I do with love." A few seconds of silence. "You should call her again."

"She'll be here. She's not used to being in such a big house."

"How do you think I should … handle her?" Hannah asked.

"How do you mean?"

"Well, her mother is gone, and I can see she's hurting."

"She'll be fine."

"I want her to like me."

"She'll like you. I know how good you are."

Harper heard them kissing and rolled her eyes.

"Do you think I should make her eat more healthily? I remember what it was like to be at that age, and no one likes a fat girl, even if she has a pretty face. I could help her get more style. To become more attractive. She could be beautiful, but she doesn't exactly use it to her best potential."

"You'll do what is best."

"We'll keep it a secret so she doesn't feel like I'm picking on her."

"Her mother was always too soft with her. She wouldn't do what's right. She always believed that a man would love a woman regardless of her flaws. It's time for Harper to get into the real world."

They laughed.

Harper stayed perfectly still, her hands clenched into fists as she heard them. They shouldn't be laughing like that. Not about what her mother thought. She'd loved all people, flaws and all.

"Oh, well, some women think that, but don't worry. I know what a real man wants. I'll take care of her."

"She'll love you like a best friend and then like a mother. Just you wait. Harper's always been a good girl. She doesn't make waves."

They sounded so happy, like their lives hadn't been touched by death.

She stared at the door across the hall. It led to the outside, to freedom, to being far away from here.

The normal Harper would walk into the room and pretend nothing had happened. Pretend that she wasn't hurting as they laughed about her mother.

Her dead mother.

Her heartbroken mother.

Facing the both of them, she didn't want to be the good girl anymore.

"I'm going out," she said, stepping across the doorway and going straight toward freedom.

She sped up, not giving anyone time to call her name as she opened the door, closed it, and walked down the long driveway toward the exit.

On the visits she'd paid to their house, she often stayed in her room, out of the way. The only reason she ever went to visit him was because he forced her to.

He'd turned up, waiting outside her mother's house, calling her mother names, saying she was turning his daughter against him. When he first started this, Harper had believed it was because he wanted to see her, and he'd not had a great lawyer to get custody of her. In the end, she saw it for what it was—he was being a bastard. He could have had custody, her mother told her. When she went home with him, he wasn't interested in her; he just wanted to hurt her mother. It was another way to bind her mother to him. She could never move on, which was probably another reason her mother had decided to end it.

Her mother never tried to turn her against him.

Not once, from the arguing to the impending divorce, did her mother turn around to her and say, "Your father is a womanizing bastard who deserves to have his dick cut off."

She acted like nothing had happened, like her husband moving on with another woman didn't even bother her. All the time, it had.

Blood.

So much blood.

Pulling out of her memories, Harper found herself walking toward the abandoned park. It was abandoned because it normally had tape around it, red tape advising, not telling, people not to go inside.

How dangerous it was.

A kid had hurt himself on one of the rides, which was why it was so dangerous.

It was still light out, and as she stared at the red tape, the sign saying not to enter, she touched it.

"Always be a nice girl, Harper. No one wants a bad girl."

Tears filled her eyes, and stepping past the red tape, she walked into the park.

Her heart raced.

To some this was just a little rebellion, but she needed this. To glide past the red tape to see what was beyond.

The swing that had snapped still lay on the ground. According to gossip in the town of Stonewall, the kid had screamed for an hour before the ambulance arrived.

Some women were so saddened by the sound. Others were pissed off that it polluted their nice ears. How dare a child scream?

Just past the park was a small wooded area. The woods, even now, was a place where teenagers made out and lost their virginity.

Having never had a boyfriend or anything, seeing the woodland called to her this time. Her rebellion was not even complete as she stepped across the park and went straight into the woods.

It was still light out.

No boy had ever looked at her, ever wanted her. Being a virgin had felt right to her.

Her mother would often say, when you meet the right boy, you'll know. You'll give yourself to him without a single care in the world.

Lies. All of it was lies.

When she heard voices and moaning, Harper didn't stop. She didn't turn around and pretend she hadn't heard them. She kept on walking, only stopping as she saw them.

The four guys who went to her school.

They didn't possess a name for their little group or gang. No one else was allowed to join, or at least, they were, but had to pass a series of tests to do so.

Others had given them a name: Fearless.

They didn't give a fuck about breaking the law, about hurting people. They were a law unto themselves, and because Axel was one of the richest kids in town, they got left alone.

Draven and Axel were both from wealthy families. Their wealth came with a lot of rumors, a lot of assumptions that it came from the mafia or illegal means.

She didn't know the truth.

Staying away from bad boys all of her life, she never looked toward them, never cared what they did or didn't do. It didn't matter to her.

Buck and Jett came from her area, the wrong side of town. They didn't give a shit about conforming.

No one would speak out against the four of them, even the teachers if they saw what they'd done, right in front of them.

Staring at them now as they stood around someone, she wondered what it would be like to have no cares in the world, to not worry about what others thought.

Draven was the tallest and biggest of them all. Girls wanted him. Boys hated him but would bow down and respect him.

They walked the school halls and owned the place.

Fearless.

Watching them now as Axel kicked whoever was on the ground, she felt her heart pound. They were kicking someone. The person on the ground whimpered, begging for mercy. She should help them.

"Please, please, I won't do it again. I won't."

Draven drove his foot between the guy's legs, silencing him.

Again and again.

"You keep your filthy cock to yourself, do you hear? The next time you think to touch a girl without her permission, you better be ready for me coming for you." Draven grabbed the guy's head, lifted up a handful of dirt, and shoved it into the guy's mouth. "You will be silent about what happened here. I hear a pervert like you doesn't do well in prison."

The guy whimpered.

"You going to be my bitch now?"

The man nodded.

"Good. There's not going to be a next time, is there?"

Another shake.

A sinister, sick smile came across Draven's face. He didn't care that he was hurting the man. All he cared about was that he was on top.

She couldn't look away.

Suddenly, as if he sensed her watching, he looked up. She stared into his green eyes, and couldn't move. With his gaze on her, he grabbed the guy's dick and started to twist it.

Stepping back, she couldn't avert her gaze.

"This now belongs to me."

The threat, the violence, all of it took her by surprise.

She took another step back and another.

Now all four guys were looking at her.

She didn't run though. Turning on her heel, she left.

****

"We need to go and stop her?" Axel asked.

Draven stood at the edge of the woods, watching the rounded ass of Harper Miller as she left the park.

She didn't run. With her head held high, she walked.

He waited to see which direction she'd go.

If she turned right, she would be heading to the police station. Not that it would do any good. The cops didn't give a fuck about people like them. They only cared about the money their parents fed to them.

Kind of a sick world they lived in.

He was the one exacting justice from the school janitor who'd cornered one of the girls in school and started to touch her tits and forced her to put her hands on him. The girl was thirteen years old and shouldn't be scared of the fucking janitor. Draven usually didn't give a shit about what went down. It wasn't his business. The janitor being a pervert wouldn't have bothered him, but today, he'd wanted to hurt someone. The janitor being into young, scared girls was the perfect outlet, and now he had a guy he could use to hurt. He wouldn't squeal to anyone because Draven knew his secret, and now he had someone to have fun with.

This town was full of darkness, and he relished every second of it.

The fear others felt toward him, he fed off it. No matter how mean he got, how evil, girls still wanted to suck his cock, and if he told them to suck his friends' cocks first, they would.

He'd seen it happen, watched them all moan and showed him mouthfuls of cum from doing exactly as he requested.

He'd heard how proud they were of themselves for sucking all four of them off. As if they could join their little clique.

He smiled, thinking about it. How he'd be sitting

in the cafeteria, his friends with him. All four of them ignoring everyone, and just eating. Some of the chicks had tried to join, and he'd tossed them on their ass.

No pussy or dick was with them. They were just the four of them. Friends for life. Each of them had each other's back.

That's what made them Fearless. None of them were afraid to step out. Because of their union, their loyalty, they didn't need a name. They were just them. The four of them. No one else.

She turned left.

This did surprise him.

Little Harper Miller. The good girl in school. The girl he'd seen with the look of disgust on her face whenever she caught them shoving people into lockers.

"No. She's going home."

He knew what had happened to her, seeing her across the woods, hands by her side. She'd stared at him, and there hadn't been disgust in her eyes. She'd looked … envious.

Was she envious of him?

Did she fancy him?

Did she want a gangbang with the four of them?

Nah, it had nothing to do with that. She was now living with her father. He knew what had happened in the past few weeks. They all knew. Her mother had killed herself. Slit her wrists, and Harper had been the one to find her.

"How much do you think the bitch saw?" Jett asked.

They all stood watching her. Jett was pissed he'd not been able to use his trusty knives.

Within the next second, she was out of sight.

"She saw enough."

Why did he find her sudden interest appealing?

THE INITIATION

The town good girl, walking into the woods known to be the area where people fucked. It wasn't even the kids either. He'd been in the woods many times and watched other men fuck their mistresses or whores.

Stonewall hid a great deal of bad shit, as he and Axel were aware.

Their fathers owned cities, but it was the towns that made hiding easier. They pushed through drugs and guns, used the women as whores, and paid the cops to look the other way as business went down.

He, himself, had been brought up on violence.

Getting hit by his father had taught him how to fight.

No son of Alan Barries was going to be a puff, gay, or a wimp. He demanded his son be strong, to fuck all the pussy he wanted, and to take. Nothing in this world came free unless you took it, unless you forced others to give you what you wanted.

He'd been taking his whole life. He was used to having what he wanted.

Axel, Buck, and Jett were the same. They didn't allow anyone to talk down to them. They always commanded respect, always expected it, even of people they hadn't earned it from.

Again, why was Harper in the woods, and why didn't she scream like the good little girl, or demand that they leave the guy alone?

She was the nice one, the sensible one, the girl every teacher called upon in class.

He knew, because he'd seen her. Some guys would be after the blonde chick, the one that flashed her pussy, wore short skirts with no panties, but not him.

They were easy targets. If he wanted a bit of pussy, he would take them, get what he wanted, and dump them. They were cum dumps as far as he was concerned.

"We'll send her a little message. She'll know not to mess with us."

"Who would mess with us?" Axel said, full of cockiness.

They all knew the answer to that, no one.

Even little miss goody two shoes wouldn't be listened to. Their families spoke for themselves.

"What business did she have in the woods?" Jett asked.

"I don't know." It was the first time Draven had ever seen her in the woods, or anywhere near where they usually hung out.

Leaving the park, he followed in the path she'd gone. He wasn't following her. Draven happened to live on the same road as her father.

Hands in his jacket, he watched everything. He saw a few curtains twitch in bedrooms as people stared out the window.

Some feared them. Others hated them.

He relished it all.

Stopping a few feet from Harper's home, he saw her. He paused, as did his friends. Harper wasn't inside her home though or even within the gates. She stood, hands clenched up at her sides, staring up at the house.

No one spoke.

Jett dropped his knife, the only sound to be made, alerting her to their presence.

Slowly, she turned her head toward them, her blue eyes dropping to the knife before lifting up to look at each of them in turn.

When she stared at him, he saw the pain in her eyes. The intrigue. The questions. She didn't run away, nor did she look away.

He kept his gaze on her, waiting to see what she'd

do.

"Where the hell have you been?" Ian Miller asked. His voice rose to a shout.

Harper finally broke eye contact, and he saw her father step toward her.

"I went out."

"Don't even for a second think about being rude. I won't have it. Not in my house."

Draven watched as Ian grabbed her arm and began to tug her back into the house. He didn't like the way her father held her, the firm grip or the anger that seemed to be simmering beneath the surface.

He moved toward the entrance of the house and cleared his voice.

Ian stopped, and Draven stared at his hand. He knew Ian, knew the kind of asshole her father was. After all, Ian was his father's lawyer. This house had been paid for by most of them. Ian's wealth came from them.

"Hello, Draven," Ian said.

He didn't speak, and Buck sniggered. Axel snorted, and Jett, being Jett, cut a branch off one of the hedges, holding it up to his face.

"You know my daughter, Harper."

Again, he didn't speak.

He saw Hannah at the house and Harper's obvious anger, but she didn't react. She stayed perfectly still, not saying or doing anything.

"See you around, Harper," Draven said.

With that, he turned away and made his way down the street to his own home.

Once at the driveway, he saw six cars parked there.

A busy day.

He knew what to expect when he walked in. The signs of a party were clear: his mother drinking straight from the bottle, semi-naked women walking around, and his father with a stripper on his lap.

"There you are, son, come here. Come and play."

With his friends behind him, he entered his father's office. This was a normal day for him. His father didn't give a flying fuck about his marriage, or about anything but his own agenda.

Draven shouldn't criticize. His mother was a pain in the ass, and they were both toxic together.

"See the tits on this one," his father said, lifting up the woman's tits.

Draven waited as he was forced to watch the display, his father groping the girl and her pretending to like it.

Once he'd done his time, he walked down to the basement, where he could hang out with his boys.

His father rarely used the basement to hurt people anymore. There was a time it was a torture chamber, but once the cops came calling a few years ago, he now took all of his *serious* work out to the warehouse. It saved him from having to cover his tracks.

Dropping down into his seat, he took the beer Axel had gotten for him and thought about Harper.

She'd changed.

No, she hadn't changed.

There had always been something about her that drew him in, that called to him. Even when they passed in the hallways, he liked the way she looked. She wasn't like other girls or women. She had curves. Some people called her fat, and in a way, she was.

At eighteen she possessed a decent pair of tits and an ass that wasn't bought from a cosmetic surgeon.

"What are we going to do about Harper?" Axel said.

"We can't let that shit slide," Buck said.

Jett didn't say anything. He held the knife in his hand, the point resting against his jeans-covered thigh. Sipping his beer, Draven saw the clenched hands, the anger.

"She's different."

"I imagine finding your mother dead changes you," Jett said.

"You got that look," Axel said.

"What look?" Draven turned to his friend.

"The one that says you want to play and see how far we can push her."

Draven smiled. Harper hadn't been on their radar for very long. He wondered what she'd do if they pushed her even a little bit.

"Oh, hell yeah, he's interested," Buck said.

"I want to know how deep that rage goes. How far we can push her?"

Axel laughed. "Come on, no chick has been able to handle what we throw at them."

"True, but none of them have been like Harper," Jett said. "She's different."

"She's changed," Draven said.

"Yeah, and if she really has, why did she run?" Axel asked. "I think you're all giving her too much credit."

"Maybe, but she didn't run, did she? She walked home, and did you see the way she looked at her dad?"

"She didn't want to be there," Axel said. "I see where you're going with this. You want to push the little princess to see how dark she can go."

Chapter Two

After an entire weekend of her father and Hannah smooching over each other, and of course them telling her how important it was to follow rules, Harper was more than happy to go to school come Monday morning. She'd have done just about anything to get out of the house, even walked to school on her own, but lo and behold, Hannah was determined to make friends with her.

Forcing a smile to her lips, Harper stared out at the large, imposing building that she still had to finish this final year before she could even graduate. Hannah brought the car to a stop, and several of the guys gave her a wave as if she was one of them.

"Boys, they always think they're all that. I remember this place. So many good memories."

"Is that why you got my father to cheat? You were just making memories?" she asked.

Hannah's face went pale. "I want to make this work, Harper."

"You can drop the act. That would be great." She opened the door, not really caring that she was waiting behind a whole lot of cars. She had no interest in getting to know Hannah or in playing nice.

With her bag high up on her shoulder, she didn't look toward anyone. She'd been a loner for a long time, never making friends.

She'd tried when she'd been younger, but there were only so many ways she allowed herself to get bullied before she gave it up as a bad job. She'd have girls or boys tell her how fat she was, how stupid, how she needed to change to make herself better. She wouldn't change just to make friends with the right crowds. So, in high school, she kept to herself.

Walking across the parking lot, she headed toward the front of the school, going through the doors. She noticed all the people whispering behind their hands as they glanced her way.

She was the weirdo who'd found her dead mom.

Good times.

With her bag high up on her shoulder, she made her way toward the locker room. Luck hadn't been with her this year as she'd been placed right next to the gym, so if she didn't make it in time, jocks and cheerleaders were always around.

She didn't like to have them point out all of her many flaws, but it was a pastime of theirs, a hobby.

Out of the corner of her eye, she noticed Draven and his little gang standing near his locker. She had forgotten he had a locker just down the hall from her.

She thought about what she'd witnessed the other night, and she kept her gaze on her locker, working the combination.

Lifting up the latch, she opened the locker and gasped, standing back as dirt spilled out.

She wasn't fast enough as plenty got on her shoes. Staring at the dry dirt, she couldn't help but look toward Draven.

This was a message. She hadn't said anything to anyone, but now, he was stating it as a fact. They'd seen her. They knew what she saw.

This was their message.

"What on earth is going on here?" Mr. Arnold asked. He taught science.

Turning her attention to the teacher, she released a breath.

"A prank," she said.

"Go to the janitor now, Harper. Get something to clean this up."

Dropping her bag on the ground, she walked right past Draven without giving him the satisfaction of seeing how pissed she was.

She knocked on the janitor's closet, and of course, no one was there. The janitor was nearing eighty and walked so slow. The other janitor was the one she saw in the woods, who always gave her the creeps. She liked the older janitor. He'd been here for a long time, and reminded her more of a grandparent than anything else. Sweet guy and he didn't mind her eating her lunch in the gym when it was empty. She opened the door and grabbed what she needed, heading back to her locker.

The teacher was still there, and so were a lot more students, including cheerleaders and jocks.

Ignoring them, she got to work on filling the trash bin she'd also picked up.

"It's about time someone calls her what she is. She's dirt."

"Trash."

"Useless."

All the time, Mr. Arnold didn't say a word. He pretended not to hear the insults. Instead, he kept his arms folded as she worked to clean the mess. Once it was all done, the bell had already rung and most of the students had gone to class.

Mr. Arnold, after another two minutes, finally left, and she finished cleaning up the mess just as the janitor arrived. He also had someone to help him carry the dirt outside.

She watched them go and stared into her locker. The few books she had were now dirty, and the jacket her mother gave her was also covered in dirt.

Picking it up, she stared at it.

Shaking her head, she put it back into the locker, grabbed her books, and spun on her heel. Only she wasn't alone.

Draven stood waiting.

She ran into him, his body stopping her from going. She stepped back, staring at him.

Neither of them spoke as they looked at each other.

It was on the tip of her tongue to scream at him, to shout, to hit him. She wanted to do something to make him realize that he'd been a dick and she didn't accept that.

Instead, she walked around him, and as she turned the corner, she heard his laughter. He found this all amusing.

Just one more year.

One more year and I'm gone.

Far away from here.

She had begged for her father to send her to another school, to get her a home away from Stonewall, but he'd not listened. She wished she had the guts to just leave, to walk away and not look back. Only, she knew what poverty felt like and knew it would be worse if she left her father behind. She had no money and no way to make a life on her own. She had to be at his mercy.

Arriving fifteen minutes late to class, she got her first detention. The teacher didn't care what she suffered. There was no excuse for tardiness in his class.

With the slip of paper in her hands, she sat down at her desk in the back, staring at it. She'd never been late, never been to detention.

She hadn't even had things put in her locker before, and yet all of that had happened within one morning.

Who knew that going to a simple wooded area would make her so damn popular?

After class finished, she shoved the detention slip

into her bag and made her way toward the next class. She passed people in the hall who'd seen what happened and thought it was the funniest thing of their lives.

Pretending they were talking about someone else, she went to each class, ignoring the ones that Draven and his gang were in. They sat in the back, and she sat in the front. There were times during those classes she was sure they were staring at her.

The temptation to turn around was strong, but she didn't.

She was not focusing on the class, taking in absolutely nothing that the teacher was saying. When the teachers called for answers, she didn't put her hand up.

First time again.

She expected to feel guilty for not paying attention, for not being the star pupil. Instead, there was a freedom in her silence. Refusing to participate felt good.

By lunchtime, she was ready to call it a day.

Instead, she went to the cafeteria, grabbed her tray for lunch, and as she spun around, Drave, Axel, Buck, and Jett were there. They blocked her path.

Staring at each of them, she turned to Draven last.

He had this smirk on his face as if he could read her mind.

Fuck you, jerk. You don't have a clue what I'm thinking. What I'm feeling. You don't know anything.

He stepped right up close to her.

"Hey, dirt face," he said. With a hand out, he slapped it down on her tray and sent everything tumbling to the floor.

Laughter erupted around them, and she gritted her teeth.

"Dude, good one," Axel said.

One by one, they walked past her.

"I'll get that cleaned up."

She didn't even know who said that.

Watching them leave, she wondered if she could plot someone's death just for pissing her off.

She had seen them, yes. She hadn't done anything to hurt them.

Storming out of the lunchroom, she went straight to the bathroom. Gripping the sink so tightly, she tried to gain control of her anger.

Why?

Fucking why?

She'd done nothing wrong. She'd gone straight home after seeing them hurt that guy. She wasn't about to make waves.

All of her life she'd been ignored. Why were they noticing her now?

She stepped into the toilet, grabbing some tissue as the door to the bathroom opened, letting her know she was no longer alone.

"Did you see that? It was so funny," Joanne said. "Damn, Draven must really have it in for her. Not that she needs another meal. She can totally skip a good couple hundred."

Through the crack in the door, Harper saw Joanne making fun of her.

"That Draven is hot though. I'd love for him to pay attention to me. The right kind of attention though," This came from Louise. "What I would do to ride him. I've heard he's rough in bed. He loves to fuck a woman and make her scream for days."

"I hear he fucks married women as well and that even husbands want to kill him because his cock ruins it for everyone," Charlotte said.

All of them were cheerleaders, wearing little skirts that showed off a great deal of thigh.

"Could you imagine Harper trying to ride

Draven?" Joanne asked. "It would be so funny. The girl's a pig. I can't believe she didn't just slit her wrists. I bet that's why her mother did it. She looked at her dirty ugly ass and said no more."

"Joanne, that is bad."

"So what? It's the truth. Anyway, I hear that Draven makes you fuck his friends. That's why they don't have any girls in their club. The initiation is brutal. They like to fuck and play, and no girl can put up with all four of them."

Shaking her head, Harper gritted her teeth. How much longer were they going to be talking about all the slutty things Draven wanted his girlfriends to do?

For another five minutes they kept on talking.

Finally, once they left, Harper made her escape.

She'd heard about the supposed *Initiation.* Draven and his gang had been inseparable for as long as she could remember. Axel and Draven lived close together where Buck and Jett lived in the old neighborhood where she used to live.

There were all kinds of rumors that surrounded them.

Stonewall wasn't exactly a safe haven for anyone. Look at Mr. Arnold that morning. He wouldn't have done anything. She'd seen fights break out, and the teachers walked to break it up.

No one dared to make waves in their small, shitty town. They were only happy to keep the money in their pockets, and to survive another day.

Leaving the bathroom, she made her way to her locker and stared at it. Would she find anything else waiting for her? She opened up her locker, and nothing was inside.

No books. No jacket. Nothing.

Glancing up and down the corridor, she saw no

one. Closing the door, she rested her head against the metal. For a Monday, this had to be her worst day ever.

She didn't care that anyone had broken into her locker. What she cared about was someone had stolen her jacket. The last thing her mother had given to her.

The thought of finishing up the rest of the day didn't thrill her. She wanted to go home, only there was no home.

Hannah and Ian's house wasn't where she belonged.

Kicking her locker, she turned on her heel and went to class. She wouldn't let anyone think they'd won. She was a fighter. No matter what her dad said or Hannah tried to do, or even these dickheads at school, she wouldn't fall.

Squaring her shoulders, she headed back to class.

The giggles and laughter that followed her rolled off her shoulders like water. She didn't pay attention to any of them.

After all, they were just children, and she didn't need their approval.

****

"Did you see her face? That was fucking priceless," Axel said, laughing.

"Dirt and no lunch all in one day."

Draven stared down at the jacket he'd taken from her locker. A couple of the jocks had decided to follow them, and he'd caught them attempting to steal shit from Harper's locker. They'd only just gotten the lock open when he found them.

Seeing five jocks piss themselves had been kind of amusing, but he'd been left with a broken locker, and the temptation of taking her stuff.

"Do we burn it?" Buck asked.

"We don't want it," Axel said. "She's way too

dull. All she has in her locker is shit for school. No pictures. Nothing. She's, like, the most boring chick in the entire history of the school."

Draven searched the pockets of the jacket and came up empty. It was dirty from the mud they'd stored in her locker.

It wasn't well worn either. The jacket looked new, cheap but new.

"We're not burning her shit," he said.

"What is it with this chick?" Buck asked, dropping her books onto the ground.

"I don't know. I find her pretty interesting right now." He folded the jacket, leaving it on his knees as he stared at his friends.

"You do realize you've announced her as public enemy number one with what you did in the cafeteria?" Jett asked, once again playing with his knife. Jett had so many wounds up and down his arms from tossing the knife and catching it wrong. Still, it didn't stop him from holding it.

Draven knew it was because of one of his many stepfathers. Jett had been used as punching bag, and some of the wounds on his back showcased how his stepfathers liked to beat him up, slash at his skin.

Since he, Axel, and Buck put a stop to it three years ago, Jett carried a knife with him. No one came at any of them.

They had each other's backs. It was what made them different from the cliques within their school. All four of them had seen how shit the world was, and still, they kept bouncing back. They kept on fighting for one another.

"Let's see how she handles it."

"Are you auditioning her for our group?" Axel asked, all trace of laughter dying in his eyes.

"I'm curious about her. She came to the woods last night, got detention today. She hasn't run to the cops, and not once did she burst into tears. She's … entertaining to watch."

"It was kind of funny watching all that dirt spill out of her locker."

He looked at her books that were on the ground. Some of them had notes inside, while others were aged. Nothing before him had any personal value apart from the jacket.

"Why don't we jerk off to it, cover her shit with our spunk?" Axel said, already reaching for his belt.

"You're fucking disgusting."

"I'm out of here," Jett said. "Got a job to do."

"You're still working in that fucking DIY place?" Axel asked.

"Got to pay the bills."

"Doesn't your mother whore herself out?" Buck asked.

"She's all dried out. No guy wants to fuck a dry cunt. Later, guys."

Draven watched as Jett left the woods. It was still light out and one check on the time, and he saw it wouldn't be long before detention was over.

"I'm heading out," he said. "Catch you later."

He didn't wait to see what Axel and Buck were doing. They could amuse themselves for hours by playing catch or gambling on some chick.

Climbing into his car, he took off back toward the school.

When he arrived, only a couple of cars were parked in the lot. He tapped his fingers against the steering wheel. None of those cars belonged to Harper. She hadn't been able to afford a car or driving lessons.

He locked his car and headed inside to see what

was taking her so long.

She wasn't at her locker, and as he stood out of line of sight, he watched as detention came to an end. A couple of guys headed out, and Harper was the last one to leave, apart from the teacher.

She looked … lost.

He watched her, curious as to what she was doing. What was going on in that head of hers? She looked at the time, and instead of going straight to the parking lot, she didn't. She went into the bathroom.

His curiosity was always a problem. He followed her inside.

The jacket he'd taken from her was inside his car.

Why was he testing her, pushing her?

Being a bully hadn't been part of his MO. He never taunted anyone. The guys who got in his way, he made sure to take care of, and the chicks always knew only his dick was on offer, nothing else. He still didn't understand why he was sticking around with Harper. She was nothing special. They'd been going to the same school since nursery school.

When it came to her, he wanted to push her, to see how far the good girl went.

Stepping into the girl's bathroom, he saw her at the sink.

She turned her head, and the blue fire in her eyes should have struck him dead and cold.

"What are you doing here?"

He leaned against the wall, folding his hands over his chest. "I'm curious how detention was."

"Wow, really? Have you ever been to detention?"

"No."

"I bet you got a slip though, right? The teachers don't give a shit what you do. You've got the right last name. The kind of name that even teachers don't like to touch."

He smirked. "You jealous of my last name, Miller?"

"Leave me alone."

"Is that an order?"

"It's a request."

"I don't take orders."

"What do you want?" she asked.

"To see … something."

"So I'm the target this year for your amusement, is that it?"

"You clench your hands often?" he asked, looking at her tight fists.

"You're so weird."

She went to pass him, but he put his hand out, stopping her from going.

"Seriously? What?" She folded her arms over her chest.

The glare she gave him turned him on. He'd never seen her look so ferocious. He blocked her exit, watching her.

"I want my stuff back."

He smirked.

"Why did you take it, huh? Did it get you off to go inside a locker that's not yours? You know what? I don't care."

She went to pass again, only this time, he caught her shoulders, pressing her up against the wall. At first, she struggled against him. He watched the fight in her gaze, how she tried to overpower him, but he wouldn't let her go.

The truth was, he didn't have a fucking clue what he was doing or even why. Only that he had to.

"Let me go." She went to strike him, and he caught both of her hands, pressing them above her head.

She growled the moment he did it.

Still, he didn't speak even as she fought him, her body arching against him. The thrust of her tits pressed on her shirt.

He was used to women being all over him, used to the female sex wanting him and willing to do whatever he said.

This, with Harper, was new.

He didn't mind it. In fact, he found it rather refreshing. She wouldn't give in, wouldn't allow him to have what he wanted.

Staring into her sweet blue eyes, he remembered them the first day of kindergarten. How scared she'd looked as she watched the other kids. Like him, she observed. She waited to see what was coming her way.

Where he had three friends, she had none. No one wanted to be her friend.

He'd watched her over the years. Seen her grow up, again, always alone, never one to join the crowds.

Always good.

He wanted to break that goodness, to shatter the innocence within her.

He'd never been allowed to be free, to be good, to be strong.

She was everything he'd been ordered to avoid.

Now, though, after her mother ended her tragic life, there was a darkness swirling within Harper. Shadows clouded her once clear gaze.

"Don't you have some teenager to screw?" she asked, fighting him.

"You want to take the job?" He finally spoke, and seeing that spark of anger flash within her gaze turned him on.

"Fuck you, Draven. Let me go."

"I'll let you go when I'm good and ready." He

kept her hands locked above her head. He wondered what she'd do if he caressed down her body, touching her tits before cupping her between her thighs. She'd probably come.

So much repressed rage.

He could tutor that, help it come out.

Leaning forward, he stroked his cheek against hers, feeling how soft her flesh was. "We're going to have a lot of fun together, you and I."

He stepped back, releasing her.

She stayed perfectly still by the wall, glaring at him. Slowly, she lowered her hands down to her sides.

"Asshole."

He laughed as she made her escape. Maybe he was an asshole; he never claimed to be anything but. He liked seeing her run though.

He followed her out of the bathroom, watching as she darted out of the school.

Walking in the same direction, he saw her stepmother was waiting. Heading to his car, he stopped and watched.

Hannah with her bleached blonde hair and fake tan, looked the part of a trophy wife to fit within the street she lived. Even his own mother had the same look, including fake tits. They had to look a certain way.

Harper didn't fit.

With her wild, raven hair, so like her mother's, and shocking blue eyes, to Draven, she stood out. She didn't belong in their world. It's what set her apart from everything he knew.

She wasn't fake enough. Harper epitomized everything real and true in the world.

He waited as she paused near the car, clearly not wanting to go with her new stepmother.

Hannah gave him a wave. They'd met a few

times at a couple of the parties his father threw. He didn't wave back as Harper glanced back at him.

The indecision stopped as she opened the door and climbed right on inside.

Hannah had propositioned him a few times. Belonging to Ian Miller hadn't stopped her whoring ways. He knew she'd come from one of the many clubs his father owned. She'd been presented to Ian as a gift.

The fucker had fallen in love, or thought he had. The truth was, Draven's father owned her. If it amused him, he could order her to a party in front of Ian, and force her to fuck every single guy there and present her cum-filled pussy to her husband.

He'd half expected him to do it, but so far, Ian Miller must have clearly been a good dog for his dad.

Climbing into his car, he saw a couple of texts from Axel and Buck. They were at Axel's place, partying with a couple of cheerleaders. He opened up the pictures and saw they'd gone straight from a party to a gangbang.

He rolled his eyes. He didn't know why his friends found it completely necessary to text him shit from their party.

Heading home, he ignored the pull to go and visit Harper. Her stepmother would let him inside the house.

His time with Harper would come soon enough. All he needed to do was be patient.

Parking his car in the driveway, he made sure to give himself plenty of space to leave if necessary. Walking up to his front door, he closed it behind him, and stopped.

"That's right, baby, you sniff it up. Good girls like you always get the good stuff."

Draven stood in the entrance to his father's office. The door was open. A brunette was kneeling on the floor as his father held her, forcing her to snort each strip of cocaine.

From the look of the debris on the table, she'd already snorted five lines already.

He counted the lines quickly and saw fifteen laid out perfectly.

This was new.

His father had gloves on his hands, but the girl, she was lapping up his attention, wanting him to be proud of her.

It wasn't unusual for him to see this. Drugs were not something he delved into. After witnessing how bad people got for a taste of the drug, he wanted nothing to do with them.

"That's right. You don't have to worry anymore. You or the baby."

"I love you, Alan. So much. I want to be with you." Her words slurred as she spoke.

"I know. Keep on sniffing it up. The baby needs it."

Draven turned on his heel and left. Entering the kitchen, he found his mother, swallowing some pills and swigging them down with some scotch.

"Classy."

"Classy? Your father got another whore pregnant and she thinks she can come and take my place. She has got another think coming."

In a matter of minutes, his mother's competition would be dead.

Draven grabbed himself a glass and filled it with water. This wasn't the worst he'd ever seen.

Staring down at his hand which held the glass, he saw he was shaking. Why the fuck was he shaking? He took a quick swig, finishing off the glass and walked outside. Ignoring the security guards, he took a seat and stared out across the garden.

The girl would die, and in a few months' time, something else would happen.

Running a hand down his face, he leaned back, closing his eyes, and all he pictured were the sweet, terrified blue eyes staring right back at him. The judgmental gaze shooting fire at him.

He wondered what she'd think if she saw something like this? Would she throw fire or accusations his way? Blame him for how bad the world was?

Harper Miller was filled with ideals, with stupid fucking fairy tales, and he intended to end every single one of them.

Chapter Three

"You look so beautiful," Hannah said. "See, I told you, showing off a bit of flesh wouldn't hurt. A bit of work on your legs, and we'll have you in tip top shape."

Harper stared across the table at her stepmother. They were on another shopping trip, a trip her father had organized to get her out of the house, and one she hated just as much as the last one.

Their baby was in the tender arms of a babysitter, and Hannah acted like she was a single lady.

She noticed her stepmother liked to wink and flirt at all the available men, or even the ones that were taken.

Some ignored her. Others looked interested.

"I'm going to monitor the food you eat, Harper. It's for your own good." She watched as Hannah pulled out a pink, fluffy notebook, sliding it across the table. "I want you to document everything you eat in here. Everything. Don't leave a thing out. We're going to have all the guys drooling for you before the year is out. You won't have to worry about college. All you'll need is to know how to handle those guys, and you're dealing with an expert." Hannah giggled. "I know all the tricks. Just look at your father. He's so in love with me." She flicked her hair and laughed.

Right now, I want to die.

Rolling her eyes, Harper pretended the book wasn't even near her. This entire outing with Hannah had sucked. The clothes she'd been told to wear revealed too much skin, and given the option, she'd rather shred them.

As it was, her father and Hannah hadn't been able to find her old clothes. When she realized they were getting thrown in the trash each time she put them in the laundry, she now made her way into town, just to wash her clothes.

She no longer cared if someone from school even noticed her. Since Draven had put her on the map, people made her life at school a misery every single chance they got.

There was no point in using her locker as most often, it got broken into. She got shoved and pushed in the hallway, and if she went to the cafeteria, her lunch ended up on the floor.

She carried her bag with her at all times. The books she needed for the day were stuffed inside along with a packed lunch, which she made when Ian and Hannah went to bed.

Gone were the days of laughter and love. Her mother's beautiful singing voice.

"I've got a thing. I'll be back in a minute." Getting to her feet, Harper left the salad bar where they were eating lunch, and headed off toward the diner where she'd seen an advertisement for employment.

They'd passed the diner on the way to shop, and she'd gotten the idea to apply for the job just so she could save her own money and not have to rely on her father anymore. Hannah seemed more than content to have all the men admiring her, and now was Harper's opportunity to get away.

Entering the diner, she went to the only waitress there and told her she wanted to apply. Ten minutes later, she had the job, and would be starting tomorrow night. The uniform was within her grasp, and feeling rather smug she turned back toward the salad bar only to stop.

Hannah was still there. The only problem she had with her new job was she had to make sure Hannah didn't pick her up after school.

A lie would keep her away.

She'd never lied. Her life was full of a bunch of firsts. Seeing Hannah now didn't make her pause though.

Draven, Axel, Buck, and Jett were sitting at their table, and Hannah was lapping up the attention.

Why were they there?

She wanted to turn on her heel and leave. Only Draven saw her. The question in his eyes was clear. The mocking look grated on her last nerves. She didn't run away, not from the challenge.

Stepping back up to the table, she stared at Draven, who sat in her seat.

"You're in my seat," she said.

"Harper, that's not nice," Hannah said.

She refused to look toward her, instead glaring down at Draven.

He leaned back, legs spread out, looking like he owned the place. He probably did own the place, and it pissed her off. No one would force this guy to go on a diet, or make him do what he didn't want to do.

"Be nice to me, Harper."

She heard the rest of the guys snickering. Between her mother, her locker, having her jacket stolen, living with her dad, she'd had enough.

Grabbing what was left of her Coke, she picked it up and tossed it in his face. "Screw you."

"Harper!" Hannah cried out her name, but she was already leaving.

The clothes she'd purchased were on the floor, probably covered in Coke, at least she hoped so, and if she had any luck, were completely ruined.

Rushing out of the mall, she didn't care that it was a three-hour walk back home.

She wanted to walk. Once outside, it had started to rain, and she lifted the hood of her jacket over her head.

She'd just thrown Coke in Draven's face. Covering her own with her hands, she groaned.

A drink in the face, to many, didn't seem like much, but to her, it was a rebellion she hadn't anticipated.

It felt good to just throw it at him. As she did, she'd pictured her father's face. The cops who came to her house. Every single person who pissed her off until finally, she settled on Draven.

Good girls wouldn't do that.

Good girls wouldn't make waves.

Good girls didn't have to hold their dead mothers in their arms, or deal with their father screwing a woman too young for him.

She heard the car as it pulled up next to her on the side of the road.

Glancing at the car, she cringed. It wasn't Hannah's. Chancing a look inside the car, she saw it was Draven, alone.

He didn't have his buddies with him, and that made her stop.

The window went down, and she stepped back. "Get in the fucking car," he said.

"Screw you."

"I'm sure a little virgin like yourself wouldn't even be able to handle me."

"Leave me alone. Don't you get it? I don't want to get in your car, or even register that I exist to you."

"Ah, but you do, and you have your mother to thank for that."

"Hannah's not my mother."

"I know what Hannah is. I'm talking about your actual mother. You know, the dead one."

She started walking.

Behind her, she heard the car brake, the car door open, and then she gasped as he lifted her with ease. She wasn't a light person, by any means.

"Put me down."

He had her over his shoulder, and she slapped his ass. He didn't put her down until he threw her in his passenger seat. How he managed to do that without hitting her head, she didn't know, but it pissed her off.

With a slam of the door, she was closed inside. She tried the handle, and lo and behold, it was locked. Slamming her hands against the window, she tried to escape.

It was no good. She was trapped, locked within the car.

Alone.

"Let me out."

Draven climbed behind the wheel, and seeing him look so calm and relaxed, she wanted to hit him. In fact, she raised her hand to do so.

"You hit me, I'll fucking hit you back." He glared at her.

The rain was dripping down his face, just as it was hers. Her hood had fallen, and she hated him, so fucking much.

Lowering her hand, she sat back in the seat. Going against Draven meant certain death.

He didn't take threats lightly, and as she locked her fingers together, to stop the temptation to hurt him, she knew it would be so easy to fight him, to have him hit her, to feel the brush of pain.

She'd watched him fight plenty of times. He fought just for the fun of it, or at least, it always looked that way.

"You shouldn't bring up someone's dead mom. It's rude."

He laughed. "I imagine she's nothing more than a ghost in your house, right?"

She wasn't allowed to talk about her mother, or

have a single picture right now. Not responding to him, she expected him to take her home, but he didn't.

He parked at Stonewall's well-known make-out parking lot. She had no intention of making out with him.

"Don't worry, Harper. I only like my women begging, and one day soon," he said, leaning in close. His breath fanned across her face. "You're going to beg."

"You think I want to be a member of your gangbang, dream on."

"Don't worry. We've got plenty of willing women to take dick."

Her cheeks were on fire, but she didn't back down.

"I know. The cheerleading squad are willing to make your every waking juvenile dream come true."

He laughed as he stepped out of the car.

She tried the door, only to find it locked.

He locked his door, slamming it closed. Draven took his time walking around the vehicle until he got to her side.

"Let me out," she said.

She had no desire to be trapped in his car. In the past week, she'd already spent too much time near him, and all she wanted to do was to go home. Even though her place with her dad wasn't home. Far from it.

It was just a pit stop. A place she had to be. It wasn't a home. A home was welcoming. The place she lived at wasn't that. It was a prison.

"Do you promise to be good?" he asked.

She folded her arms and stared out the window ahead of her, ignoring him at hers.

"Fine, have it your way." He turned on his heel, about to walk away.

"Hey! Don't leave me, asshole."

"Asshole, you're calling me an asshole?" he

asked. "Ask me nicely."

She shook her head, and again he went to leave.

"Wait!"

He stopped but didn't turn back to look at her. Gritting her teeth, she wanted to tell him to go and fuck himself, to leave her alone.

Instead...

"Please, let me out."

"Say pretty please."

"Are you for real right now?"

"Totally real. As real as a heart attack."

"Pretty please, let me out."

He walked back to the car, and she watched as he put his key inside, opening the door. He held his hand out for her to take.

Would it be so wrong to hit him and run?

Draven wasn't full of empty threats. He'd hurt her just for the fun of it.

Climbing out of the car, she pulled her hand out of his the moment she could. Shoving them into the pocket of her jacket, she stared at him.

"Now what?"

"You're not very trusting, are you?"

"Not with you."

"Not with anyone would be my guess." He laughed.

"You've made it your life's mission to annoy me this week. Forgive me for not giving a fuck about what you think right now."

"Look at you, being all tough." He suddenly took her hand and marched her through the woods.

She didn't have a clue where they were going. Rain fell down all around them, making visibility almost impossible.

"Draven, stop!"

He kept on going.

"I mean it. Stop."

He still didn't listen. She didn't know how long they walked before he finally stopped, spinning her around.

"Go on, tough girl, have your best shot."

"What the hell is all this about?" she asked. Anger flooded her as he slapped his hands against his chest.

"Come on, Harper, you know you want to. You want someone else to feel the pain that you're going through. To know what it is that makes you get up in the morning and not slit your own fucking wrists."

"Stop it. You have no right to go there. No right at all." She shoved her hands against his chest.

Draven didn't budge. He didn't give her a chance as he put his hands on her shoulders and shoved her back, hard.

She fell into the wet dirt with a gasp. The pain rushed from her ass, spreading through her body from the impact. Her pants were dirty and soaked from the water.

"You better learn to stand up for yourself, Harper. You want people to leave you alone, you better keep that good girl image at the door."

Tears filled her eyes. This was the last thing she wanted to do today. Getting to her feet, she faced him, summoning the memory of his smirk as dirt fell from her locker, the food tray he'd purposely shoved out of her hands.

"I'm done." She tried to brush the dirt off her pants, but it was no good.

Turning on her heel, she went to leave, only, Draven caught her arm and pressed her back up against the nearest tree.

She tried to fight him, but he held her hands

above her head. His body pressed against hers.

It was the first time she'd ever been this close to a guy before, and for a split second, against all of her own sensibilities, she liked it, liked the feel of Draven controlling her.

Get a grip.

No way in hell will you ever like Draven Barries. He's a first-class asshole.

"Don't you ever throw shit at me again."

"What's the matter? Can't handle it when people fight for themselves?" she asked.

She'd enjoyed throwing her drink at him and even more so, the shock on his face that she actually did it.

"Baby, I got no problem playing this game. You want to fight, I'll more than happily give you something to fight against. For too long now, you've been too nice. It's time to dirty you up a bit, and I know just how to do it." He leaned in close.

His lips nearly brushed against hers, and she couldn't help her gasp.

Angry at herself, she drew her knee up, taking him off guard. This time, she ran. She ran back past the car, and went to her house. Her heart raced, and she wasn't used to having to fight to get away from someone.

Just as she was about to cross the road to her home, his car came veering to a stop.

She stared at him through the windshield.

Panting for breath, she waited as he pressed on the gas, revving his engine.

The sound of another car approaching had her turning her head to see Axel driving the other. She caught sight of Buck and Jett as well.

The four friends. Fearless. Dangerous. They all had each other's back.

Had Draven called them?

Staring from one car to the other, she did no more than step out into the center of the road.

Crazy.

So fucking stupid.

What the hell are you doing?

They could kill you right now, and no one would care.

The only person who ever cared is dead.

She left you.

Hands clenched tightly, she held them out and turned, letting them know they could have her. Part of her wanted one of them to do it. To push the car at her. To knock her down and take her life. To put her out of this fucking misery.

None of the cars made a move as she waited.

Not one nudge, nothing.

Time stood still as she challenged them, waiting for them to give in. To just drive to carry out their threat.

Finally, she faced Draven one last time, and waited.

He wasn't going to do it.

Lowering her hands, she stepped off the road and didn't even look back. What was the point? She just realized that no matter how far he pushed her, or they pushed her, they weren't going to kill her.

Entering her home, she only had to wait a few seconds before Hannah was there, touching her.

"Oh, Harper, I was so worried. They told me to just go home, and I brought all of your things for you. They're in your bedroom. I'm getting soup ready now."

The house smelled like boiled cabbage.

"Why did you do as they told you?" she asked.

"What do you mean?" Hannah's smile looked a little unsure.

"They're kids. You're a grownup. Why did you do as they were told?"

Hannah went pale.

"Y-you know how it is. It's just easier to do as you're told than to be in the line of fire. Your dad's going to be home any minute. Get dressed. He'd like to see you in your new clothes."

Harper watched her leave and walked up to her room.

So, talking about Draven and his cronies sent Hannah in the opposite direction. It was good to know.

****

"What the ever-loving fuck?" Axel asked.

"Were you going to run her over?" Buck asked, a hint of a smile on his lips.

"Of course he was. He thought about it," Jett said.

"What he said," Draven said.

Jett chuckled. "Classic."

"Okay, is anyone else curious as to why she didn't fucking run screaming?" Axel stood in the center of the room, hands outstretched.

They were at Axel's house because the truth was, Draven didn't want to go home. He was fucking wired. Harper didn't react how he anticipated her to. She'd stood in the center of the road, looking all powerful.

Challenging him.

Her gaze had screamed for him to just drive the fucking car, to charge at her. When she realized he wasn't going to do that, she'd looked disappointed.

He was many things and had done a lot of bad shit, but killing Harper Miller wasn't at the top of his list of things he wanted to do to her.

Right now, in this very moment, fucking her *was* top of that list. To see her writhing as he took her.

"She doesn't give a fuck," Jett said. "That's why

she didn't run screaming. Why run when she's not even afraid?"

"How could she not be afraid? The threat was there. Maybe she's just fucking weird."

"Or maybe there's more to her than meets the eye," Draven said.

They all turned to look at him.

"You've been pretty obsessed with this chick in the past week. Why?" Axel asked, taking a seat.

Sipping at his beer, he thought about Harper. He'd watched her for years. His obsession wasn't just the past week. His friends didn't know because he'd never told them. It hadn't been important then, as in the past Harper didn't have what it took to suit them, and he would always put his friends before his dick. Only now, as he saw the darkness swirling inside her and the need for someone to notice, did it even mean anything. There was a chance for him to finally have her, and he was going to take it. She'd be a good bond for him and his friends, one who would fit in their group.

"I want her on our team," he said.

Silence met his request.

He stared at each of his friends in turn and waited for the shit to hit the fan. This was the first time he'd ever wanted another to join their little club. Not that they were a club with actual sponsors or anything.

They all had each other's backs and took care of one another. When one of them called, the others came running. It was how it was supposed to be for all of them. He knew without a shadow of a doubt he could count on them.

"Are you shitting me right now?" Axel asked.

"That's not possible," Buck said.

"You're talking about pristine little goody Harper. There's no way she has what it takes to be part of our group. We have to rely on her. She's got to be willing to have our backs." Axel shook his head and stepped away from the group. "Look, I get that she's different from a lot of the other chicks in school. Can't you just fuck her and get her over with?"

"She needs us," Draven said.

Axel and Buck snorted.

"I'm in," Jett said.

He turned toward Jett, who shrugged.

"Why not? She's interesting. She made my dick hard the way she just stood there, watching us."

"We don't know if we can even rely on her," Axel said. "We've got to think about this."

"I've thought about it. I want her. She's going to be part of us, Axel. Trust me."

"How? How can you know for sure that this girl won't just spill to the cops at the first opportunity?"

Draven sat back, smiling. Stonewall was quite a big place. Harper wasn't going to run to the cops. She knew what to expect. Living with her father, he doubted she'd run to anyone or anything but her room.

"She won't."

Axel threw up his hands. "I give up. One of you two talk some sense into him."

"If you want to take her for a test drive, then that's what we'll do. She's strong," Draven said. "She hasn't spilled her guts so far. She hasn't faltered."

"She's not got a dick, Draven," Buck said.

"Okay, let's put it in a way that you'll understand. Harper Miller belongs to me," Draven said. "She's mine to do with as I please. I want to play with her, but ultimately, I want to join her with us."

"You know the rumors that come with us," Axel said. "You really think she can handle that?"

"I know she can handle a whole lot, Axel. Trust

me."

"I do trust you. I just think you're making a mistake."

"I don't rush anything. You should know that." He finished his beer. "We'll start tomorrow. You'll all follow my lead."

None of them argued, but he saw Axel really didn't like where this was going.

Shaking Axel's hand and slapping his back, Draven didn't even try to offer him reassurances.

"Yeah, yeah, whatever. I've got your back, always. I know you've got mine."

He left Buck and Axel alone, walking with Jett back to his car. He and Axel were the ones that owned the cars. Buck and Jett always came for the ride.

Climbing behind the wheel, he waited for Jett, not surprised as the knife he always held was once again within his grasp. School was the only time he had to put the knife away. The tip of the blade rested against his knee.

"You wanting to shove that in someone anytime soon?" Draven asked.

"I got a feeling it's going to go into the new stepdad," Jett said.

"He slapping your mother around?"

"Nope. He keeps giving me the eye as if he wants to fuck my ass."

"Shit. You want to stay at my place?" Draven stopped the car, willing to have his friend over.

It wasn't like Jett hadn't seen his father killing a whore he'd impregnated. There had been a lot of shit his friends had seen over the years.

Axel's dad and his own were pretty much BFFs, if you could ever call two raving lunatics BFF material.

"Nah. I can't wait for him to come in my room,"

Jett said, licking his lips as if it was the best idea around. "It's been too long since I got to hurt anyone."

To most people, this would freak them the fuck out, but Draven wasn't most people. He pulled away from the curb and drove in the direction of Jett's house. It wasn't his job to monitor Jett, only to have his back.

"This thing with Harper, you've been wanting her for a while, haven't you?" Jett asked.

Draven didn't answer.

Jett chuckled. "That's fine. I don't expect you to be honest about it. It's your feelings after all. I'm not looking to take the piss or to laugh. Just saying, the guys haven't seen the way you look at her."

"And you have?"

"I noticed whenever she walked into a room, you'd watch her. It wasn't even a conscious thing you did either. You'd watch her, and wait, and it was kind of strange to see at first. All the chicks that throw themselves at you, why you'd even want to be with someone like Harper."

Draven waited.

"Then I realized how different Harper is from all the others. She doesn't wait for anyone. She's always been alone. No friends. No connections. No waiting around for someone to laugh and giggle. Then when her mom killed herself, she's been forced into a situation she hates. She's struggling. The good girl versus the rebel."

"You've got a poetic spin on shit, haven't you?"

"I read a lot. It passes the time. What I want to know, Draven, is what you want to tell this girl? Is she going to be yours, or belong to all of us?" Jett looked over at Draven.

"You've noticed her, haven't you?"

"Kind of hard not to. She doesn't try to draw attention to herself, and that's what she does without doing it. She doesn't cry my name and giggle at the first sign."

"I don't know what I want. All I know is, I want her. I want Harper."

"Then you're going to have to take her."

"We're going to be doing this my way," Draven said, pulling up outside Jett's house.

"I know. Let's hope you can handle a chick like Harper. Something tells me she's going to be pure fire." Jett climbed out of the car and the knife had gone away.

Draven waited a few minutes after Jett had entered his home before driving back to his place.

He didn't end up going back to his home. Instead, he pulled up outside Harper's home. It was late and dark.

Staring up at her place, he wondered where she slept, what she was thinking about, and if he'd completely lost his mind this time.

Harper was a different woman from the kind they always played with. None of the bitches that came to them, begging to be part of their clique, actually got tested. They were there to fuck, nothing else.

Sure, he'd tease them, pretending that if they took all of their cocks, then it was a game changer.

It wasn't a game changer.

They didn't have any special instructions on how to be initiated into their group. Since they were kids, they'd come together. Their families had been connected through work. His and Axel's fathers were the bosses whereas Jett and Buck's fathers had been mere soldiers. Grunts. Jett's father was killed in a shootout with a gang in the city. He didn't leave Jett with anything but a whore for a mother, and this knife fetish he loved so much.

Shaking his head to clear the fog that came with Harper, Draven drove home.

Rather than come in through the front door, he

THE INITIATION

walked toward the back, and wished he'd gone in the front. His father was riding the cook again.

This was the same cook that had been with them all for twenty years, according to his mother. Her food was awesome, and no matter what, she wasn't allowed to leave the house.

Draven didn't let his presence be known, especially as he watched his father. He'd seen him fuck plenty of times before. It's what his dad demanded.

Standing in the shadows, he watched as his father pulled out of the cook, spreading her legs wide, tasting her pussy.

What made Draven pause though, was the love he saw on his father's face. At no other time in his life had he ever seen that look before.

Watching him now, he saw the truth. His father was in love with the cook. The cook who'd been with them over twenty years.

His father had married his mother twenty-five years ago. They had tried for a kid but had three miscarriages within that first year.

Staring at the two in the kitchen, Draven wondered if his mother had gotten pregnant again or if he was in fact the result of the cook and his father?

It would make sense.

Stepping away from the shadows, he entered through the garage and snuck up to his room.

One thing his father always taught him was to always be prepared for anything. Right now, he had some ammunition. He just needed to know when to use it.

Chapter Four

Harper's locker was still empty. She slammed the door shut, pissed off.

That jacket was the only thing she had left of her mother, and she wanted it back. They could keep all the textbooks and other stuff. The only thing she wanted back was the jacket.

When she stepped away from the locker, the whispers still followed her as she made her way down the hall.

She went straight to the cafeteria even though there was a sandwich in her bag to enjoy. She'd sneaked into the kitchen last night to make it. The lunch Hannah prepared for her didn't exactly leave her wanting to eat. Going vegan was the last thing she wanted to do.

Standing in the doorway of the cafeteria, she checked the tables, noticing the nerds, the jocks, the different groups of people, all of them in their own little circles. She'd never wanted to join.

It pissed her off to see them all looking so happy, so in control of their shit.

Above all else, it pissed her off that they whispered about her and judged her.

Spotting Draven and his little friends, she stormed over to them. He noticed her first and didn't even move a muscle. He looked almost bored.

"Give it back," she said.

"What?"

"You know what. You can keep the books and shit. You certainly need it, but I want my jacket back."

"I don't have it. Wow, you really have lost your mind."

"Fuck off, Harper. We don't have time for dirt like you," Axel said, laughing.

She glared at Draven. "I want it back."

"It's good to want things, princess."

Glaring at him, she was very much aware of people watching her. "You're not going to give it back?"

"No."

"Fine."

She stormed away. She went straight back to her locker and glanced over at Draven's.

Don't do it.

Be the good girl.

The girl that no one expects to make waves.

Be nice.

Be polite.

Don't cause trouble.

Blood.

So much blood.

Her mother's lifeless face staring up at the ceiling. Bad things happened to good people. Her mother didn't deserve to die.

She stepped away from her own locker and stood in front of Draven's. He was there every single morning. She was always aware of him, of his gaze following her.

She wanted her jacket. He had it. She wanted it. He'd just take what he wanted. Lifting her foot up, she slammed it against his locker.

It hurt. The pain rushed through her entire body as she brought her foot back up and did it again, then again.

Over and over, she kicked his locker, seeing a dent form. The metal wasn't strong and in fact quite fragile.

Suddenly, she was grabbed and pinned against the locker. Draven had his fingers wrapped around her neck, but he didn't squeeze.

The threat was there.

He wanted to hurt her.

"What the fuck do you think you're doing?" he asked.

People were watching, but she didn't care. Something shifted inside her as she glared at him.

"Taking what I want."

"And what you want is that fucking jacket?"

"Yes."

He glared at her. She glared right back. Neither of them moved.

"What the hell is going on here?" Mr. Arnold said, walking down the long hallway.

That's right, teach, don't run. You may have to intervene.

"What is the meaning of this?" Mr. Arnold didn't even ask for Draven to remove his hands from her neck.

"We're talking here," Draven said.

"Yeah, we are. Back the fuck off, people. Can't five people have a convo anymore without you nosy bastards listening in? Get gone," Axel said.

She wasn't talking to anyone but Draven.

"Give it back."

"What are you willing to do for it?" he asked.

"It's mine. I'm not willing to do anything."

"Finders keepers."

"Seriously, is that what you want? To dress up in my jacket?"

"I'm attached to it."

She grabbed his arms and attempted to throw him off her, but he wouldn't budge. "Let me go."

The teacher had disappeared, and once she glanced over his shoulder, she saw they were alone.

"Seriously, who are the ones in charge here?" she asked.

"You're looking at them."

She grabbed his wrist. "Get your hands off me."

She didn't expect him to push his entire body against hers. His fingers were still wrapped around her neck.

"Stop it," she said. Her heart started to pound as she watched him. The bag on her back was digging into her as he kept her flat against the lockers.

"You know we've hurt people for less," he said.

"You filled my locker with dirt. I wasn't going to tell. You didn't need to do that."

"How do we know you won't tell?"

"I'm not a damn rat. I know when to keep my mouth shut," she said.

"You know all of our dirty secrets?" Jett asked.

"I don't want to know anything. I just want to finish up this year and go."

"What if we can make it a little more fun for you?" He stroked the flesh of her neck, right next to her pulse. He smiled as her pulse seemed to jump against his touch.

She didn't like this one bit.

Being trapped against his locker, being under his spell, liking how he felt against her body.

She was better than this.

Gripping his shoulders, she tried to push him away. Suddenly, Buck and Jett were there. Their hands gripped her wrists, pushing them flat against the locker.

The threat was there. Against the four of them, she didn't stand a chance. They were always together, always working as a team.

"You know I've hurt guys for less than what you've done?"

"What's the matter? Not used to a girl pissing you off?" she asked.

"I'm used to them being on their knees

worshiping my cock."

"You're a pig."

"And I want to hurt you right now. You've dented my locker."

"You've taken something of mine, and I want it back."

"I stopped some fuckers from taking shit from you."

"Give it back."

"No."

She pressed against Jett and Buck and still couldn't get free. Draven leaned in close, the tip of his nose brushing her cheek.

The action took her completely by surprise. She froze in place, not really sure what to do.

"Tell you what, why don't we make a trade?" he asked.

"I'm not trading anything."

"You want your jacket back, you come to me at my place Friday night. You don't, you don't get it."

"Are you demented?"

"A little." He leaned back, smirking. "The deal is on the table. A jacket for one night."

"One night doing what?" she asked.

"That is up to me." He let her go. Jett and Buck stepped away.

Draven stared down her body and back up again. "Those clothes are not you."

The jeans she'd been forced to wear were too tight, and the shirt enhanced her tits. She hated the clothes, preferring the sizes that were too big for her.

Ignoring him, she folded her arms across her chest.

"Why me?" she asked. "You can have anyone you want. A lot of girls would love to play this game with you. Why me?"

"Why not you? It's the last year of high school, Harper. It's time to live a little and have some fun."

He walked away.

She watched him go.

This wasn't living and having fun.

She left his locker, because there was no way she could fix the dent, and now that all the anger that had left her, she was shaking. Heading outside to the football field, she sat on the top bleachers, looking out across the field.

She pulled out her peanut butter sandwich that had seen better days. It was all squished from being pressed up against the locker.

Was this what people felt like after experiencing a death of a parent?

She felt reckless, stupid.

But in need of someone who'd fight back.

Her father didn't want to know or talk about her mother. He only wanted to talk about Hannah and get up in his new, pretty wife.

She hated Hannah and hated the way she was living just because she couldn't leave home.

Once she finished her sandwich, she went through the rest of her classes, ignoring all the ones that Draven was in.

She didn't need to watch him or see him to know he kept looking at her. Some of the girls were giving her dirty looks, and that was fine. It wasn't like she'd ever been popular before.

Now though, he'd made her the enemy because he liked to steal things from her. She couldn't help but smile thinking about him wearing her very feminine jacket.

By the end of the day, she still didn't want to go

home, and she had the best excuse ever, work.

She'd been going to the diner for the past week. She liked the work. Taking meal orders, serving them, pouring coffee, filling salt and pepper, all of it was so enjoyable, and for a short time each night she got the chance to forget how much she hated life and all that it entailed.

Instead, she worked. It soothed her soul. When she arrived at the diner today, it was busy. Men and women, families, friends, loved ones, they all frequented the diner, all loving the food that was presented to them. There were burgers, fried chicken, pasta, and so many other dishes that made it a rather popular joint.

As she got near the end of her shift, she walked out of the kitchen and froze.

In the back booth sat Draven. They were in her section. Why couldn't they leave her alone? Was it worth quitting so she didn't have to serve them?

Why can't I catch a break?

She'd never been one to back down, and so, back straight, she walked right over to them, her little notepad in her hand, and pen at the ready.

"What can I get you?"

"Well, well, well, isn't this interesting?" Axel asked.

She stared at him and took a breath. "Have you all come to your senses and brought my jacket with you?"

"Nope," Buck said laughing.

"How long you been working here?" Draven asked.

"None of your business."

Draven took a picture of her.

"What the hell?"

"Tell me, or I mail this to your father. I wonder if

he knows that his daughter has a job."

"Are you for real right now?"

"Five."

"How do you even have his number?"

"He's a lawyer, four."

"I can't believe this."

"Three. You better hurry."

"Two."

"Fine, fine. I've been working here a week. That's all, a week. Don't text him." She reached over, trying to grab his cell phone, but he pulled it out of the way. "Don't text him, please."

He'd make her quit, and this was the one thing she could call her own.

"You're a strange one, aren't you?" Draven said. "What is it about this job?"

She shook her head, and he held the cell phone in his hand as if it was some kind of magical weapon.

"Stop, stop. Fine, I work here because I like it, and I hate being home. Happy?"

"I think she caved too soon. Her dad is a real sticking point, huh?" Axel asked.

"He and I don't exactly see eye to eye."

"Does that have to do with your stepmother?" Draven asked.

"You mean how he cheated on my mother with Hannah and now I've got to pretend she doesn't exist? Yeah, that will really piss a girl off. Do you want to order?" she asked. Her hands were shaking.

"We could beat him up for you," Draven said.

She glanced over the notepad, really tempted. "He's not worth it."

"He makes you angry."

"A lot of things make me angry."

"Like what?" Buck asked.

"Like the fact you guys are holding my jacket hostage. I miss it and want it back."

"We've told you how to get it back," Jett said.

"Look, whatever this is. I want no part of it. I have no interest in fighting with you or sleeping with you, or whatever it is you're planning. I just want to get through the next year, what's left of it. Now, let me take your order."

You're a liar.

You want more than to take their order.

You want to scream.

To fight.

To punish everyone who has ever hurt you.

To have someone you can rely on. Who won't hurt themselves.

You're alone.

She took their order, and she went and put it through. Coming back with the drinks, she placed them in front of the guys.

The sound of the doorbell had her turning and groaning. She'd avoided most of the groups at school. Today was her unluckiest day as a group of jocks took a seat opposite Draven.

"You don't serve them," Draven said.

"If their waitress is on break, which I see she is, I've got to serve them."

The manager had been clear. The customers all came first. You stuck to your area, but if the waitress was on break, you served the table until she came out.

They all had each other's backs. Walking through her tables, she served them, not wanting to deal with the jocks but seeing she didn't have much choice. She finally stopped at their table.

"What can I get you?" she asked.

"Well, well, well, look at you, Harper. It's about

time dirt like you knew your place."

Gripping the notepad in her fist, she stared down at Ben. He was the captain of the football team and a real asshole.

Many times, when he walked past her, he either shoved her into a locker, a wall, or forced her to spill her books. He'd poured soda all over her bag one year.

She fucking hated him.

"What will it be?" she asked.

"You, on your knees, sucking my cock, dick-face." He burst out laughing and held his hands up for his boys to slap.

****

"Don't do it," Buck said.

"Don't start shit over them just talking," Axel said.

Draven watched as Ben, hero of the football team, told another joke that involved Harper being on her knees for him.

He kept watching as Harper did nothing.

She took their jokes and their order, spinning on her heel to go. They whistled at her ass, and Ben stood up, grabbing his dick as if it made him look cool.

Draven wanted to hurt him, to feel his knuckles slam against the flesh and snapping his arm or even a leg. He'd love to send a message to the jocks to leave Harper alone.

She came back to their table, their food in her hands, and she leaned over the table, putting their burgers in front of them. The angle gave him a perfect view of her cleavage, which was pressed up against her uniform.

Those tits were for him and only for him.

"Is that all?" she asked.

"Don't serve them," he said.

"I've got no choice. If their waitress isn't out, I

have to serve them."

"Harper, you only have to do what you want."

"Isn't it fun for you to just do what you want? Screw you, Draven." She turned on her heel and left.

He picked up his burger, watching for the jocks' waitress. She didn't turn up, and he waited as Harper brought over their food. She leaned over the table as none of them were willing to pass the plates. As she did so, the skirt of her dress rode up a little, showing more of her thigh.

Draven didn't mind. He made a note to buy her some shorts, and force her to wear them. What pissed him off was Ben.

The piece of shit ran his hand beneath her skirt and squeezed her ass.

She let out a scream, and as she tried to get away, his team held her in place, stopping her.

He'd seen enough. None of his boys tried to stop him. Draven jumped over the table, and grabbed Ben's hand, twisting it so that he let her go.

Axel, Buck, and Jett were at his back. They pulled Harper up, drawing her between them.

"You don't touch what belongs to us," Draven said. He still held Ben's hand.

"Are you for real? Seriously? You weren't fucking joking. It's Harper. You can have better pussy than what she has to offer."

He'd heard enough. Slamming his first against Ben's face, he used the momentum to grab his head and slam it on the table, once then twice.

The rest of the team got up and rushed toward him. Drawing his foot up, he kicked one in the nuts. He didn't need to look to know that his boys had his back. They would always have his back. It's the way they were.

"Stop this, right now. Stop!"

He didn't listen. Ben was up now, nose bleeding and looking pissed off.

"You can't share, Draven."

"She's mine. She belongs to us."

"So no one can play?" Ben asked.

"You know how it is."

Slamming Ben hard, he pushed him out of the window. The glass smashing seemed to freeze everyone in place.

Draven had gotten his message across.

The cops would be here and then his father would know. Most of the time he didn't give a shit about his father finding out, but right now, the last thing he wanted to deal with was his father.

Grabbing Harper's hand, he took off, knowing Axel, Buck, and Jett would get the hell out of dodge.

As they ran around the corner of the mall, he saw the cops heading their way. He rushed her into the stairwell. She didn't fight him, running with him as they escaped the cops.

Once they were clear and inside the parking lot, he opened the car. Harper got in the passenger side without arguing.

Climbing behind the wheel, he pulled out of the parking lot, just as he saw Axel and the others entering the parking lot.

His knuckles hurt from the punch he'd landed to Ben.

"I can't believe we just did that," she said.

He glanced over at her and was surprised to see a smile on her face.

"You never ran from the cops before?"

"No." She scoffed. "Some of us don't make it a habit of being thrown in jail."

"I've never spent a night or even an hour in jail."

"You're lying."

"When you've got my last name, it takes a lot of balls for cops to be willing to throw me away. Besides, your dad is one hell of a lawyer."

"Great."

"You got an issue with the old man."

"It's none of your business."

"You like to say that a lot." He whipped his car around and came to a stop outside an abandoned garage. There was no one around, and he sat back, turning off the ignition as he waited for Axel to arrive.

"I left my stuff back at the diner."

"You're not working there again."

"You're not the boss of me. Don't even try to tell me what to do. I don't like it." She opened the car door and got out.

He rolled his eyes, doing the same.

She folded her arms and stared up and down the street. "Which way is home?"

"I'll take you home when I know the others are here."

"I can walk."

He stepped up toward her, trapping her against the car. He liked doing this, loved the shocked look that always appeared in her eyes whenever he caught her off guard. When she went to touch him, he captured her wrists and held them against the car.

Once again, he saw her jaw clench. The anger was just beneath the surface. He wanted her to get angry, to stop holding it in, to stop accepting that this was her life.

"Let me go."

"Make me."

"Fuck you."

"You keep saying that. One day I might. One day we all might."

"I'm not one of your gangbang whores, Draven. I don't even know why I'm suddenly of interest to you."

"What makes you think you haven't always been interesting to me?"

She rolled her eyes, those blue eyes that reminded him of the ocean.

"Please, you and I, we don't mix. We'd never mix. I'm from the wrong side of town."

"Last time I checked, you lived on the same street as me. You're fighting. I wonder who told you to be the good girl. Your dad? Did he tell you to always be Daddy's special girl?"

"You have no idea what you're talking about."

"No, it's not Daddy. I bet if he told you to be good, to be nice, you'd do the complete opposite because you hate his guts." He smiled. "I'm going to guess … Mommy."

She started to struggle against him.

"Yeah, you've got no friends. No one else in your life who'd tell you to do the right thing. The only person left is the woman that killed herself. The woman your father won't allow you to have even a memory of. Those clothes you wear, your mom didn't pick them out. Hannah did."

"How do you know Hannah?" she asked. "I saw the way she was with you guys. Something is going on there."

"In our world, there is always something going on. Let's not change the subject though. Did Mommy want you to be a special little girl? Did she tell you how right it was to be good? To always tell the truth. To make Daddy proud."

She pushed against his hold, and when she went

to draw her knee up, he dodged that. Stepping right up against her, he spread her thighs, resting his between hers, drawing it up her legs. He didn't touch her pussy even though he wanted to.

He wanted to turn that fire to passion. Her anger and rage bubbled beneath the surface, threatening to spill out. She'd been feeling this way for a lot longer than he would have guessed.

"Let me go," she said.

"No."

"Now."

"No."

She thrashed in his arms, and still, he held her still even as she screamed.

He watched her unleash all of her pain. Her anger. Her rage.

It was so beautiful. He marveled at being the one to bring it out. She was perfection. Not once did he let her go, or did he regret holding her here. She belonged to him.

Forever.

She'd match all of them so perfectly, so well. The beauty she displayed wasn't easy to find, but he would nurture this part of her. He'd find an outlet for her rage and allow her to break free.

Axel and the others arrived as she came to a stop. Her voice was hoarse as she asked him once more to let her go.

He still didn't. Stepping close to her, he breathed her in.

"You shouldn't keep that shit inside," he said. "It's toxic."

Locking their fingers together, he gave her space, tucking her against his side as Axel, Buck, and Jett stepped out of the car.

"I got her shit," Jett said, lifting up the bag.

"Is that why you weren't fighting?" Draven asked.

"Yeah, he's too much of a pussy to get his hands dirty. Always thinking of the ladies." Axel laughed.

Harper remained tense at his side, waiting for one or the other to turn their aggression on her.

"You shouldn't have started that fight," she said.

"It was fun, and Ben had it coming. Fucker has been messing with us since the start of the year. Thinks he's better than us because he drives a fancy car and can stick his dick into anything he wants." Buck shook his head, looking sick.

"Even those that are not willing," Axel said.

He stared at his friends, and it felt right to have Harper by his side. She didn't pull away or cause a scene.

He imagined she was exhausted.

"I'm taking her home," he said.

"Usual meet area?" Axel asked.

He nodded. There were a few things they were going to have to discuss. Ben would try to retaliate at some point. There's no way he'd accept taking a beating like that because of Harper. Besides, he had a feeling his boys wanted to talk to him.

Helping Harper back into his car, he nodded at his friends as he pulled out of the abandoned garage.

"Are you going to get into trouble?"

"Nope. I don't believe in ever getting into trouble."

"You know what I mean."

"Do me a favor, don't allow yourself to be alone. Quit the waitressing work."

"Why?"

"Because I said so."

She shook her head. "I enjoy it."

77

"Find something else to do. I don't know, take up a hobby."

"No. Don't be a dick about this. I'm going to work, I enjoy it."

"I'll tell your dad."

"Don't be a dick."

He smiled. "It's my middle name."

He pulled up outside of her home and saw Hannah getting out of her car. She looked over, giving a little frown before waving at them.

"What is the deal with you guys and her?" Harper asked.

"Don't have a clue."

"You're lying to me."

"I don't lie."

"You're lying about lying."

He laughed. "I'll tell, and it'll end badly for you."

She climbed out of the car, and he watched her ass as she walked. He liked her ass. He'd been admiring it for several years.

Pulling away from her house, he set off toward the group's private meeting area.

It wasn't in the woods, or even at any of their usual places. The place they met was an abandoned factory. It had been condemned years ago, but they still broke in. Only assholes would even try to spend time in the falling-down building. For the most part, they had gotten away unscathed from any damage to the crumbling building. They liked to live dangerously.

Axel, Buck, and Jett were not inside when he pulled up but were in fact leaning against Axel's car.

"It's about time you showed up. Are you fucking her already?"

"You sound jealous, Axel."

"I'm not, and you know it. I want to know what

the deal is. We don't start fights like that, especially not with so many fucking witnesses. What the fuck?"

"He was touching her," he said. "No one touches what belongs to us."

"Belongs to us?" Buck asked.

"Just last week you were picking on her. We stuffed dirt in her locker and now you're saying she's part of us? Part of our group?"

"You really think she can be fearless?" Jett asked.

"Or even a banger?" Buck did some weird thrusting hip action. "You know, to have one you to have to have us all."

"You can't tell me that when you look at her, you don't see," Draven said. "She has a place right here."

"It has been the four of us since the beginning. We have each other's backs, and we agreed any chick that comes between us has to belong to all of us," Axel said.

Silence fell between them, and Draven stared at Axel.

They had rules.

They'd seen men, strong men, torn apart because of a woman's pussy. They had all agreed to be above that, and part of their initiation, was to fuck them all. To be one of them, they had to fuck them all.

So far, no woman had ever met up to their expectation.

Sure, they had fucked their way through their share of women, but they'd all been willing and none of them would take a hit for any of them.

"I don't care what you say, Harper's the one."

"This has to be a vote we all agree on," Axel said. "I don't think she's the one."

"You don't."

"The way she looks at us, she wants to hurt us,"

Buck said.

"Scared she'd bite your dick off?"

"She's too good," Jett said. "We can't have a law-abiding citizen in this group. You know that. We need each other, and we're always there for one another. If she's part of us, then she has to be willing to lie, cheat, and steal."

"Otherwise your dad will put her on the cutting block," Axel said. "You know that. You've got to be prepared to train her. It's not just us. Our folks will deal with any problems they don't think we can handle."

Chapter Five

Harper sat at her desk, flicking the pen she'd been using between her fingers, trying not to think about Draven, or about any of them. Her body kept on remembering how good it felt to have him so close, to feel his body next to hers.

Draven, Axel, Buck, and Jett.

Four guys.

She couldn't remember a time when they weren't a group, a gang. The moment they were in school, no one was willing to tear them apart. Boys had tried to get between them, had tried to become part of their crowd. No one had ever succeeded.

Even girls had wanted to be with them.

So many people had tried and failed.

No one knew how to become one of them, and she didn't even have a clue as to why she was thinking about it now.

Being trapped against Draven with him holding her in place, letting go, screaming, it had felt rather liberating. Twirling the pen around her hair, she stared out the window.

She spun around as Ian cleared his throat. He stood in her doorway, the sleeves of his shirt rolled up.

"Evening," he said.

"Hey." She stood up to face him.

Had Draven told him?

He entered her bedroom, and she waited as he reached out, picking up a picture that had been placed on her wall.

The only photograph she had of her mother was inside her drawer beside the bed. Every single item that reminded them of her mother, she'd gotten rid of or had been taken from her.

She hated the way they both seemed to just pretend she didn't exist. Her mother was part of her. There were times she looked in the mirror and saw her.

"We've not had much time to talk, Harper. I've been so busy with work. I feel we should talk."

Staring at him as he took a seat on the edge of the bed, she made no move to join him. Why talk? Why do anything?

"Hannah wanted me to talk to you."

"About what?" She folded her arms across her chest, hating that he started a conversation with her.

"About the fact you're older and guys and I was wondering—"

"You don't need to have that conversation with me."

"What conversation?"

"Sex. Boys. Mom had it with me."

"Harper, I think it best I talk to you about this. Me and Hannah."

"Why? Because you can't stand to know that Mom was there for me?"

"Hannah's worried. She noticed a couple of boys hanging around you, and she wanted to be there for you."

Harper laughed. "You still won't acknowledge that she existed, can you? Is it, like, just a mistake, is that it? You can't stand the fact that Mom got things right, and you didn't."

"Your mother didn't know enough."

"She knew that if you put a cock inside a pussy and climax, there's a risk of a baby. There's also a risk of that cock being infected because they don't know how to keep it in their pants. What more do you need me to know?"

"That is enough from you."

"Why? Can't handle being the infected dick of

the story?"

Ian slapped her around the face. The action took her by surprise. Her cheek hurt, and as she covered her face, her heart raced.

Blood.

So much blood.

"When the right man comes along, you'll know. Also, don't waste your life on a guy that will move on to the shiny new toy. Men do that. Men can't handle getting old."

Her eyes had been open when Harper found her in the tub.

The pain in her cheek didn't even compare to the pain in her heart.

Drawing her fist back, she let it fly, connecting with her dad's face. She didn't linger though. Running for her bedroom door, she ran downstairs, shoving Hannah out of the way as she left her home.

She didn't look, didn't even care where she was going. She had to get away.

To stop seeing the blood.

To stop feeling the pain within herself.

Before she realized what was happening, she found herself standing at the gates of her old home, in her old neighborhood, in pajamas. Her slippers did not really offer her any protection against the wet pavement.

The house had been bought by a young couple with a couple of kids. Staring up at her old bedroom window, she felt tears spring to her eyes.

"You shouldn't be out by yourself."

She turned to see Jett beside her.

"What are you doing here?" she asked.

"I live here. You ran past me as I was taking the trash out."

They both stood beneath a streetlight. He put a

finger beneath her chin and lifted her face up to the light.

"Did Draven do that?"

She touched her cheek. "No. My dad."

"Your dad hit you?"

"It's the first time. I did call him an infected cock, so I guess we're even."

"Why would you call him that?" Jett asked.

"He wanted to talk about sex."

"Is your dad a pervert?"

She laughed. "No. I don't think so." She rubbed at her temples. "He didn't think my mother had the right qualifications to talk about sex. I guess, he was wrong. I got angry. I'm not allowed to talk about her or to have anything of hers."

"Is this why you're obsessed with the jacket?"

She nibbled her lip. "It was the last thing she gave me. It means something. If I took it home, they'd probably destroy it. It's like they're trying to kill off every single memory of her I have. I'm sorry. I shouldn't be talking to you about this."

"It's fine."

"No. It's really not."

Jett laughed. "I play with knives because my stepfather likes to try and rape my ass. There, that's an over-share. We're even."

She froze. "Really?"

"A long story, short. I'm good with a knife."

Rain started to fall around them.

"We got to get out of the rain," he said.

She looked up to the sky, wanting to have the rain fall all around her rather than go back home.

"Come on." He held her hand and walked her back to his place.

The lawn was overgrown, and the paint on the outside of the house was flaking. She'd passed this place plenty of times but didn't know it was Jett's.

He didn't use the front door, instead going to the window at the front and prying it open.

"This is your room?" she asked.

She'd never been in a guy's room before.

"Welcome to my humble abode. I don't sleep upstairs. It's easier to make an escape here."

She noticed the bedroom door was bolted, and he closed the window.

Wrapping her arms around herself, she felt the chill settling in her bones.

"You're cold." He had a blanket in his hands and was wrapping it around her.

She shouldn't be here. She knew it but didn't ask to leave. Going home wasn't an option. Taking a seat on his bed, she watched as he started to type on his cell phone.

"You're not calling my dad, are you?"

"Not all of us have your dad on speed dial," he said.

"Who are you calling?" she asked.

"Don't worry about it."

Staring around his room, she was shocked by what she saw. Jett's room was … clean.

He sat down in his chair opposite her, knife in hand, resting the point against his flesh.

"Don't you ever hurt yourself?"

"Sometimes. What's a little pain though, right? It makes you feel so alive."

"I never thought of it like that."

He shrugged. "No one ever does."

"I didn't mean to … invade your space."

"You really are a little too good for everyone, you know that, right?"

Heat filled her cheeks, and she stared down at her

lap. "I think I broke my dad's nose."

"No shit."

"I hit him, hard."

"Good."

"How is that good?"

"He hit you. You hit him back. It's fair."

"That's not fair. I shouldn't have argued with him."

"And he shouldn't have cheated on your mom. Can't handle the truth, don't do it." Jett shrugged. "You need to get over your shit, otherwise you're going to spend the rest of your life miserable."

"Why do you hang out with the others?"

"They're my friends."

"They're horrible."

Jett laughed. "You think I'm not."

"You're being nice to me."

Again, this made him laugh harder.

"That's because I know something you don't know."

"And what's that?" she asked.

"It's a secret." Jett's gaze went to the window. "And here is another secret."

The window opened, and sure enough, Draven climbed on through.

She had nowhere else to go as he cupped her face, lifting her chin up. "What happened?"

"Stop. It's fine. You don't have to worry. It's all handled."

"All handled? I went past your house and saw a cop there, Harper. How is that handled? You've got a bruise on your cheek. What happened?"

Her father had called the cops?

For real?

She found herself telling Draven exactly what had

happened. She didn't even know why she was being this open with him.

"I don't know if I can go back home," she said.

"You shouldn't hide. One look at your face and the cops will know what happened."

"I can't believe he called them."

"Hannah may have," Draven said. "I'll take her back home."

"No problem. Enjoy."

Draven climbed out of the window, and she put the blanket, folded, back on the bed. "Thank you."

"No problem, Harper. Remember, don't apologize for everything. It's not all your fault."

She nodded and climbed out of the window. Draven was there, waiting, his car parked against the curb.

How strange, the four guys she'd avoided had been the ones to stick by her side. Once at the diner and now here. Of course, Axel and Buck aren't around, but she had a feeling with one call, they would be.

For the multiple time in a matter of days, she sat inside Draven's car. The ride back to her home was short. The cop wasn't there when they pulled up outside of her home.

"Do you think you could take me to the bus stop or something?"

"You're not running away. This is your home as well."

He got out of the car, and she hated him for it. Why couldn't he just help her and let her get out of Stonewall?

Her mother had died here. She'd seen her mother's heartbreak here, and it was all because of the man she had loved.

Draven took her hand and together, they walked

up to the door. She expected Draven to ring the doorbell. He didn't. With his head held high, he stepped over the threshold.

Hannah and Ian rushed to the doorway.

Draven held her hand tightly.

Her father's nose was covered in a bandage, and she was taken aback by the damage. Already his eyes looked bruised because of it.

"Did you call the cops?" Draven asked.

"I did," Hannah said, stepping forward. "Harper ran out, and I panicked. I didn't want her getting hurt. I'll call them now to know that she's fine."

"If they come to take her away, I will hold you personally responsible and you know what my dad is capable of," Draven said.

"Don't you dare talk to my wife like that inside my house," Ian said.

Harper cringed.

"Are you forgetting yourself, old man?" Draven let go of her hand and stepped up to Ian.

"It's fine. It's fine. I shouldn't have hit him," Harper said. She let out a squeal as Draven grabbed her and lifted her face up to her father.

She held onto Draven's wrists, hating being manhandled by him.

"Go ahead, Miller. Call the cops. Let them see what you did to your own daughter. Such a big, tough guy hitting a girl."

Harper pulled out of Draven's arms.

"Go to your room, Harper," Draven said.

She looked from him to her father. The power here confused her. Was her father the one in charge or Draven? She didn't argue as neither turned toward her. Going to her room, she closed the door and collapsed onto her bed.

What the hell do I do now, Mom? I hit him. I hit him, and it felt good.

I liked it.

Touching her cheek, she got to her feet and took a look in her vanity mirror to see just how bruised her cheek was.

She looked like a battered daughter.

Falling back to the bed, she tried to listen to what was going on downstairs.

****

"Leave my house," Ian said.

Draven smiled. "Your house?" He put a hand on the wall and ran his fingers up and down it. "You don't own this house. We own you, Ian. Remember that." He stepped up to Harper's father.

"You're nothing but a little punk, Draven. You don't scare me."

He acted.

Men like Ian were all mouth and no action. Wrapping his fingers around Ian's throat, he slammed him up against the wall.

To a lot of people, he was a punk-ass kid. They underestimated him. He was Alan Barries's spawn. His blood ran in his veins, and ever since he'd been old enough, he'd been taught how to fight, how to be ready to take over.

Even as Ian clawed at his wrist, Draven didn't stop. He didn't want to stop. He liked that Ian fought him.

It was pointless.

He knew what he was doing and had been fighting for as long as he could remember. Hurting people was second nature to him. His talent came in hurting people.

Hannah entered the hallway and gasped.

"Please, Draven, don't."

"Listen, whore, get on your knees, and show this cocksucker who the real man is here."

"Draven," Hannah said.

"Now!"

He'd seen his father command her. Hannah went to her knees.

"You see her. She belongs to us. She's our property, and we allow you to use her because it amuses us. She's nothing but a cunt and ass designed to take cock. She was your reward for a job well done. We can take it all away. The house, the car, the bitch, all of it. You ever put your hands on Harper again, and I will make you pray for death long before I grant it. Understand?"

"Yes," Ian wheezed out.

Releasing him, Draven stepped back. "Don't step out of place again." Without another word, he shoved Ian to the ground.

"Fuck him, whore."

With that, he made his way to the stairs and went to find Harper.

He guessed right, finding her flat on her back, staring up at the ceiling. The moment he closed the door, flicking the lock into place, she sat up.

The pajamas she wore were so cute. They had shapes of ice cream cones on them.

"What are you doing here?" she asked.

The bruise on her cheek pissed him off. Ian shouldn't have hit her. She got to her feet, and he stepped up to her, inspecting the bruise.

"It's fine."

"It's not fine." He shook his head. "Don't ever make excuses again."

"What about you? You were happy to hit me

back."

He smirked. "I'm not your dad." He stepped back. "So this is your bedroom. It's not very you."

"No, it's Hannah."

"That explains it." He stared at the artwork on the wall. "She likes to spend your father's cash."

Draven often wondered if the kid she'd been carrying was even Ian's.

If his father decided to pay her a visit, it tended to end with him being balls deep inside her. He knew, he'd seen it happen.

Sitting on the edge of her bed, he opened the drawer.

"Hey, what the hell?" She rushed toward him, closing the drawer. "You can't come here."

"Why not?"

"Because, I said so."

He grabbed her wrist, tugging her down on his knee. Putting a hand on her stomach, he reached into the drawer and withdrew the picture of her mother.

"She's really pretty," he said.

He'd seen Harper and her mother out around Stonewall plenty of times. They were both alike, both with raven hair and blue eyes.

He recalled going to their house one time. Harper hadn't been awake. He remembered her because his father had gone to Ian's house to see him to talk business, only Catherine had opened the door. Ian hadn't been there, and not long after, Hannah had been given to Ian. Draven wondered if the reason Alan had given Hannah to Ian was in order for her to keep an eye on him. With Catherine, Alan had no control, but through Hannah, he did.

Harper took the picture from him and put it back inside the drawer.

"Why don't you have it on display?"

"I can't. They'll take it from me."

"They can't take away the fact she's your mother."

"I know that, but I don't think they do."

She looked so incredibly sad.

"It's time for you to get some sleep," he said.

"You've got to leave."

He lifted her up off his knee, and he stood. "Not happening."

"Draven!"

"Harper, get into bed and stop being a pain in the ass." He removed his jacket, kicking off his sneakers and pushing his pants down so he only had on a pair of boxers.

"What the hell?" Harper let out a little squeal, covering her eyes. "Stop. Put some clothes back on."

"I'm not even naked here."

"This is not happening."

He climbed into her bed, putting her blanket over him and snuggling beneath the covers. "This is nice."

She opened her eyes. "Get out of bed."

He wriggled a little more, and she glared at him.

"That's my bed." She tried to push him out.

He held her wrist, pulling her across him and gripping her ass tightly. He loved the feel of her soft ass. It would feel even better nestled against his cock.

She tried to heave her body off him, and he laughed. "So cute. You know that."

"You're not going to budge?"

"Nope."

"You're impossible."

"Actually, I'm cute. I've been told so many times."

"I doubt that."

She rolled away from him and started to put some pillows between them. Each one she placed between them, he put back near her head.

"Just stop," she said. "Does my dad even know you're here?"

"Yes. He saw me come right up here. He probably thinks I'm fucking your brains out right now."

"I hate you."

"Hate me all you want." He tugged her down onto the bed, putting her into a position that was comfortable for him. He sighed, pressing his face against her neck.

"You're a pain in the ass," she said.

"Don't worry, one day you'll love me for it."

"Yeah, right."

She sighed, and she was still tense, even five minutes later.

"I'm not going to hurt you."

"I know."

"Then why are you tense?" he asked. He cupped her hip and leaned up so that he could look down at her.

She turned her head to the side, and he stared at her plump lips. They were designed to be kissed.

He didn't kiss her.

"Tell me."

"I've never had a guy in my bed before. Forgive me for not being used to … this."

"Sweet, little virginal Harper."

She tried to pull away from him, but again, he wouldn't let her go.

"You're not getting away from me that easily," he said, trapping her on the bed.

During the slight struggle she gave, he'd somehow managed to move between her thighs, nestled close to her pussy.

"Will you stop doing this to me? I'm getting bored."

"Then stop trying to run from me. You're going to learn one day that it's not going to help you either way."

She rolled her eyes.

"Cute, Harper, real cute."

He leaned down so that his lips were close to hers. He waited until she was focused on him.

It wouldn't be so hard to kiss her.

Just a brush of lips against lips, only, he didn't do it. He pulled himself away and sat back.

"Get off."

"No reason to get pissed at me." He wrapped his arm around her waist and settled back into bed.

"Aren't you worried that my dad will come in and shoot you?"

He laughed. "Please, that asshole won't even try."

"You're insulting my father. It's really not fair."

He snorted. "You think I give a shit? He hit you. You need to learn not to defend those that will hit you, Harper. They don't deserve your time or your energy. They're worthless."

"How can you talk like that? He's my father."

"Who hit you. He doesn't have a right to even get to register in your guilt. He's not worth it."

"He's still my father."

"Is that the kind of defense you're going to give him? What would your mother say?"

"Don't bring her into this."

She made to leave, but he wouldn't let her. Keeping her in place, he stared into her eyes. So filled with pain.

He regretted bringing her up.

"Don't … mention her."

"You can't hide from her forever, Harper."

"I'm not hiding. I'm just not giving myself the chance to …"

"You're not allowing yourself the chance to miss her."

"I can't," she said.

He hated how sad she looked, how lost.

"She was a good mother," he said.

She sniffled and tried to turn her head. He cupped her cheek, stroking away the tears that spilled out of the corner of her eye.

"She killed herself while I was at school. She's not a good anything."

"She loved you."

"You don't know that. If she did, she'd still be here now, and I wouldn't be alone. She wasn't strong enough. She didn't care enough."

"You're not alone."

"I punched my father because he wanted to talk to me about sex and wouldn't listen when I said my mom had already covered it. I also insulted him about having an infected dick."

He laughed. "Good."

"That's not good, Draven. It's disrespectful."

"He doesn't deserve you. He left you and your mother. Never forget that, and don't allow him to think that he can have better than you. He's just a guy with a loose dick."

"Who is Hannah?" she asked.

"No one you need to concern yourself with."

"Have you fucked her?"

"Look at you, speaking all big girl words."

"Don't mock me."

"I'm not." He moved off her, missing the warmth of her legs. Pulling her against his chest, he snuggled in tight.

"You should go home."

"That's not going to happen."

"Why not?"

"You need this."

"Draven, I don't need anything."

"Keep saying that to yourself. I know the truth."

He imagined her rolling her eyes, and he smiled against her neck.

"This is nice," she said.

"Be careful, it won't be long until you're begging for me to sleep with you."

"That won't ever happen. You sleep with everyone."

"I don't actually."

"Please, I've heard the girls at school talking. You're a man-whore."

He snorted. "I don't sleep with them. I fuck. It's completely different."

"How?"

"I don't hug them, and my dick is always inside them. Afterward, I kick them out."

"Seriously?"

"Yep."

She sighed. "I don't think I like you."

"That's okay. I don't always like you either."

She laughed. "Thank you."

"For what?"

"For picking me up. For being here. I'd have gone by now."

He held her even tighter.

"If you ever think of running, I want you to come straight to me, understand? If not then, Axel, Buck, or Jett."

"That will never happen."

"Promise me."

"What do I get in return?" she asked. She sounded so sleepy.

He had nothing to give her. "I'll be nice to you."

She chuckled. "I don't mind you being mean. It's kind of fun."

"You're a weird girl, Harper Miller."

"Says the guy who was shoving dirt down a guy's throat not long ago. Night."

He felt her relax against his body seconds later.

Running his fingers through her hair, he pressed a kiss to her neck. It felt oddly … comforting to have her in his arms.

He'd have to talk to his dad about what had gone down here. He didn't know what Alan would make of what happened. Last time he checked, Alan didn't give a shit about Harper or her mother.

Tightening his hold on her, he vowed to protect her.

To not let her go.

To always be there for her, to be strong so she didn't have to be.

He'd made Axel, Jett, and Buck a vow.

Harper Miller didn't know it yet, but she now belonged to all of them, mind, heart, and body. She could keep her soul. He didn't want it.

Chapter Six

The following morning Harper woke alone. She touched the pillow where she was sure Draven had slept the night before. There was a mark where he'd been, so she didn't feel like she was going crazy.

Pushing the covers off her, she climbed out of bed, quickly got ready for school, and headed downstairs.

Normally, Hannah would greet her, looking all perky with a nice, healthy breakfast that always tasted like dirt to Harper. Their baby would be in the high chair, playing with her toys.

Nothing.

No sign of Hannah or her father, or even the new baby that she'd not seen that much of, and had no intention of ever getting close to.

Not even a note.

She checked each room.

Finally, a little panicked in case they'd left her, she made her way upstairs to their room. Before going to Ian and Hannah's, she went to the baby's room. Pushing open the door, she saw the bags were gone, and no sign of the baby.

There was no reason to linger here

At the door, she took a deep breath, remembering how her mother cried when he finally left for good. The bedroom they had once shared, her mother would no longer sleep in because it had too many memories.

Opening the door, Harper stepped inside, and the first thing she noticed was the overwhelming stench of perfume.

Closing the door behind her, she stared at the bed that looked like it hadn't been slept in. Checking the desks, drawers, and the bed for a note, she found nothing.

Just as she was about to take a seat on the edge of

the bed, the doorbell rang. Rushing downstairs, she opened the door without checking to see who it was.

Axel waited for her. This made her pause.

"Oh."

"Wow, chick, don't sound so happy to see me."

"It's … why are you here?"

"I'm your ride for the day."

"Where's Draven?"

"Busy. He's got a thing to do."

"A thing?"

"You talk a lot."

"Don't have much of a choice. You're not exactly helping me out here."

He laughed. "Good one. Come on, school awaits."

"I can walk."

"And I can carry you. Come on, sweet cheeks, it's not that hard."

"Why are you being nice?"

"I'm always a nice guy."

"Not to me, you're not."

"Okay, fine. I like being a nice guy to you, is that fair?" he asked. "Don't make this too hard, and don't overthink everything that is going on right now. It's not very ladylike or becoming of you."

She rolled her eyes. Grabbing her bag, she took one last look inside the house and for the first time felt extremely nervous.

With no sign of Ian or Hannah, she didn't relish the thought of coming home. Closing and locking the door, she noticed Axel kept staring at her face.

"It's nasty." He pointed at the bruise. "He must have hit you hard."

"Does everyone know what happened?"

"No, I'd own it in school though. It will make

you seem pretty badass to me." He whistled, and she rolled her eyes; not going to even try it.

Climbing into his car, she noticed no one else was there. Buck usually rode with Axel.

He climbed into the car and turned on whatever music he was listening to. It sounded like constant noise to her, and then they were on the road with Axel bobbing his head to the beat of the music.

She ignored him and stared out of the car. Where would Hannah and Ian be?

She didn't like to worry about them, but right now, it wasn't like she had much of a choice. Biting her lip, she tried to think of where to look. She didn't even have their cell phone numbers. The day she had detention she ended up going to the office for them to call Hannah to give the message for her to not come and pick her up. She'd gotten a couple of funny looks over that. How can a daughter not know her dad's contact details?

This girl didn't have a clue.

Running a hand down her face, she saw plenty of girls and guys staring at them as they arrived at school.

Axel had never brought a girl to school, at least not that she recalled. The four of them were always together, either arriving in two cars or the one. She hated herself for looking for Draven's car.

"We're here, madam," Axel said.

She climbed out of the car as he rounded the vehicle, coming to stand beside her. He placed an arm around her shoulders, and together they started walking into the school.

"What the hell are you doing?"

"I'm protecting you."

"Axel, I don't need protecting. Not by you or Draven."

"Or Buck or Jett. Don't forget, we come as a

foursome."

She rolled her eyes.

He didn't let her go until they'd gotten to her locker. Much to her surprise, Draven was already waiting for her. Buck and Jett were also there.

"Safe and sound and completely under control," Axel said.

She noticed Jett wasn't carrying a knife. Both of his hands sat by his sides, and she quickly glanced to Buck.

He was the joker of the group.

Axel the loudest.

Draven the deadliest.

Jett the quietest. The way he looked with those knives, she would never underestimate him at all.

Running fingers through her hair, she blew out a breath.

"So, loving the bad chick look," Buck said.

"You should do it more often," Axel said.

Looking from one to the other, she saw no judgment of her black eye. Nothing. Taking a deep breath, she looked at Draven and again, nothing.

"I'll catch up with you guys in a minute. I'll make sure she has everything."

"Adios, suckers," Buck said, stepping away and waving at them.

She forced a smile to her lips and looked at Draven. "You snuck out?"

"Nope. I walked right out the front door. You were pretty out of it."

"Did you sleep at all last night?"

"Yes. Some. Not a lot. I don't sleep a lot. I never have."

"Right, of course." She tucked some hair behind her ear, feeling … odd. "Did you see Ian or Hannah?"

"You're calling him Ian now?"

"I don't know what to call him."

Draven laughed. "I've got a few ideas. You're not going to like it."

"Tell me why you're all being nice to me," she asked.

She'd seen enough movies to know this wasn't going to last. There was always an agenda, always a reason for something like this happening. She didn't like it nor did she trust it.

"We voted on something."

"You did?"

"Yes. It's a pretty intense something." He winked at her.

She glanced around the corridor and saw they were being watched. "Everyone cares about what you do," she said.

"That's because they're assholes and rude and don't know when to look away. Want me to hurt them?"

She shook her head.

"You got to drop the good girl routine, Harp. It's not good. I'll be seeing you. Don't allow yourself to get hurt today. Stay in one piece."

"What happened to my dad and Hannah?"

"They took a road trip. Don't worry. They're alive and busy. You're going to be alone for a couple of weeks. Ian got a … promotion."

"But he didn't take me along with him," she said.

"Would you really want him to after what happened?" He pointed at her eye.

She touched the spot around it and winced. "You've got a point."

"Remember, Harp, don't let everyone walk all over you. You'll end up hurt otherwise." He gave her shoulder a squeeze. "And ignore all those that will stare at you. They're fucking rude."

"My name's Harper."

"I know. Harp sounds musical." He winked at her and off he went, leaving her alone.

Girls were all staring at her, some in shock, others in wonder.

Ignoring all of them, she glanced over at Draven's locker and saw the dent was no longer there. He'd gotten it fixed. She didn't know why that made her happy, but it did.

She worked the combination in her own locker and opened it up slowly. She still didn't trust them to not mess with her in some way.

Nothing fell out, but she stopped as she looked at the jacket. It was neatly folded inside.

Lifting it up, she inspected it, checking all around it and finally, breathing in the scent. It had been washed, but that was fine. There were no more dirty stains.

Knowing she had it back filled her with … hope.

It was kind of weird to be full of hope just from seeing a jacket that was given to her by a woman that killed herself, but that was the way it was.

Putting her books back into her locker, she decided to trust it again. Carrying around a bag full of books was great if someone decided to attack her. Not so great for her shoulders.

Closing her locker, she stepped away and headed to class.

Whispers followed her. Even as she sat in the homeroom, she pulled out a book, one she'd started reading weeks ago, and still she heard them.

"She arrived with Axel."

"I heard she went from bed to bed last night."

"The whore. She's sleeping with all four of them."

"She's being initiated."

"What is so special about her?"

"Look at the black eye. I heard Axel gave her that."

"I heard it was Draven."

"Nah, it had to be Buck."

"Nope, I bet she's been cut as well. Jett."

Ignoring all of them, she went from class to class. Whenever she passed Draven, Axel, Buck, or Jett in the hallway, they'd always stop and look at her. Draven would reach out, touching her hand.

She didn't pull away from him or fight his touch.

Biting her lip, she found herself searching for them all.

There was no sign of Ben, but there were a few jocks around. She kept a wide berth from them. When Ben had grabbed her ass at the diner, she'd been so fucking angry. How dare he touch her. Her body was her own.

No one had a right to touch it but herself, and she wasn't going to give herself to a damn jock. Or to anyone.

By the time lunch arrived, she was starving. The thought of heading home that evening didn't exactly thrill her. She hated going home to an empty place.

Arriving in the cafeteria, she stood in line, waiting to get something to eat. She didn't have time to make herself something that morning. She'd been too busy snooping around.

Within seconds, Draven had his arm across her shoulder. "We've got you lunch."

"What?"

He pulled her out of the line.

"Hey."

"You should have some faith, little Harp."

"Will you stop calling me that?"

Her cheeks flamed as right there, in front of everyone, he marched her toward their table within the cafeteria.

No one sat with them. No one. Not even any girls they were sleeping with were allowed near their table.

In front of everyone, Draven walked her to their table and forced her to sit down.

"You guys really don't take no for an answer, do you?" she asked.

"Only when it counts. Chick says no cock, she doesn't get it," Axel said.

"Are you serious?"

"Totally. We don't joke around about sex. It also has to be safe. Speaking of which, is it true you're a virgin?" Buck asked.

Looking from Axel, to Buck, to Jett, who was biting into an apple, she turned to Draven last.

"Am I awake?"

They all burst out laughing.

"Here, eat this." Draven pushed her plate toward her.

There seemed to be pizza and fries, also an apple pie of some kind.

"It's not poisoned nor does it have laxatives in it," Buck said. "Dude, we should totally do that to the football team. That would be so funny."

"Spiking their drink with laxatives?" Jett asked.

Buck nodded. "Right before a game. You know. Right when they have to be running they'll be squirting all over the field. Game of shit." Buck slapped the table and burst out laughing.

She wrinkled her nose, picking up the pizza. She couldn't help but inspect it … just in case.

"Your food is fine," Draven said.

"Yeah, well, fields of shit is not what I expect." She took a tiny bite, tasting the dull tomato sauce and greasy cheese. It was good. Well, as good as school pizza could be.

"So, I hear we're all camping out at Harper's tonight," Axel said.

"I'll bring the beer."

"Wait, what?"

"You're home all alone, and we're the good guys now. We're going to protect you from the boogeyman. Don't worry. I'll be the one taking you home."

"I've got work," she said.

"Oh, that. You're already fired." Draven reached into his pocket and pulled out a folded envelope. "Here you go. Last payment."

"I barely worked there."

"I know, and you made a lasting impression. When the owner realized that we'd be there every single day to take you home and we wouldn't allow anyone to touch you, she decided to cut her losses," Draven said. "You're jobless."

"And my dad is out of town."

"Oh, here you go." He reached into his other pocket. "I knew there was something I needed to give to you."

She took the envelope and opened it up. Like the other one, money was inside. This one had a lot more within it though.

"What is this? How long is he going to be gone?"

"Just a couple of weeks. Maybe longer. It depends on how well this promotion goes."

Buck, Jett, and Axel snickered.

"Enough with all of this. Tell me the truth, what is going on?"

No one said a word.

"Hey, Draven," Joanne said.

Harper turned to see the blonde cheerleader at their table. She stood so close to Draven.

Any laughter the guys had vanished. They looked pissed off.

"So, I was thinking you could take me out on a date tonight."

"Be warned, boys. She's *thinking*. It could end badly for all of us," Buck said.

They all started to laugh, and Harper stared at her food, trying not to laugh. The cafeteria had gone quiet at Joanne's approach.

Harper wondered what they were all thinking. She glanced over at Draven and saw him watching her. Biting her lip, she didn't look away, even as Joanne tried to step closer to him.

The tension mounted.

"So, how about seven, my place? I'll make it worth your while." She went to reach out and touch him.

They all stood. Draven grabbed Harper's hand, and she had no choice but to stand also.

"Fuck off," Draven said. "No one wants your used-up pussy. Go and serve the football team."

With that, he pulled her along and made sure everyone saw that he was holding her hand.

She got a little thrill at that, especially when Axel, Buck, and Jett moved up behind them.
****

"You want to tell me why my lawyer has taken a case in the city."

"It's good for his career," Draven said.

He sat in his father's office. He wanted nothing more than to check the time to see how long he'd been sitting here. It wasn't like Alan was even paying him any attention. He had a woman behind his desk, servicing his cock.

Knowing how many women he liked to fuck, it made him wonder about the cook and whether or not he'd even seen emotion on his father's face as he fucked her. Clearly not, otherwise he wouldn't have someone else servicing his cock.

"I got a call from Ben Carnes's dad today."

Draven smirked. "What about it?"

"He asked if I was going to pay compensation for his boy being thrown through a window."

"He tripped and fell."

"I was told it was over a girl."

Draven shrugged.

"Does this have anything to do with that Harper girl? The one I hear you're around all the time."

It shouldn't have surprised him that his dad had a spy at school.

To take over the Barries name, he needed a son that was fierce, loyal, and independent.

"What goes on in my life isn't your problem."

"True, and I have to say for most of the pussy you've had in your life, Draven. I wouldn't care. Women in our world know the score. I remember Harper as a child." Draven tensed up. "Sweet little thing, if I remember from the few times I saw her around town, but like all bitches, they have a price. What I do know is she's not part of this world, Draven. She's not even close to it. You continue with her, it'll be a big fucking mistake."

"You've got nothing to worry about." He wasn't going to let Harper go, not even with his dad's warning.

"I'm not worried about me. If you're taking this girl on, the four of you, which is what I know you're all about, then you better make sure she knows to keep her fucking mouth shut if she knows what's good for her. Be warned, Draven, I'm watching this play out. Her mother didn't have a fucking spine, and look what happened to her."

With that, he waved his hand, telling him to go.

He wasn't even out of the office door before the woman servicing his father was spread out on the desk. Draven guessed that was how he dealt with everything. Fucking every single woman within reach.

His mother was, as always, sitting on the stairs, drinking from her bottle of vodka.

"He's a sick bastard, and you're growing up to be the same. Using girls like they're trash. All of them can do better than you. All this town is going to burn for turning a blind eye to what you do."

Ignoring her rants, he left his home. Driving to Harper's place, he took his car even though it was a ten-minute walk away. Axel's car was already there, and he headed inside.

The music was clearly Axel's choice. Draven entered the sitting room and saw his boys had already trashed the place.

"Come on, Harper, live a little." Axel took her hands away from her ears and started to dance with her.

She wouldn't budge. "This is horrible. Absolutely horrible."

Buck rolled his eyes and turned it onto the latest love song. She lowered her hands and sighed. "Ah, peace."

Seconds later the head-banging rock music played.

She groaned. "I need an aspirin."

She walked away, and Buck turned the music down.

"How are things with the old man?" Buck asked.

"Fine. He knows about her." He nodded his head

in the direction she was going.

"We need to make amends for sending his precious lawyer to the city?" Axel asked.

"Nope. You heard anything from your dad?"

"My sire doesn't even want me in the house tonight," Axel said. "There's an auction going on." He twisted the cap off a bottle of beer.

Draven snagged one, doing the same.

"What kind of auction?" Buck asked.

"The kind that sells women. Young women."

"Isn't that a little dangerous? You know, doing it at the house?"

"Why? It's not like cops give a shit about that. Most of the women have been walking around the place naked. Whenever Dad says drop and service, they do. They're trained slaves. It's what they've been working on all summer. Any that try to escape or make waves, end up dead, or hurt in such a way that they don't fight back." Axel shrugged.

Axel lived in the biggest house of Stonewell. If Draven's dad was the muscle, Axel's owned all of it. The town, the land, the people, all of it.

Draven rarely got the chance to see Axel's dad as he was always making deals, always advancing, always building.

He was a deadly son of a bitch that you didn't cross. One day Axel would own all of that. They would all own what they'd been born into. Apart from Buck and Jett. They were going to make them kings just like them.

"Dad doesn't like me being there when the shit hits the fan. There's a lot of perverts, and I'm a pretty boy. He doesn't want to start a war when he refuses to sell his son's ass to a prospective buyer, and I do *not* want to know if I have a price tag." Axel shrugged. "This place is nice."

"Thanks," Harper said, joining them. "Hannah did everything from what I recall." She stared at all the artwork, the furniture with disdain.

He smirked. The disdain was a good look on her. It really brought out the ice within her eyes.

"In that case." Jett pierced the cushion beside him and drew the blade up.

"What are you doing? You can't do that?"

"Why not?" Jett asked. "It's not your money, and Hannah rode your dad's dick when he should have been at home with you and your mom."

He kept on stabbing the blade right in. Then Jett stood up and walked toward her. "Give it a try."

Draven watched as Jett handed her the knife.

She shook her head and held the knife as far away from her own body as was physically possible. "I can't do this. I don't … no."

"You want to, Harper. The good girl inside you is fighting. What do you think when you see Hannah?"

Silence met Jett's words.

Draven sat and watched her. She'd tucked her raven hair behind her ears. The clothes she wore clung to every curve and served to enhance her figure. They were not the usual baggy clothes that hid everything from sight.

"I hate her," Harper said. "I hate her smile and the fact she thinks I want to go on a diet. How she controls everything and I can't even complain to my dad because he believes I'm being difficult on purpose."

"Then stab that perfection," he said.

She stood over one of the cushions, and he watched as she slowly placed the tip of the knife against the pillow.

She held herself still.

He waited. Sipping at his beer, he watched her.

The good girl, fighting with the one in pain. The one that had seen her mother.

"What do you see when you think of your mother?" Draven asked, invading the moment.

Harper turned toward him, the ice in her eyes shining right back at him.

She was breathing heavily, her tits pressing against the band of her shirt that seemed to enhance her cleavage.

"Blood. I think of blood."

"She killed herself."

"I don't even know why she did it. Why she picked that day. What had happened for her to give up?" She took a look at the pillow. "There was so much blood. It turned the water red. She laid in the bath, naked. The water was so cold. Her lips, blue. She looked … looked so sad even in death. I held her even as I called an ambulance. They took so long."

He watched as the tears spilled down her cheeks as she told them what happened. There was pain in her voice as she relived that moment.

She lifted up the blade and hit the cushion. She attacked each cushion, stabbing the blade once inside it. When she finished the last cushion, she picked up the lamp on the end table and threw it across the room until it shattered on the floor.

Draven watched her commit destruction, seeing the pain that she'd been hiding. This was just beneath the surface of her, threatening to come out. She needed them, all of them.

She grabbed a picture frame, one of Hannah and Ian's wedding photos.

She slammed it against the side of the table, and it shattered. She stepped back from the chaos she'd created, and his dick was so hard just watching her. She was a sight of beauty and power as she ran her fingers through her hair.

"I can't believe I did that." She took a step back, escaping the room.

None of them made a move to join her. Draven heard her feet on the stairs as she ran to her bedroom.

"Wow, that was intense," Buck said.

Jett picked up his knife. "Anyone know why the mother offed herself when she did?"

"She saw Ian and Hannah at the park," Draven said. "Not the abandoned park. The one near the supermarket across town."

"She had seen them a lot though. They were always around town," Axel said.

"They had a kid with them," Draven said. "The perfect happy family."

"How do you know this?" Buck asked.

"I heard him telling my dad about it. It was the last time he saw her. Later that night he got the call. Harper was at the hospital."

"Why a trip to the park though?" Buck looked at all of them. "Unless she was, like, seriously depressed how the fuck could that have sent her off?"

"He never went to the park with Harper," Axel said, speaking up. "Remember as kids, Harper and her mother were always there together."

"You remembered quite far back," Draven said.

"Come on, out of all of the moms there, Harper's was always the prettiest."

He couldn't deny it there, but he'd rarely looked at her mother. Finishing off his beer, he told Axel to turn the music up. He got to his feet and headed upstairs to see how Harper was doing.

Entering her bedroom, he saw her clothes were on the floor. Sitting on her bed, he turned toward the bathroom and waited.

Seconds later, she stepped out and let out a gasp, her hand holding the towel in place, covering herself.

"What are you doing in my room?" she asked.

"I rather like it." He lifted his feet up and leaned back. "Ah, the peace."

"I need to get dressed."

He sat up again. "I'm not stopping you."

She didn't move. Those eyes of her gave him a glare that told him in no uncertain terms, to piss the fuck off.

He didn't.

She may think she wanted privacy from him, but it was the last thing she was going to get.

"Please, Draven. I don't know what the hell is going on, but I'm not interested."

He stood up. She didn't back down or even look scared. He took a step toward her.

This time, she took a step back. They kept doing this dance until he had her pressed up against the wall in the bathroom. Putting one hand above her head, he smiled at her.

"You're embarrassed," he said.

"I don't know what it is you think I'm capable of, but you're wrong."

"I don't think you're capable of anything, but if you keep denying your anger, if you keep locking it up tight, you're going to lash out and hurt someone."

"So I should just be like you and like them? Just give in to what makes me angry?"

"You held your mother's dead body. Even when she was dead, you still held her. I don't care who you are, that will fuck with a person's head."

"You think I'm crazy."

"No. I think you're angry and scared."

"And you've decided to be the one to help me?" She tilted her head to the side.

The scent of lemon was heavy in the air.

"Do you know what makes us strong? Me and the guys."

"You're fearless?"

He laughed. "No. Not even close. We have each other's backs. That's our secret. That's what we don't tell anyone else. We have each other's backs, and it is a beautiful thing. We know that no matter what fight we get into, we'll always have each other."

"Why are you telling me this?"

"We're offering you the chance to have us at your back."

She stared at him, and he saw he'd surprised her.

"You want me to be part of your group?" she asked, frowning.

"That's what we're offering." He reached out, stroking a finger down her knuckles. "It's not easy being part of us. You're going to have to learn to fight. To not back down, and above all else, to ignore that need to be the good girl."

"My mom told me to be that."

"And you're going to have to ignore it if you want to survive. Once you become one of us, there's no backing down. There's no out. There's only us."

"Do I get a say in all of this?"

"Yes. It's your choice if you're in or not." He teased the fabric of her towel. She didn't push him away even as he touched flesh.

"What is all this then? The cafeteria, taking me to school, being at home with me."

"We're giving you a taste of what could happen. Of what it would mean to have us on your side." He placed a finger inside her towel and gave it a tug. She caught it before it fell from her body.

He didn't get to see anything.

"We do have certain … rules and recommendations."

"Rules? You guys have rules?"

"Yes, and you only get to hear them when you agree."

"I have to agree to this?"

"We take consent very seriously, Harper. It's one of our hard limits." He was so close to her. Her lips looked so inviting. He'd been wanting to kiss her for a long time now.

Harper Miller had been someone he'd wanted, but they were so far apart.

She the good girl.

He the bad boy.

They came from different lives. If she decided to do this, then she'd have to be prepared for everything they threw at her. Cupping her cheek, he tilted her head back.

"If I could take back what you saw, I would. No one should have to see that."

"Have you ever seen a dead body?" she asked.

"Yes."

He saw the tears in her eyes.

"I get nightmares at times. I think she's there, begging me to save her. To arrive home on time. I … I get so angry," she said.

"I know. You have to get angry. She left you."

"She's dead, Draven."

"I know, but that doesn't mean you can't be angry. Get angry. Don't lock it inside."

"No one likes it when they get angry."

"I'm not like most guys." He'd love to see her get angry, to finally let go and to not conform like the good girl she'd been trained to be.

Chapter Seven

The next week was a little surreal for Harper. Between her four new friends, which was quite a stretch considering she didn't know all that much about them, they didn't leave her alone.

From school to home, then back again, someone was with her at all times, not once leaving her alone.

If it wasn't Draven, it was Axel. They were the two drivers. Buck and Jett took turns babysitting her at night.

Still no word from her father, and she couldn't help but feel guilty for hurting him. No matter how many times Draven told her to not feel that way, she did. Hitting him went against everything she'd been taught. Violence didn't solve anything.

Ben and the rest of the jocks were also back in school. Out of all of them, Ben looked the worse for wear.

One look from him and she wanted to run and hide. Draven, again, wouldn't let her. He made her sit with them every single dinner time.

If they had the same classes, she no longer sat alone. The teachers didn't call on her to answer questions. Her life had done a complete turnaround.

Late one Friday night, she sat alone. Jett had been with her until an hour ago when he had to leave after getting a phone call. She picked up a slice of pizza and was watching television when Draven arrived.

All of her *new* friends had keys. They let themselves in. Most of the time they crashed in the sitting room, or took one of the spare bedrooms.

She always went to her room, and if Draven was staying the night, he slept in her bed. It was kind of a weird setup.

She found herself enjoying his company more and more, which again, was weird.

He put the keys in his pocket and collapsed onto the sofa.

"You changed the sofa," he said.

"I wasn't going to live in a mess. I doubt Hannah will like it."

"Who gives a shit about Hannah?" He took a slice of pizza, and she watched him chew.

"What is the deal between you and Hannah?"

"Nothing. Why?"

"You know her, and she's strange around you."

He smirked. "That's one of the things you'll know if you join us."

She sighed. None of them had pressured her, even though each day they gave her a tease of what it would mean to join with them. She'd never had someone she could call her own before.

The thought of having all four of them was kind of … nice.

"Do I have to kill someone?" she asked.

"Can't tell you that. Those are the rules."

"You do know rules suck."

"They don't. They're pretty fucking great if I do say so myself." He winked at her, and she got up, putting the uneaten pizza back in the box.

"I don't know about this. I can't even make a decision if I don't know what it is I'm getting myself into." She ran fingers through her hair and grabbed a bottle of water out of the fridge. Draven had followed her, watching her every move. "I don't know what I'm doing here."

"Why do you feel like you have to know what you're doing?"

"Up until a couple of weeks ago, I didn't even

register to you as a person. Now you're saying you want me to join your club, even though no other girl has ever been allowed to. They've had sex with you. I've given you no reason whatsoever, why you'd want me in your little gang." She took a sip of water.

"You know we could rectify that one problem," he said, stepping up toward her.

She didn't move away as he touched her elbow.

"I'm not having sex with you."

"You want to remain a virgin forever?"

She kept her lips sealed. Staying a virgin wasn't on her list of plans. What she refused to give into, was that curiosity he had her feeling.

"You're wrong," he said, stroking his finger up her arm, grazing across the curve of her breast.

She didn't pull away, nor did he stop or go any further. The touch was light, almost an accident, only, she knew better. Draven didn't do anything by accident.

"What am I wrong about?" she asked.

"That I didn't notice you. I did."

"Really?"

"Really." He leaned in close, his lips stroking across her neck, and she held her breath.

Pleasure rushed through her body. She wasn't immune to his touch. She was stronger than this.

"I noticed you, Harper, since kindergarten I noticed."

"You're lying."

"Oh, I'm not. I noticed, but the difference here, is you're good and I'm not."

"What changed?"

"You. You were unreachable to me. Too goody-goody for an asshole like me, like us."

"Us?"

"There's a darkness in your eyes, and no one else

can see it. They expect you to forget what happened, to move on. I know that it's not so easy."

"You've seen death."

"I've caused it. You're not an idiot, Harper. You know what Stonewall is like. It's why you've stayed so far away from us all. Axel, Buck, Jett, myself, we're a toxin that is so ingrained in this town, no one can get rid of us. You've watched the cops look the other way. You know, deep down inside, that if I was to take your body right now, rape you, no cop would come to me in the morning. I'm untouchable."

"No one should have that kind of power."

"Just because it shouldn't happen, doesn't mean it doesn't happen. Unfairness in the world is always there. You got to learn to fight for your place, or always be pushed over, beat down."

"You're giving me the option to run with sharks."

He laughed. "Sharks don't run. We wait for our prey to come to us willingly, and we snatch it up."

His lips were so close.

She felt that connection between them, the draw that tugged her. She'd never been kissed by a guy, and right now, Draven was very much taking pole position.

"Are you the leader?" she asked.

He smiled.

"Technically, Axel should be the leader, but I'm the one that gets shit done. That's all you get to know for tonight."

"Can we have a deal?" she asked. "Sorry, can we make a deal?"

"A deal. You want to bargain with me?"

Surely, how hard could it be?

"Sure, why not?"

He smiled. "I can't wait to see what you have to offer or what it is you even want from me."

"Okay, erm, it's quite simple. I'd like to know more. One thing a day before I make a decision."

"You don't get anything in this world without me getting something in return."

"What would you want?" she asked.

He smiled. "How about I tell you what I want on the day."

"I can't do anything illegal," she said, knowing deep down, she could. "Or wrong."

He laughed. "I'm not that bad, Harper. Have a little faith, and I believe you can do whatever you want to do. Don't underestimate yourself."

"Kind of hard to do right now."

"True. I've never claimed to be a good guy. I'm not a good person. I do bad things. It's what I've been designed to do. You know the rumors. I won't lie to you."

"You won't tell me the full truth either."

"The truth can be really overrated." He sighed. "So, we're at an impasse."

"No. I still want to know. One piece of information and in return I'll give something to you or do something. Conditions are, nothing illegal or anything that can break the law and end with me in jail."

"You know that gives me a lot of things to work with."

"I know. It's quite a thing, but I'm willing to try." She wanted to know more before she committed to anything.

She hated being alone, and right now, that was exactly what she was, alone. She missed the times that she didn't mind being on her own.

"You owe me something right now," he said. "How will you pay me?"

"That's up to you."

He stared into her eyes, waiting. Time seemed to stand still. "I know what I want."

"What?"

"I want a kiss."

"Seriously? That's it?"

"That's it. One kiss," he said.

To him it was just one kiss. To her, she'd never been kissed before.

"What is it?" he asked.

"Nothing."

"If you decide to join us, Harper, you can't keep secrets."

"None of you have any secrets, at all?"

"None that matter. I don't need to know who Axel is screwing or what Jett's thinking. The important stuff we tell each other. It's why we're so close. No secrets. Always sharing."

There was something in the way he said sharing that made her want to ask him exactly what he meant.

She didn't.

"I've never been kissed," she said.

"Not at all."

"No."

"I'd be your first kiss?"

"Yes."

"That's quite a responsibility," he said.

"Stop mocking me." She went to hit him, but he caught her hand.

"I'm not mocking you."

"I bet you've kissed a lot of girls."

"Are you jealous?"

"No."

"You sound jealous."

"I don't even know you, Draven. I can't be jealous of someone I don't know." She pulled her hand away, but he wouldn't let her move.

"I'm going to kiss you. I'm not going to mock you, but don't even try to hit me again."

One of his hands went to her hip, and she felt frozen into place with nowhere else to go. Draven was the one in control right now, not her.

His gaze went to her lips, and she couldn't help but lick them. Her mouth was so dry, her heart racing. She couldn't think. It was crazy.

He cupped her cheek with the other hand, sliding back to grip her neck.

Breathe.

Breathe.

Breathe.

You can do this.

Don't panic.

Don't screw this up.

"Don't think about it, Harper. Let it happen."

"*Good girls don't have sex until they're ready, Harper.*"

"*Everyone prefers a good girl.*"

"*Bad girls are hated.*"

"*Don't be a bad girl.*"

Blood.

Watery, cold blood.

Lifeless eyes.

Her mother dead.

Her mother had been a good girl, and she ended up killing herself in the bathtub.

Heart racing, she gripped Draven's arm as his lips crashed against hers. The first touch sent a thrill down her spine.

Ignoring the warnings in her mind, she focused on the pleasure of his lips. He pressed her back against the kitchen counter as his grip on her hip tightened.

His body slid against hers, every hard inch making her very aware of how much he liked being close to her. There was no mistaking the length of his cock as he rested against her stomach.

She moaned as his tongue slid across her lips, and opening her mouth, she caved to the pleasure of his kiss.

He held her neck, tilting her head back and showing her what he wanted. Plundering her mouth, he slid the hand at her hip, up until it grazed beneath her tit. So close. So intimate and yet not pushing her boundaries.

She wanted more.

His thumb slid up across her nipple, and she cried out. The instant pull of pleasure went straight between her thighs from that single touch.

She'd never known how good it was to be a little bad. Good girls didn't kiss boys that didn't belong to them. Draven wasn't hers, and yet she didn't want him to stop.

All too soon, he pulled away. He held her arms, keeping her steady, which she was thankful for, as she didn't think she'd be able to stand on her own.

She'd nearly lost it all because of a kiss. She should be mortified, and yet, she was … thrilled.

Licking her lips, she was sure she could taste him, the lasting impression of his lips.

Her first kiss.

Draven Barries.

One quarter of Stonewall's bad boys.

He cupped her cheek, and his thumb ran across her lips. "I think I've just found something I enjoy doing."

"It was just a kiss," she said.

He chuckled, leaning in close, and she wondered if he'd kiss her again.

He didn't.

"You can think that, but I know the truth. I totally rocked your first kiss, bad girl." He took the water from her and tipped it back.

She watched him drink, fascinated by him.

Get a grip, Harper.

It was one kiss.

That was all.

Nothing special.

Nothing life-changing.

She only hoped she didn't lose herself in this process.

****

Draven stood in the warehouse with Axel and their fathers along with several soldiers.

For a Sunday morning, this was not how he wanted to spend his day, but the needs of the Barries and Cook children meant they had to be there.

Two men were hung upside down, and a woman was bound to a chair. Blood covered the floor.

He wished this was the worst thing he'd ever seen in his life, but it wasn't. The auctions, where some of the merchandise got tested, were among some of his worst-ever memories. Still, it was all work, and if he showed any sign of weakness, his father would make his life a living hell.

He had no reason to allow that to happen.

Standing in the warehouse while they exacted vengeance for stealing dope and trying to run, was not going to get him a punishment he didn't deserve.

Axel was on his cell phone.

One look at his screensaver, and Draven snorted. There was a picture of the five of them together, taken during their lunch break last week.

Harper looked petrified while the rest of them looked smug.

"She made a decision yet?" Axel asked.

Seeing as he and Harper shared a connection, the guys had left it up to him to deal with her, to bring her into the fold, or to threaten her to silence. While he did that, they were working on her trust with them.

He knew she had a bond with Jett. They were quite happy being alone together, and nothing seemed to scare her when it came to his knife fetish. In fact, she'd started bringing him fruit so he had an excuse to always have it in his hands.

Buck made her laugh, even when she clearly didn't want to.

What Draven had come to see with her, was if they didn't help her through her craziness, she was constantly sad. The darkness clung to her like shadows refusing to move on.

Fortunately, for the most part, the pointing fingers and whispered rumors were no longer circling.

Which brought him back to now.

Buck and Jett were with Harper and per their father's instructions, he and Axel were watching torture, to prepare them.

"No decision yet."

"You think she's going to accept what we have to offer?"

"Only time will tell." Part of him still expected her to run screaming. Himself, and his three friends. The four of them, bound to one woman. United as one. It was a long shot. A couple of women had enjoyed playing with them, but long term, he doubted it. Besides, they all came with their baggage.

Part of it was this: if Harper wanted to leave Stonewall, she wouldn't be able to once she accepted the four of them. Being part of them meant her life would remain here. She'd never go without, but her life would never be the same.

"Please, I'm begging you," the woman said. "I'll do anything."

Draven watched as Axel's dad slid the blade across her neck. Blood seeped down from the wound, coating her dress.

"I don't allow scum to live."

The woman died seconds later, her body jerking as the last bit of her life's blood leaked out of the cut. The bitch had only been trying to steal dope while the men had wanted more, and tried to make a deal with the cops.

For the men, Draven waited as they were hacked to pieces while they were still alive. They started on their dicks, removing their balls and shoving them into their tongue-less mouths.

"This is gross," Axel said.

"Yep."

Once it was over, the lesson was learned and they were free to go.

Climbing into Axel's car, they took off, heading back to Harper's house. Neither of them spoke while they traveled the first half an hour. They didn't need to talk as they processed what they'd seen.

Their fathers were also giving them a warning. Taking on Harper was fine, but she needed to learn to keep her mouth shut or she'd suffer the consequences just like them.

"You ever wonder why our dads haven't killed our moms?" Axel asked.

"No reason to? Boredom? They're worth more to them alive than dead."

"I've seen the way my dad looks at my mom," Axel said. "He spends most of his time wanting to murder her."

Draven thought about the cook.

No matter how many women Alan fucked, he always came back to her, to the cook. To the woman he wouldn't allow to move on. He also knew that his mother wasn't allowed to be mean to her either.

Strange.

He hadn't really thought about it until then.

"It doesn't matter why they don't kill them. They're useless to them anyway." His own mother was often on drugs or halfway down a liquor bottle. It wasn't like she was part of the conversation or even the world half the time.

"What are we going to do about Ben and the jocks?"

"Wait and see what their attack is going to be. Keep an eye on Harper. I saw the way Ben was looking at her. I don't like it."

"Harper's really fucking beautiful."

"You sound shocked," Draven said, laughing.

He pressed the button to push the window down, pushing his arm out to the wind as Axel drove.

"I guess I've found easy chicks more … entertaining."

"You're not wanting blue balls. That's all it is."

"True. True. I like to have my dick serviced. You think this is going to work with us? The four of us, one of her."

"With time. She's broken at the moment and needs time to heal." He had no doubt she still saw her mother's lifeless body, even when she didn't want to. That kind of shit stayed with someone.

"Do you think her father will stay away?" Axel asked.

"You're full of the questions today, aren't you?"

"I just watched a guy have his dick chopped off,

and dismembered. It affects a guy's head. You know that shit always does. I don't even want to think about it, and yet it's the first thing I see right now."

Draven smirked. "Think about all the chicks you're not going to fuck."

"We're weird. You know that, right. Real fucking weird."

"That's our charm."

They arrived back at Harper's place. Her father would arrive soon enough. For now, Draven had made sure he knew not to touch Harper again. He'd already fucked up her life enough. The least he could do was not strike her.

The bruise on her face had started to fade, but it was still a reminder of the fact he'd hit her.

Entering her home, he heard music playing and laughter coming from the sitting room. Axel closed the door behind him, and he stood watching, Buck and Jett dancing with Harper.

She wore a dress, shock of all shocks. It was the kind that lifted up when she gave a little spin.

Her raven hair was bound up on top of her head, and she looked beautiful, happy.

"Look who are back," Buck said.

"It's about time you came back," Jett said.

Harper stopped dancing. Jett wrapped an arm around her waist and held her against himself. He forced her to keep on moving.

Draven watched her. His friend was holding her, protecting her. It's the way it was supposed to be. Stepping into the room, he took her hand, gave her a twirl and settled her ass against his dick.

Axel stepped forward. The song changed, going into a slow beat, one filled with seduction and promise.

"Did you miss us?" Draven asked.

"A little bit." She wrapped her arms around Axel's neck.

He didn't let her go as she pulled Axel in closer.

"You look a little hungry there, Harper," Axel said.

Draven watched as Axel cupped her cheek, his thumb stroking along her lips.

Leaning forward, he kissed her neck. This was not new to them. Harper was new because rather than use her, they wanted her to be part of them, to be exclusive to them, to accept that darkness, which curled within them, drawing them close to hell.

All four of them held the devil, a source of evil deep within their souls. Jett was raped and abused by men who should have protected him. Buck had been tossed out of his home and forced to live on the streets before he was able to come back. He and Axel were the ones that were the devil. They lived with them, thrived under their tutelage. Every single day, they had to learn more to be ready to take over, to be forced into a world that they neither chose or wanted.

Yet, Harper still held that light, but he saw the darkness festering beneath the surface begging to come out. She only had a cloud above her head, the pain of finding her mother, the death of her innocence.

She belonged to them, and they would protect her, care for her.

"What do you say to getting your second kiss?"

"Draven?" she asked.

"Axel, why don't you kiss our girl?"

"I have to hear it from her lips first. I don't take what is not freely given."

Kissing her neck, he flicked his tongue across the pulse and waited. She didn't tell him to stop or beg him to leave her alone.

Harper may think they were the ones that held the power, but she was so wrong. The only person with any power here was her. She controlled them, all of them. Harper would be the one to bind them together forever.

"Yes," she said.

Axel cupped her cheek, and suddenly his mouth was on hers.

Draven watched as his friend stroked his tongue across her lips.

Taking hold of her hands, Draven held her still, getting her to submit to Axel. She wasn't bold in her kisses. They were tame, unhurried, new. They would teach her all she needed to know, so long as she gave herself to them.

Seconds later, Axel broke from the kiss, and Draven recognized the lust shining back at him. He'd felt it long before this. Banding his arm around her waist, he turned toward Buck.

"It's your turn, Buck."

"Draven, I don't know," she said.

"If you don't want to taste him, don't. Remember, this is about you. What you want to do." He kissed her neck again.

"Okay," she said.

"You want Buck to kiss you?"

"Yes."

She didn't sound so sure, and Buck took his time getting out of his seat. "I guess it's left to me to do this properly," Buck said. Harper chuckled. "Be prepared to have your mind blown."

"Already blown."

"Well, I'll have to do even better, won't I?" Buck smirked, and suddenly, his hands were on her face, and his lips were on hers.

Out of all of them, Buck had the least finesse. He

nibbled her lip, and Draven laughed as he pulled away.

"Mind blown," he said.

Buck walked away, and Draven turned her toward Jett.

"I'm going to be called a slut."

"Ignore what the whores say at school," Jett said, getting to his feet. "They're jealous. Given the option, they'd love to be in your place." He didn't rush. He leaned in close and brushed his lips against hers. "I hope you decide to come into our fold, Harper. I think you'd be surprised."

He spun her around and had her dancing with him.

They ordered more pizza and partied in her home. All the time, Draven didn't let her go. He needed her close to him, and releasing her was no longer in his plans.

Chapter Eight

"Good girls don't skip class."

Harper skipped class. She followed Draven out to the woods where she'd witnessed him feeding a guy some dirt. He held her hand as they walked across the ground. Since it had been raining there were patches of really soggy mud. The sneakers she wore were already covered, and some had gotten into one of them.

Gross.

They were alone, not that she'd complained. Since kissing all four guys, she'd felt shy. Had they all compared notes on her kissing? She hated the thought of them doing something like that. Surely, they wouldn't.

She hoped not.

Oh, well, she'd soon find out.

"I'll make a bad girl out of you yet," Draven said, pushing her against the tree.

"I didn't get given a choice here. You grabbed my hand and walked me out of school. Teachers saw. I'll get another detention."

"You'll get nothing of the sort. They know you're with me."

"Do you really think you've got that much power with them?"

"Teachers are paid to turn a blind eye."

"I don't like that. No one should have that much power."

"We own Stonewall and everyone in it."

"You don't own me," she said.

"True. I guess that is a decision you're going to have to make."

"Decisions." She tilted her head to the side. "Tell me something more." Even as she asked, she knew it would come with a cost. With Draven, she trusted him.

He'd never force her to push too far. She could handle whatever he had to throw at her.

"I can tell you anything and everything. There will be a price."

"I know, and I'm ready."

"You are?"

"Yes."

"Tell me what you want to know. There's a lot for you to take in, and you've got to be ready for it."

Staring into his green eyes, she waited, trying to think of what she wanted to ask. "What will I have to do?"

"You'll need to prove your loyalty to us and us alone. Be willing to fight with us, not against us. You know my family are not good people. You're going to have to be willing to break your own code when it comes to them. Belonging to us, means belonging to them."

She opened her mouth to speak, but he tutted and pressed a finger against her lips. "No, not your time to speak. All will be revealed in time. You need to pay the toll."

"What do you want?" she asked.

"Tonight, at your place, I want you to get naked."

This made her pause. "What?"

"I won't have sex with you or take advantage."

"This is a pretty big leap from a kiss to seeing each other naked."

"It's a good leap. I'll be naked as well."

"Yeah, that makes me feel so much better."

She tried to move away from the tree, but he wouldn't let her.

"I need you to trust me to do the right thing," he said. "I'm not going to push your boundaries."

"My boundaries are already being pushed."

"Then you don't want to be a part of us."

"I didn't say that."

"We're offering you something we've never given anyone a chance to do before. It is up to you if you take it."

"This is not fair," she said. "I didn't ask for this."

"Then tell me to walk away. Tell me no and I'll let the guys know you don't want to."

She held onto his arms, refusing to let him go. She didn't want him to go and stop this process. Being part of their group hadn't been in her life choices, and yet, she couldn't bring herself to tell him no.

"I haven't made up my mind yet. I don't want you to go and tell them no. A deal's a deal, and I'll see it through."

"Don't make it sound like I'm forcing you."

This made her laugh. "You're not forcing me. It's all just new. I wanted to know something, you told me, and now I must pay the price. Fair is fair, even if I don't like it. I recognize this place."

"I know."

"You were feeding that guy dirt. You really didn't have to put it in my locker though. I could have done without the dirt."

"It was fun."

"Not for the guy eating it."

"He was touching girls he shouldn't. We're bad guys, but we also have our limits."

"So you're bad guys with morals?"

"Something like that."

"I think that's pretty interesting," she said. "What do people do when they cut class?"

"Your mother really did a number on you, didn't she?"

"She told me how important it always was to be a good girl. To be nice, to be kind. To always do the right thing."

"And now?"

"She always did the right thing, and she hated her life." She shrugged. "It's hard. I just want to do things to make her proud, but at the same time, I'm so angry. How can I make a dead person proud?"

"You can't."

"How do you do it?"

"How do I do what?"

"Not care? Not think about what others are saying behind your back?"

"The problem you have, Harper, is the fact you care. You give a shit. I don't. I stopped giving a shit a long time ago. No one cares about us, not really. Teachers, cops, social workers, they're all there to do a job. You know what I realized?" She shook her head. "Every single person I've come across has a price."

"A price?"

"Yes, a price. An amount they're willing to take to do bad things. Once you realize how fucked they all are, it makes you stop. Your mother had a price."

"Draven, don't."

"You don't want to hear it because it's true. Her price was your father's love. Everyone else could go fuck themselves. She didn't think about you or what it would do to you when she hurt herself."

Pain flooded her as she stared up at Draven.

His words were so … right, and she hated him for it.

Anger filled her. She wanted nothing more than to hit him and to hurt him. Only, she couldn't do it. Why hurt *him* when it wasn't him that pissed her off? It was her mother. She'd killed herself for selfish fucking reasons, and it angered her, even now.

"Let it out," Draven said.

She shook her head, stumbling away from him. Breaking from his body and the tree, she walked through the dirt, slipping in a wet patch until she fell to the ground. Taking in deep breaths, she tried to think of everything and anything that wasn't her mother.

Cutting off the image of the blood.

She knew he was right.

Her mother's price had been her father's love. Ian had walked away from the both of them, cut them both off as if they didn't matter to him. Passed them over for Hannah. She still didn't know who Hannah was.

Did she even want to know?

"Come on, it's time for you to get home."

He lifted her up out of the dirt. She didn't fight him as they walked back to his car. Her head pounded. Pain filled her body, and as he helped her into the passenger seat, she gave up to him, letting him guide her, take control.

One glance in the mirror, she saw how pale she was. Everything had been sucked out of her body. The truth was a hard thing to accept, but what more could she do?

There was not much to the drive home as she lived so close to the woods. She didn't even notice the passing houses as he drove. Only when she and Draven were entering her home did she finally focus.

"I'm going to call us a pizza."

"Don't worry about me. I think I'm all pizza'd out right now."

"Pizza'd out? How does anyone get tired of pizza?"

"Oh, it happens." She didn't bother going to the kitchen.

She went straight upstairs to her bathroom, removing her clothes and throwing them in the laundry basket. Stepping under the spray of water, she relished the cold chill that rushed over her from the water. She didn't turn it up, wanting to freeze. Wishing more than anything to feel the cold. To feel anything other than the pain right now.

Eyes closed, she tried to think of sunshine and long summers.

Water.

Anything but the memory of what she was trying to escape.

She let out a scream as Draven banded his arm around her waist.

"It's okay. It's just me." He pressed a kiss to her shoulder, and she tensed.

"You're naked, aren't you?" It was a stupid question. She knew it was, and yet she still asked it.

"You know I am." He stroked a hand down her arm. "You were crying."

"I was?"

"Yes. Sobbing. I've got you now."

"I don't know what the hell is going on with me."

"You're grieving. Did you even cry when you found your mother?" he asked.

She shrugged. The only thing she remembered was screaming. Of begging for help. Her hands shook so much.

"I don't remember."

"You need to let it go."

"Is that what you do? You let things go?"

"I don't cry. For anything or anyone."

"I don't believe that."

He laughed. "You should. I'm not a good person."

"You keep telling me that, and yet you're here."

"I took your first kiss, Harper. I watched you kiss

my three friends. I'm in the shower naked with you. I want you to be part of us. You don't know all that means now, but soon, you will."

"You make it sound like it's inevitable that I'm going to pick you guys."

"You'd be a fool not to."

"You're biased."

"I know what we can give you and what you can give us. You'd never be alone again. We'd never push you aside or take our lives. We'd be everything for you."

"And if I say no?"

"Then, I'll leave. We'd all leave you alone."

The thought of being without them scared her. They had helped her in the past few weeks. "I don't want you to leave."

"Then I won't leave. You're going to have to make a choice soon, Harper." He kissed her shoulder. "For your own safety."

She stared at the tiled wall. Without her father, she found it easier for her to think. With the guys around, she didn't have to think about anything. They helped to ease the pain within her.

Slowly, she turned around to face Draven, forcing herself to keep her gaze on his face.

"Was that so hard to do?"

"Not as hard as I thought it would be," she said.

He took hold of her hand and placed it on his chest.

The ink on his arms and body surprised her. "I didn't think you could get ink at our age?"

He laughed. "I know a guy that knows a guy. I can have anything I want done. All you got to do is say the word, and it's yours."

"That easy?"

"You'll learn that it is always that easy. So easy,

all the freaking time. From ink to a shoulder to cry on. To someone to dance with. We'll be there for you. No matter what."

Her palm lay over his heart, and she gasped as he touched her, his hand over her heart. She didn't move or look down. Staring at his chest, she wondered if he saw her … if he liked what he saw.

Tilting her head back, she watched him. He stared right back at her.

"I love the size of your tits."

She burst out laughing as he wrapped his arm around her waist and pulled her in against him. His body pressed against hers.

She gasped as he moved her up against the cold tile wall.

"There's a lot of things about you I like."

"There is?"

"Yes. I like your hair. How dark it is. I don't know it what it is, but I can always find you in a crowded room."

"It's kind of a weird thing to like."

"Your eyes. They tell me a story that you won't allow yourself to share."

"I think that's enough."

"Your tits and ass. I like watching your ass as you walk away from me. Hannah doesn't have many gifts, but I do like seeing your butt. It's the only thing I like though. I want to hide all of you so no one else can see what you've got to offer."

"This is crazy."

"I also like that you don't try to impress me. You've never shaken your tits and ass to gain my attention. You've always been different."

"I've always been good."

"You'll always be good. You've just got to learn

to embrace a little mean in your life." He spread her legs, and she gasped.

"I'm not ready," she said.

"I told you I wasn't going to fuck you."

"You also didn't mention coming into the shower with me and yet here we are." She put her hand against his chest.

His cock pressed against her stomach, and she tried not to panic.

"I know when to keep it in my pants."

"It's not in your pants though. It's very much out of it, and I can feel it."

He smiled. It was the kind of one that made her think of dirty things, of things she shouldn't be thinking about.

"Don't panic." His lips brushed her neck, and she closed her eyes against the onslaught of pleasure that hit her hard. "Kiss me."

Tilting her head back, she gave him the kiss he so clearly wanted, moaning as his tongue filled her mouth. Gripping his shoulders, she forgot about their nakedness and instead, basked in his kiss.

"I'm really bad at this," she said, breaking from the kiss.

"Really? I think you're actually really, really good." He took possession of her mouth again. Seconds passed before he finally broke the contact. "Besides, we can practice a lot."
****

Draven woke up the next morning and found Harper gone. The side of her bed was clearly made, and he couldn't help but smile at that. She always tried to keep everything so neat and tidy around him.

It was sweet as fuck.

So was making out with her last night.

He'd made out a lot of times, and usually, he didn't much care for it. When it came to Harper though, she completely blew his mind of expectations.

The scent of coffee called to him. Climbing out of the bed, he went and took a piss, washed his hands, and prepared for the day of school.

He figured they would have to go today. He couldn't keep on stealing her away, no matter how much fun it was. She wanted to graduate, and he didn't want to take too much from her. Her future belonged to them. The least he could give her was her graduation.

Pulling on his jeans and tugging on a shirt, he headed downstairs.

Axel, Jett, and Buck were already eating their cereal at the kitchen counter.

Harper was dressed as well, her raven hair falling all around her, and he watched as she spread peanut butter on some toast.

One look at him, and her cheeks flushed that pretty shade of pink he loved.

"Are you two going to flunk it today?" Axel asked.

"No. I've got to go. I still want to graduate, and it's pretty important that I actually attend classes," she said.

"Spoilsport."

She shrugged. "Eat something."

"Yes, Mom."

She rolled her eyes.

He watched her as she picked up her piece of toast and took a bite.

Draven snagged the other slice of toast, and she chuckled and put some more bread in the toaster.

With her back turned, he looked toward Axel, who nodded at her back.

Draven winked. None of the guys had a clue what he was meaning, and it was so funny to watch them.

"I'm driving her today."

"I can walk, you know."

"I know," Draven said.

"But it's so fun to see the evil look other chicks give you," Buck said. "Do you have any idea how many want to audition for the spot in our club?"

"I have no idea."

"Quite a few," Jett said.

"They didn't want to be part of us," Axel said. "They just wanted the reputation of banging the four bad boys."

"It didn't do them any good," Draven said.

"Why not?"

"We didn't go back for seconds or thirds. It means something in boy world," Buck said.

"Okay. I don't really know what it means, but good for you." She spread more toast, and he took another slice from her plate.

She didn't even have a clue what it meant to be with them, all of them.

"I've heard rumors," Harper said. "I don't know how accurate they all are, but I've heard them."

"What rumors are they?" he asked.

"That all of them have to sleep with all of you."

Draven chuckled.

"It's not something we force on them. Besides, half the time it's them that beg for a gangbang. We simply oblige them," Buck said.

"Is that what you're expecting from me?" she asked, looking between each of them.

Draven saw that made her nervous. "Is this another question?"

She nibbled her lip.

"Remember, a question for something in return."

"No, it's not. I'm not ready to know that answer yet."

"Chicken," Axel said, laughing.

"Very much a chicken," Buck said.

Much to their surprise it was Jett who made the chicken sounds.

"Stop it," she said. "Some things in life you don't need to know."

"Well, I'm looking forward to when your curious mind won't give you a break," Axel said. "I've got all the knowledge you need." He grabbed his junk.

"Wow." She shook her head. "It's time for us to go."

Draven finished her coffee. She didn't put any sugar in it.

Grabbing her bag, he threw it over his shoulder and walked out of the house to his car. Just as he got to his car, he noticed his father, parked up a couple of feet away, on the street.

This was the first time Alan had ever shown an interest in him.

"Get in the car, Harper," Draven said.

He handed her the bag and took off down the street. Axel, Buck, and Jett stayed near his car, protecting her.

As he approached his father's car, the driver climbed out, expecting him, and opened the door.

Climbing in, he took a seat opposite his father, who was alone.

"What are you doing here?" he asked.

"Watch your lip, boy. You may have everyone else running scared in this town, but I know where you came from."

"The cook?" Draven stopped laughing as his

father didn't argue with him.

Well shit.

"You're going to continue with the Harper business?" Alan asked.

"Have you got a problem with me and the guys picking her?"

"She's not for our world, Draven. She's dangerous, and I don't like that you're wasting my time with this. Girls like her grow a conscience, and we don't have the time to deal with her prick of need to do the right thing. That's what makes her dangerous. If she can't keep her mouth shut, she's dead. Think about who you're spending your time with."

"She's got what it takes."

"I will only make myself clear about this once. Either end this or make sure she is so bound to you and your friends that she will be loyal. Bitches like her, they grow a conscience, and I don't have time like that on my hands to deal with that. Always know there are enemies ready to take you down that will prey on you. I expect more out of you. You're my son."

"Is Axel getting the same warning?"

"Axel is not my responsibility. You are. Deal with that. Get out."

Draven left the car, and he saw his friends were watching him. He shook his head. He'd talk to them later.

"Was that your dad?" Harper asked when he got behind his wheel.

"The one and only."

"You okay?"

"I'm fine." Pulling out of the driveway, he headed toward the school.

Why was his father getting involved? Why did he feel the need to interfere now? Alan was always interested in his own business, his own future. Draven was able to do whatever the hell he wanted, and no one got in the way. However, he'd never picked a girl like had he with her. All the other women he'd been with, they hadn't meant anything to him. She did. Harper was a good girl. Her whole life she'd been bred that way, to be good, to not make waves. Glancing over at her, he saw her staring out of the window.

He also knew she was dying inside.

A lot.

Every single day.

Pretending her life was fine.

There was a real passion beneath the surface. The way she was with him, she wasn't like that with anyone else.

Tapping his thumb against the steering wheel, he pulled into the high school.

"Are you sure you're okay?" she asked. "You're, like, really quiet."

He chuckled. "Just something my father said is all. Nothing new there."

"Do you want to talk about it?"

"I really, really don't."

She nodded. "Do you know when my father will come back home?"

"He'll be back in a couple of weeks, probably." Draven had hoped Ian and Hannah would stay away. With his father already showing his displeasure at his interest in Harper, it was clear, he was going to meddle. Harper wasn't part of their world, never had been, and it clearly bothered his father for him to bring her into it.

He sat back in the car, thinking about how best to deal with his father.

Loyalty was something that was built through trust and time. She hadn't run off to tell the cops when she caught them in the woods. There were a lot of things she could have screamed at them about.

When Axel pulled in beside them, he climbed out. Harper was already out before he got around to her side of the car. Draven took hold of her hand, and they all headed into the school.

He noticed the stares and points.

When would Harper's curiosity peak and finally ask that question? She would belong to all four of them. Part of him was tempted to stake his claim now, to make her his.

But he'd liked seeing her kiss all three of his friends. This was what they had all agreed on, and he couldn't go getting greedy now.

Axel, Buck, and Jett had each talked about their kiss as well, and he knew they were looking forward to her finally belonging to all four of them.

To some, having a gangbang like theirs at eighteen was a little extreme.

No one had grown up like them. They hadn't seen the darkness within the world, the evil. All four of them knew what they wanted.

The only way for all of them to succeed, to remain faithful and loyal, was to have one woman, one woman they could devote their lives to. Having multiple women, their own personal wives, came with consequences. He'd seen it tear the friendship apart of his father and Axel's father. They worked together, and they'd once been firm friends.

They weren't anymore. That was now plagued by anger, rage, resentment, and above all, jealousy.

Entering the school, he noticed a path cleared wherever they went. That wasn't what surprised him. He was used to people getting out of his way. They were not the nicest of guys when someone stepped in their way.

As they came to a stop at his locker, he saw it. Harper's locker.

Red ink painted the surface with so many words.

Whore.

Slut.

Gangbanger.

Cunt.

Idiot.

Cum dump.

Fatty.

Ugly.

He stepped over to the locker, pushing Harper behind him. Axel grabbed her.

"Hey, stop it. Let me see." She pushed away from Axel and was suddenly moving him out of the way. "Oh," she said.

He looked behind him to glare at Axel, but he was cupping his junk.

"Who the fuck did this?" Draven asked. He slammed his hand against the metal.

Silence met his question.

"We'll find out," Buck said.

Again, no one answered. Finally, Axel got over having his balls hit.

"It'll be easy for you now."

Harper brushed past him, and he saw how red her cheeks were. "What is it?" he asked.

"It's nothing."

"Come on, Harper, don't do this now," he said.

"I need to go to the janitor's closest. I have to wash it off." She pulled out of his hold, and he let her go.

Looking at every single person in the corridor, he stood guard over her locker.

"Out of my way," Mr. Arnold said, the slowest middle-aged teacher in the history of all Stonewall.

Draven had a feeling the married teacher was having an affair with the principal, seeing as he always appeared coming from that direction and looking ruffled. Clearly sucking principal dick was more appealing to Mr. Arnold than eating his wife's pussy.

"What is the meaning of this?" Mr. Arnold asked.

"We're dealing with it," Axel said.

"I want it cleaned up, right this instant."

Buck grabbed the teacher's shirt and slammed him up against the locker. "He said we're dealing with it. You need to remember who you're talking to."

Draven didn't look back. It was loud and clear for everyone. They ruled this school. Harper belonged to them. Someone had ruined her property, and now they were all pissed off.

He was pissed off, fucking livid that she had to see those words. He would find out who it was, and when he was done with them, they were going to wish they'd never even seen her locker.

Harper appeared seconds later, a bucket and brush in her hands. He watched as she put her hand into the bucket and started scraping at the words printed there.

"I want to know who did this," Draven said, looking straight at Mr. Arnold. "Just as I'm sure you want to know who would do this to school property."

"Of course."

"Good. You better run to it then," he said.

Harper was attacking her locker, her arm moving back and forth with such speed.

Draven went to her, and, grabbing her arm, he took the brush from her hands.

"I need to clean this up," she said.

He dropped the brush into the water, cupped her face, and in front of everyone, claimed her lips for his own.

Right there, in front of people in school, he claimed her. Anyone who messed with her would have to deal with all four of them. He'd never made a claim like this in front of anyone else before.

With his father's warning in his mind, he ignored it and kept on kissing her. She tasted like coffee and peanut butter. The taste was so mind-blowing to him.

He relished her moan and sank his fingers into her hair, keeping her in place.

Once he was finished, he kissed the tip of her nose, grabbed the brush, and got to work fixing her locker.

"I can do that," Harper said.

"Don't worry about it. I'll be the one to fix it."

She didn't go to class. When the bell rang to start classes, he, Axel, Buck, Jett, and Harper were waiting. He'd cleaned her locker of all the words.

"Is it true?" she asked. "The rumors."

"I'm going to want something in return," he said. "You're ready for that?"

"Yes. I need to know."

"Yes. The rumors are true. With you, it will be different."

"How?"

"A second question."

She hesitated and shook her head. "No. I don't need to know the how."

He walked her to class, kissing her one final time before watching her go. Staring into the room, he looked at everyone, including the teacher.

"What do you want to do?" Axel asked, the instant the door was closed.

"I think it's only fair that we go and check that security footage," he said.

"Whoever it is must be shitting themselves," Buck said. "We could just follow the trail."

Draven shook his head, and went straight toward the room he needed. He'd find out who did it, and then there would be consequences.

Chapter Nine

Harper didn't see the guys all day long. Draven sent her a text to say they had a job to do and would be by later to pick her up from school. It was the first day she'd been alone. The feeling was kind of surreal. What was interesting, everyone gave her a wide berth. No more nasty words on her locker, which she was thankful for. She hated being called names.

She grabbed her food out of the cafeteria but didn't linger as Draven's table was empty. She never felt comfortable eating there and wasn't about to start now.

By the end of the day, there were no signs of any of them, and she sat on the bench near the parking lot, waiting.

Checking the time, she saw she'd been waiting for an hour and even the teachers were starting to leave.

She wasn't about to wait around for them to arrive. Walking wasn't that hard to do.

Harper: **I'm bored. I'm going to walk. Feeling a little uncomfortable. See you soon.**

She sent the message without including any kind of intimate emoji or words. Was it wrong to send a love heart? A kiss? Shaking her head, she hitched her bag high up on her shoulder, and started the walk back home.

It wasn't too bad. She usually liked walking. Her mother used to meet her at school, and they'd stop off at the grocery store on the way home.

I miss you.

Pushing thoughts of her mother out of her head, she focused on walking. That's all she could do right now. Keep on walking, ignoring the hurt she felt every time she thought of her.

She crossed the street and began walking past the woods. The quiet didn't help her right now. The words on the locker kept ringing in her head.

The way people looked at her, including the teachers, with a hint of fear as if she was going to attack them.

Draven had admitted the rumors were true.

A gangbang. All four of them.

What did that mean? Did she have to sleep with all four of them? Was it something that was required to be part of them?

She already owed Draven payment, but could she handle more of what he threw at her?

Why was she even debating this? She enjoyed being with them. Being alone today had only enhanced how lonely she felt being alone.

They had her back. Draven had taken the brush from her and cleaned the words off her locker. He was there, at her back, as were Buck, Axel, and Jett. They helped her.

She was part of them. Joining with them wouldn't be hard. It would be thrilling. Exciting.

They do bad things.

This made her stop. She knew their reputations. Some of it had to be gossip, but when it came to their fathers, it was all true.

She started walking again and paused when she heard some rustling beside her.

Was it a fox?

Shaking her head at how stupid it was to watch out for a fox, she kept on walking. Just as she made it past the clearing, someone grabbed her.

Arms wrapped around her neck, and she was pulled into the woods.

She didn't have time to let out a scream as the person cut off any sound with the strength of his grip across her windpipe. Slammed to the ground, she felt a kick to the ribs that had her gasping for breath.

Whoever it was didn't speak as he moved between her legs. His fingers were around her neck as he started to tug and attack her jeans.

She'd never been so thankful for how well-fitted they were. Her old jeans were always so big they would have pulled down easily.

Thank you, Hannah.

Clawing at the hand around her throat, she scored her nails into his flesh. He cried out, drawing his hand back and punching her in the face.

She saw stars, and tears filled her eyes as he went back to attacking her jeans.

Come on, Harper.

Fight.

Don't let this happen.

She tried to push him off, but he kept overpowering her. His hand was once against across her neck. Grabbing his thumb, she yanked, hard. He cried out, and as he released her windpipe, she took in a breath, and screamed. It wasn't enough before his hand was covering her mouth again.

No.

I don't want this.

No.

Just as he got her jeans undone and started working her legs, he was pulled off her.

Out of nowhere, Draven, Axel, Buck, and Jett were there, all four of them. She sat up, moving back, but she couldn't look away.

They dropped to the ground the man who'd been attacking her. Each of them landed blow, after blow, after blow. There was no way the man could escape.

She saw the blood as it spilled from his body.

Jett had stopped using his hands and fists and

instead was cutting him, slashing at his flesh, opening him up as if he was some science experiment.

Her stomach rolled.

When the man was silent, they all stared at each other, before Draven moved toward her. She didn't flinch away as he picked her up in his arms. Axel removed his jacket and placed it over her. It was then she realized the man had torn open her shirt and exposed her upper body in the fight.

"Thank you."

Axel nodded.

"I'll be back," Draven said.

"We'll be waiting," Axel said.

Jett didn't stay with them. He came with Draven as they carried her back to their cars.

"You found me," she said.

"It wasn't hard to do. We weren't far from the school when we got your message."

"I missed you. I didn't know what to do."

"You should have waited at the school. We'd have come for you," Draven said. "Next time, wait there."

"Don't leave me then. Trouble seems to find me quite easily."

"No kidding." He helped her into the car, and she held Axel's jacket against her body.

Jett climbed into the back. No one spoke. Silence filled the car, and she found it even more strange that no one was talking about what had just happened.

She wasn't about to speak. Her body shook. She was in shock.

Draven arrived at her home, and once again, he carried her inside. He didn't dump her and leave. He took her upstairs, and she was very much aware of Jett following them this time. Draven set her down on the toilet seat as he filled her bathtub.

With Jett watching, Draven stripped her of her clothes, and then helped her in the bath. She still held Axel's jacket in front of her. It gave her a little modesty but not much.

"I'll be back," Draven said. "Watch her."

Jett nodded. Harper stared at Draven. He'd taken her clothes with him. Jett sat on the toilet, his gaze on her.

"You don't have to stay."

"You're in a bit of shock. No one will leave you alone."

"I'm fine."

"Stop trying to be a hard ass, Harper. It doesn't suit you."

She smiled. "You were all gone today."

"Did you miss us?"

"Yes. I'm not used to missing anyone."

"I know the feeling."

She held Axel's jacket to her body and sat up. Jett made no move to stop her.

"Did you find out who ruined my locker?"

"Yes. We know who it was."

"Are you going to tell me?" she asked.

"When you're ready."

She averted her gaze, closing her eyes. Her head hurt, but then, she did have it punched so she figured it was more than fine for her to be hurting right about now.

As she rubbed her temple with the tips of her fingers, her stomach turned. A wave of sickness rushed over her, but she didn't throw up. In the next second, it settled down, and she eased back in the tub, trying to relax. Every time she closed her eyes, she saw the guy.

"I didn't even know who he was."

"He was a loser, trying to take something that

didn't belong to him."

"I … how can it happen?"

"It happens a lot, Harper. Don't think about it. There are a lot of assholes in this world. Sick perverts as well. We wouldn't let anything happen to you."

She laughed. "I didn't think it was safe hanging out on the school bench. The school gives me the creeps."

"So instead you walk past a creepy woods that can have anyone and anything inside. Makes total sense."

"I was walking toward the good part of town. You know, where all the money is."

"Let me give you some advice, Harper. Just because someone has wealth and prestige, doesn't make them good. It only means they can pay to hide their true self. Nowhere is safe."

She opened her mouth to speak, but then she heard the door.

"I'll go and check and see who it is."

With him gone, she climbed out of the bath, replacing the jacket with a robe.

Jett came back seconds later and didn't look impressed. "Your dad and Hannah are back."

Great.

****

Draven parked his car near the wood and found Axel and Buck waiting. Both of them were playing games on their phones.

"You recognize him?" Draven asked.

"Didn't he work for your dad?" Axel asked.

"Yes. He did."

"And he gave you a warning today?" Buck asked.

"Yep."

The man who'd been attacking Harper was dead. Draven didn't know who dealt the killing blow, but he had a feeling it was Jett. The blood coated the ground.

"What do you want us to do?" Axel asked.

Heading to the trunk of his car, Draven grabbed out the tools he'd need.

Laying the sheet on the ground, they all rolled the dead body onto the blanket. Carrying it back to his car, he tossed it in the trunk.

Closing and locking his car, he walked back into the woods and picked up a shovel.

"Dig the blood in. We don't want anyone to see this."

"Got it," Axel said.

"Where are you going?" Buck asked.

"I've got to pay the old man a visit."

"I don't think that's wise." This came from Axel.

"Why?"

"He's given you a warning, and you're about to go and shit on all of that. It's not good."

"I know it's not, but I'm also not going to let him get away with thinking I'll allow him to hurt our girl. He can give warnings all he wants, but this is our decision, not his. You good with this?"

"Yep," Axel said.

Leaving his friends there, he got behind the wheel and took off home. There was a fancy party at his home.

No one there was a law-abiding citizen. All of them had secrets.

Rage flooded Draven as he got to the trunk and stared down into the lifeless face of the asshole who'd been trying to hurt Harper.

If he'd not heard that scream, he wouldn't have found her.

He imagined the instructions were pretty simple. Find Harper, rape her, kill her, and be done with it. His father didn't want the mess of dealing with a civilian in their world. If she went missing after being seen with them for so long, it would open up questions that he really didn't want to deal with. Tough shit. Draven had no intention of following his father's rules. This was his life, and he wanted Harper. Besides, the damage had already been done, and he wasn't about to leave her alone. He was his father's son and wouldn't let anything get in his way of what he wanted.

He needed to protect Harper. These kinds of instructions only came from his dad, and now he was so pissed.

Axel and Buck were digging the blood into the mud and checking the area so there was no lingering evidence they were there. Picking up the dead body, he ignored the crushing weight and entered his home. The man on the door looked like he was going to shit himself.

It was all good fun. The sound of music and laughter filled the air from the dining room. That was fine.

One glance into the room, and Draven recognized most of the people there. Some of the women were whores, others mistresses. His mother wasn't there though.

Walking into the room, he went right up to his father and dumped the body on the table.

Silence rang out at his challenge as he stared at the man whose blood ran in his veins.

Alan Barries was an asshole, a monster.

Draven had seen all that he had done, and had ignored it. It was what he did, turned the other way.

"What is the meaning of this?" one of the guests demanded.

Draven picked up his dad's glass of wine and took a sip. The woman closest to him, he shoved her out of a chair and sat down.

"That's what I'd like to know," Draven said.

"This kind of business is done in private. Forgive my son, he doesn't know how to be polite."

Draven picked up the knife and slammed it into his father's hand, the blade going straight to the wood.

Alan let out a yell. Right now, his father was the enemy. He needed to be dealt with, and walking away wouldn't work.

"Get out," Draven said.

"Sir?" another guy asked.

"Get out, all of you." His father growled through gritted teeth.

Draven wiggled the knife. "I hope I didn't go through any bones."

"You little shit. You think you're so tough where you're sitting."

"No. I think I'm so tough because I'm doing what my father taught me to do. Harper is mine. She belongs to us. You tried to have her fucking killed."

"My strict instructions were for him to have fun with her."

Draven started to twist the knife, and he took pleasure in hearing his father's scream.

Seconds passed, and Alan chuckled. "You're exactly my kind of son."

Out of the corner of his eye, Draven saw the cook near the doorway, a tray of food in her hand.

"Come in," Draven said. "Come in. Join the fun."

He saw his father lose his cocky edge. Out of all of the women his father bedded, raped, and fucked, it would seem he had a soft spot for the cook.

Draven smiled. "I have this feeling that my mother couldn't have kids and you knocked up the cook. Sit the fuck down!" The cook looked ready to run, but she took a seat on the opposite side of the table.

Draven picked up another knife and walked around toward the cook. His father grabbed the knife that was in his hand, and pulled. The knife was sharp so the wound was a clean one.

Draven smirked. Putting the fresh knife against the cook's neck, he stared at his father.

"I don't give a shit who you are. You'll leave Harper alone."

"And if I don't?"

"Then I'll make sure you wish you didn't have a son."

Alan Barries smiled. "Fuck! That's what I'm talking about."

"Leave her alone!" Draven wasn't going to give up until he heard the words spoken.

"You prove to me that she's not a liability and I will. You have a great deal to protect, son. It's not worth losing it all over some cheap pussy."

"Done." He released the cook, who got to her feet and ran back to her little kitchen.

"When are you going to let her go?"

"Never. She's mine."

Alan wrapped his hand up, but he looked … happy.

"You're weird, you know that right." They were the exact words Harper had said to him.

"This is a work of art, Draven. One day, you're going to put us out on top."

"You want to overthrow Cook."

"He's getting old. His judgments are not the same as they used to be. This, makes me happy. You're willing to do whatever it takes to get the job done."

"Anyone who comes after Harper, will all meet the same fate. Not just from me, from the four of us."

Alan stared at him. He'd wrapped his hand up in

a piece of cloth he'd torn from the table.

"Come to my office." Alan got to his feet, grabbing his glass of wine.

Draven wanted to head back to Harper's home, but he couldn't, not until he satisfied his father. Once inside his father's office, he waited as Alan poured him a drink.

"Take a seat."

He did.

Alan sat behind his desk and sighed. "I know you have this deep loyalty to your friends, and that is … acceptable. It's good to have people you can rely on."

"But?"

"There comes a time in every single man's life, when you need to know when to cut the pack loose. They all look to you for guidance. You tell them what they can do and not do. You're the leader of the pack." Alan got up from his chair, and walked around the desk to lean against it. "All of this is going to be yours one day. Men and women will look to you. You've got to be fearless."

"And you think my friends make me fearless."

"You don't have friends, Draven. All you have are men that are not your enemies yet."

Draven stood up. He put the full glass down. "If you keep cutting off your friends, you'll end up with no one. You'll be weak."

"Cook's not going to last much longer, Draven. This world, it will kill you if you let it. Fight while you have the chance and think about what I said." He watched his father take the last swig of wine. "Good chat, son. Good kill."

Turning on his heel, he left his house without a backward glance.

Getting into his car, he drove to Harper's. Seeing Ian's car in the driveway, it pissed him off.

Jett: **Had to bail. Dad's home. He didn't see me.**

Axel: **Looks like party time is back at my place.**

Buck: **What we doing now?**

All three texts had come in within seconds of each other.

Draven: **Checking on our girl. Meet you at our spot.**

Turning off his cell phone, he climbed out of his car, locking it. He didn't go to the front door. Instead, he walked to the side of her house, and began the walk up to her window. It was locked, and he gave it a tap. The curtains were drawn.

She didn't keep him waiting long. He saluted her, and she pulled the window up.

"What are you doing?"

"I wasn't going to start shit with your dad, not yet. Are you okay?"

He climbed through the window, stood and tilted her head up so that he could get a better look at her face.

"It's fine. Really."

There was a bruise on her face, and he gritted his teeth. The son of a bitch had died early. "I'm so sorry we got there too late."

"It wasn't too late."

"He hit you."

"He wanted to do a hell of a lot more. You saved me." She wrapped her arms around his back and pressed her head against his chest.

Cupping the back of her head, he breathed in the scent of her. He'd not taken the time to just hold her, not yet, not really.

"I missed you," she said. "Jett kept me company until an hour ago."

"I know. I got his text. Have you made a decision yet?" The threat posed from his father was a real one. He didn't know how long he'd be able to keep him at bay. They needed to move quickly, as otherwise he'd lose her.

"It's a lot to take in. I need a little more time."

He twirled her hair around his fingers. She pulled away, and he stared into her eyes.

She licked her lips. "Don't I owe you something?"

"You want to pay up?"

"There's no time like the present."

He chuckled. "I'm going to shower first. I'll be back."

Pulling away from her, he entered her bathroom and took a quick look at his appearance. He looked a fucking mess, no doubt about it. His hair was all over the place, and his clothes were covered in dirt. Stripping down, he stepped beneath the cold spray of the water.

He had no doubt one day he'd be following in his father's footsteps. He was a Barries, and with it came a shitload of responsibility.

Memories of what his father did, starting with the girl he knocked up and fed her drugs until she killed herself, filled his mind. At eighteen, he'd seen a lot of bad shit. Auctions with women and kids. Even men and boys. He'd watched them be put up for sale, even witnessed them being used. All in the name of business.

Not one of them was given money for the use of the body and lives.

His life had been filled with so much blood. He'd witnessed his first murder at age five. One of the nannies that had been assigned to him over the years was stealing from the safe. She'd been caught, and as she played tea parties with him, his father had walked up and shot her in the head.

He'd watched dogs trained to savage people, their flesh being pulled, tugged, and yanked from their bones without a care in the world. Alan liked to also drown people. There was a well on their land, out near the forest. He'd strap men and women to it, and dunk them under until he got bored and leave them to rot.

Each memory served to reinforce his manhood.

Alan Barries wanted a son who could take over, a monster. Someone ready to do whatever it took to get the job done.

He used Harper's soap. The scent of her helped to rid him of the memories of all he'd done. Once he could no longer stand the spray of the water, he climbed out, wrapped a towel around his waist, and entered his bedroom.

Harper sat on the edge of the bed. She wore these cute shorts and a crop shirt. The buds of her nipples pressed against the front, making him want nothing more than to suck on them.

She stood up, and he stepped right up close to her.

"Are you okay?" she asked.

"I'm fine." He teased her hip, sliding his fingers beneath her shirt, touching her flesh.

"Draven."

"I will never do anything you don't want me to do. I won't hurt you. I'll always take care of you." With his other hand, he placed a finger beneath her chin, tilting her head back to look at him. "But I need to kiss you. To feel you against me."

She nodded.

She wrapped her arms around his neck, and he groaned. Her sweet tits crushed against his chest. He wanted her so fucking badly, he could taste it.

"You drive me crazy, you know that?"

She shook her head.

"I think about getting you naked, sliding your legs open, and fucking you. I want to take that cherry, Harper. To make it mine."

He captured her lips once again, and she moaned his name. He silenced her, moving her back to the bed until she had no choice but to fall back. Draven slid his knees between her thighs, opening her up to him. She didn't fight him, kissing him back as he pushed her shirt up.

Trailing his lips down her neck, he lifted the shirt past her tits and took a nipple into his mouth, sucking on the hard bud. He bit down, and she cried out.

He reached up, placing a hand over her mouth. "We can't have Daddy hearing you."

She moaned. He flicked his tongue back and forth over her nipple. His cock pressed against the front of his pants, and he felt the tip already leaking pre-cum.

He wanted inside her so fucking badly. To take her virginity. To make her his. Putting most of his weight on her body, he slid his other hand down, inside her shorts.

She wasn't wearing any panties, and as he opened the folds of her pussy, he touched her clit. She was soaking wet.

Using two fingers to work her pussy, he stopped licking at her tit and watched her. She wriggled beneath him, and he kept her mouth covered. He'd only let her go when she came, when she flooded his fingers.

"You ever have someone touch your pussy?"

She shook her head, and he smiled.

"Good. Me, Axel, Buck, and Jett, we're the only ones allowed to touch you. To fuck you. To take you. Understand?"

She moaned, and he smiled.

Within a few strokes of her clit, she came. It wasn't long, but for her first time, she looked utterly shocked. Removing his hand from her pussy, he sucked her nipple into his mouth. Taking his hand away from her face, he leaned up.

With the hand that he'd touched her pussy, he began to work his length, going up and down, staring into her blue eyes as he worked his dick.

Gritting his teeth, he felt his climax so close to the surface.

He'd not taken off the towel, and as he spilled his cum, the towel soaked it up. Collapsing over her, he wrapped his arms around her, holding her close, hugging her.

He'd never let her go.

Chapter Ten

Harper once again woke up to no Draven, which wasn't a surprise. After last night, she didn't know if she'd ever be able to face him again.

His touch had set her on fire.

She got out of bed, went to the bathroom, used the toilet, washed her hands, and winced. The guy who hit her yesterday had left a huge bruise on her face, not to mention her neck.

Tilting her head back, she saw the bruises, some of them the shape of fingertips. She'd been so afraid yesterday.

Draven, Axel, Buck, and Jett had come for her. They'd saved her.

Shaking her head, she left the bathroom, changed into a pair of jeans and shirt, grabbed her bag, and headed downstairs. Hannah was nowhere to be seen, but Ian was in the kitchen.

"You're back," she said.

He turned to look at her. The bruising was still there but not as bad on his nose.

"What did I tell you about causing trouble?" He slammed his cup down on the counter.

"I didn't mean to hit you, Dad." At least not that hard, but she didn't add that.

"This, look at you. Your face. I asked for you to be a good girl. To be a lady and you're getting into fights."

"I was attacked yesterday. You'd have known if you were ever home."

"Oh, so now it's my fault, is it? Maybe you should consider what you're doing. Just like your damn mother. You never know when to keep your mouth shut. The two of you were always fucking useless. Always. No wonder she killed herself. Best thing she ever did."

Harper stepped back.

Even Ian looked guilty for what he said.

"I didn't mean—"

"Yeah, you did. You meant every single word. I was walking home yesterday, and a guy attacked me. I didn't get into any trouble." With that, she turned away and left her home. Running sounded like quite a good thing to do.

She didn't linger on her driveway waiting for a ride. Harper turned the corner and started to walk in the direction of the school. She'd hoped she and her dad could find some way to forgive. He had a new family, and she got it. He didn't want to be reminded of her or the woman he'd been married to.

Tears filled her eyes as she thought of her mother, the pain she must have gone through. He didn't want her around. He wanted his new life. She had nothing. No one.

You have someone.

Four someones.

This made her pause.

Draven. Axel. Buck. Jett. They were four guys that wanted her, who'd been there for her.

Join them. Never be alone again.

She turned her head as a car pulled up beside her. The window wound down, and she stared at Buck. Draven drove the car, while Axel and Jett were in the back.

"Hello, beautiful. Want a ride?"

She nodded. Jett climbed out of the car in the back, and she slid in, moving into the center.

Glancing over at Draven, she saw his pointed look. He'd been gone this morning. Jett climbed back in, and they were heading to school.

Would it be so hard to join them?

She'd have to quit being the good girl.

They already had her back. Would it be wrong to have theirs? She stared at each guy in turn.

"I want in," she said.

Draven brought the car to a stop. The school was just up ahead. They all turned to look at her.

"What?" Axel asked.

"I want in. Whatever it takes to be part of your gang or club, whatever, I want in." She pushed some hair off her face. "I'm ready."

Draven spun the car around, and they didn't go back home. He made a right, then a left, taking off out of town. She looked behind her as the town started to disappear.

Axel and Jett each put a hand on her leg.

She didn't tell them to remove their hands.

Staring out of the window, she couldn't figure out where they were going. Silence filled the car, and the longer it went on, the more uncomfortable she got. Before she caved and asked one of them to talk, to say or do anything, Draven pulled up outside of a condemned building.

"Welcome to our office."

They all got out of the car, and Harper had no choice but to follow. Jett took her bag from her, and threw it back into the car. "You won't be needing it."

Draven grabbed her arm, and they walked into the building.

"Isn't it dangerous?"

"Come on, Harper, live a little," Buck said.

As she entered the building, the scent of decay and urine filled her nostrils.

They cleared the main ground, and she saw beams that had collapsed. As she looked all around at the broken windows, she saw that the walls seemed ready to fall down. It didn't appear stable at all.

"Why do you come here?"

"No one else will," Draven said.

"We don't stay for long," Jett said.

She noticed they'd formed a circle around her. She spun around, looking at each of them. They were all staring at her.

"Okay, I am getting a little freaked out, right now." She spun around again until her gaze landed on Draven.

"Once you become one of us, Harper, there is no getting out."

"Unless you die," Buck said.

She turned to him and nodded.

"We are not good people. We don't come from good people, and by being one of us, you belong to us," Axel said.

"This is why no matter who auditioned for the role, they were never going to get it," Jett said.

She turned as each one spoke.

"It's not a gangbang or a club. It's us, for life. We made the decision who we wanted," Draven said.

"And you're it." Again, back to Buck.

"Our word becomes your law." Axel's turn.

She looked to Jett. "No one else but us at every single turn."

"One betrayal, and you're dead," Draven said.

"You will belong to all of us." Axel again.

"Your mind," Buck said.

"Heart," Jett said.

"And body will be ours. You'll belong to all of us. We will own you." Draven stepped forward. "And in return, you will own us. That's what we're offering."

"All four of you?" she asked.

"Yes. We will protect you, Harper. Offer you safety, kindness, everything you could ever want," Axel said.

She swallowed past the lump in her throat. Spinning around, she looked at them. "Do you even ... fancy me?"

They all laughed.

"We all took a vote," Draven said, stepping up to her. "And you won. It's why we're here now. We've just been waiting for you to catch up."

She took a deep breath.

"This is your last chance. Once you start this, there's no turning back. We'll tell you everything, and in return, you'll keep our secrets, be loyal to us. We offer you forever."

"We're eighteen," she said.

"And we know what we want," Axel said. "This wasn't some quick decision with us. We know how to survive. Without each other, we'd be dead anyway. This is what we offer. It's up to you if you take it."

The words on the locker came back to her. She stared at each of them, wondering what the hell to do.

You want this.

You want to be part of it.

Stop being the good girl and take what you want.

There was no getting out of this town. One look at each of them, and she knew she was with them every single step of the way. She wouldn't back down, or leave, or betray them. She was part of them.

"I'm in," she said. "All the way. I won't back out."

"Good. We know who wrote those words on your locker. She's not our problem. She is yours," Draven said.

"We need to know that you're able to handle

yourself," Axel said.

"Your training is going to begin tonight," Jett said.

They all started to head toward the exit.

"Wait, what is going on?" she asked, watching them leave.

"We're not staying here too long. It's fucking dangerous," Buck said.

Within seconds they were back in the car and heading to school.

"Can someone answer me? What is going on?" she asked, completely confused by the new turn of events.

"It's simple. You meet us at Axel's place tonight. We'll be waiting, and your training will begin," Draven said, pulling into the school parking lot.

No one was around.

She turned toward the school, and sure enough, people were watching her. Jett held her backpack on his shoulder.

"You better know now, they're all watching you. They all want to know what it is you've got that none of them have," Buck said.

Axel put his hands across her shoulders. "School is about to get so much more interesting."
****

Later that day, Draven waited with Buck and Jett for Axel and Harper to arrive. He stretched out his muscles, tilting his head from side to side, and swinging his arms.

"You think she just made the biggest mistake ever?" Jett asked, taking a long draw on his joint.

Draven stared at Jett, and he breathed out a mouthful of smoke and chuckled.

"Where's your knife?"

He held it up. "Always got it on me. It's my security blanket."

"Dude, you are fucked up," Buck said.

"It's some good shit."

"Seriously, you're going to take a hit today of all days," Draven asked.

"We have been working nonstop all summer. Harper is a magnet for trouble, and we've just declared to the entire school she's ours. I think I can take a hit. Especially as all I've done is kiss her," Jett said.

"With that kind of attitude, that's all you're going to do. I'm not a magnet for trouble," Harper said, entering the small condo at the bottom of Axel's property.

It was originally slept in by the gardener, but from what Draven remembered, the gardener liked to take what didn't belong to him.

Harper had a bag on her shoulder, and she looked a little flushed. Axel looked pissed.

"Did something go down?" Draven asked.

"Her dad wasn't there. Hannah was," Axel said, taking the pot from Jett.

"Now that I've declared myself as one of you guys, tell me the truth. Who is she?" Harper dropped her bag on the floor, arms folded, looking mightily sexy.

Draven's dick twitched at the sight.

"Hannah works for my dad," Draven said.

"Works, as in, still does?"

"Your dad did some good work for us, and seeing as my father likes to reward in the most weird of places, he used Hannah. She's a whore. Plain and simple. If my dad told her to, she'd fuck the entire town and, still with cum dripping down her thighs, would go and suck her husband off. She's there to keep Ian in place and to warn my dad if something happens."

"Wow. My dad left my mom for that."

"He only knew recently what she was."

"It doesn't make it okay."

"Never said it did. It is how the world works."

"The world is a shitty fucking place."

"That I agree with you," Draven said.

She pushed her hands into her pockets. "So, how is this training going to go?"

Draven smiled and shoved her hard.

With her hands in her pockets, she fell to the floor. This time, he put his hands in his pockets as she glared at him.

"That wasn't funny."

"I'm not laughing."

Her gaze went to Axel, Jett, and Buck.

"They're not going to help you. In fact, they're going to help you train."

"This is training?"

"You got to learn to take a hit. It's what we need from you," Draven said. He didn't offer to help her up.

She got to her feet, and he went for her again, only she spun around.

Axel was waiting. One by one, they circled her.

"To have our backs, we need to know that you can fight back. So, fight us, Harper. Don't be afraid, and don't hold back. We can take whatever you've got."

Two hours later, exhausted and sweating, he didn't back down, but Harper was a strong fighter. She took everything he shot her way.

They taunted her, showed her how to defend herself, and played with her, pushing her, shoving her. They forced her to fight to be free of them.

When pizza arrived, they took a break. Harper sat on the floor, legs folded as she ate a slice of pizza. Her hair was piled on her head, and she looked so alive. Her eyes sparkled with life.

"So, you guys, you do bad things, right?"

"Yes."

"Have you all killed someone?" she asked.

"Yes."

"So, what do I have to do then?"

"You need to prove yourself to us. We'll show you each step of the way. You'll be tested. One of us will have to be with you at all times," Axel said. "It'll be fun. I know right now it sounds like the last thing from fun, but it will be. Sometimes our dads enter us in fights, or we have to help them out. Being part of the team, you'll have to be there."

"Wait, actual fights?"

"Yes. The real deal, you can't back down. Losing is not acceptable," Draven said.

She released a breath. "I have really brought this on myself, haven't I?"

"It's not going to be that hard. So long as you want it, you'll get it," Buck said.

"How did you all come together? Is that top secret, or can this loser girl find out?" she asked.

Draven was the one to take the lead, telling her how they all met. How they were all born within the same month, and how their families brought them together. Their life was bound together for eternity. Their lives and those of their children would be forever born into a world of death and blood.

"And how did you come about sharing? I mean, am I going to be the first woman of four?"

"No," Buck said.

"We've seen our families torn apart because of a woman. No offense," Jett said.

"None taken."

"When it comes to a woman, look at your parents.

Your dad screwed up big time, and we realized that we didn't want that. We didn't want to have to fight to get what we wanted, so we agreed to share. One woman for us all." Jett finished the explanation.

"And you all decided on me."

"It was a hard decision, but you came out on top," Axel said.

"You've all shared before?" She licked her fingers but didn't reach for another slice of pizza.

"Yes," Draven said.

"And you enjoy it?"

He saw her curiosity.

"Are you wanting to take a test drive?" Axel asked, grabbing his junk.

She shook her head and sighed. "One day, maybe." She turned toward Draven.

He thought about last night, feeling her pussy on his fingers as he worked her to orgasm. She'd been more than ready last night.

"It's time to call it a night. I'll take Harper home," Draven said. "I'll be back to pick up my car later."

Getting to their feet, Jett, Buck, and Axel each hugged Harper.

"It's good to have you on the team."

She nodded, not saying anything.

Following her outside, he took her hand, and they walked out of Axel's gate. He made sure to take her the long route.

"You're not driving me today."

"You just agreed to belong to four men and to allow us to share you. I think it warrants a walk. You can clear your head. Talk to me."

"Talk to you. You'll go back and tell the others though, right? Harper's having second thoughts."

"Are you?"

"Not about being part of, you know, this. I want this. I want to belong, and I'm tired of being alone. I've enjoyed being around you guys, and after everything I've been through so far, you guys are the only ones that understand."

He tugged her close, stopping her, and pushing her against a lamppost. He tilted her head back, staring into her eyes.

"You don't have to hide from me. We get that you've been through a lot."

"You've been through so much." She placed a hand on his chest. "Your fathers are some kind of mafia bosses?"

He laughed. "In a way. We're not Italian or Russian, but we're a family, a group. Axel and I are the oldest sons, so we've been forced to learn the ropes."

"What about Jett and Buck?"

"Soldiers. They're trained to take a bullet."

"And my dad helps get you off the hook?"

He nodded.

"And if you didn't do this?" she asked.

"It doesn't mean it would stop. Drugs, guns, sex, and death all sell, Harper. Someone has to do it."

"All of you have decided to do it?"

"Yes. It's the way we've been born to do it. We're together, we're a team. It's what we do." He tucked some of her hair behind her ear. "I understand if it's too much."

"It's not just that. I just feel a little overwhelmed. I know I should be afraid. The last thing I should do is join, to be with you guys, but I don't want to run away."

He took her hand. "Good. It's not going to be easy."

"Did you kill that guy that hurt me?" she asked.

Draven stopped and watched her. "Yes."

"Good."

He smiled. "See, you're getting all bloodthirsty already."

They started walking back to her home. The street was so silent. Draven was used to the silence. Inside each house would tell a different story. His own home told a big story, a story of death, of chaos, and of pain.

He turned to look at Harper. They were both so young. She could go away to college, to get out of Stonewall, to be as far away from them as humanly possible.

She'd be safe. His father wouldn't hurt her. She didn't know enough and could walk away. His father didn't want the risk of having her close to them. But Draven didn't believe for a second she'd walk away.

The thought of letting her go filled him with such pain.

All of his life, he'd gone without. He'd watched her from afar. Loving the girl he'd seen with her mother. She was the one who would push her daughter on the swing, even though it was too high. Who was always there to pick her daughter up from school, and took her out for ice cream. Who held her daughter whenever she cried.

The day he heard of her suicide, Draven had been shocked. None of the guys knew he'd driven past her home in search of answers. Harper hadn't been there. The house itself had been empty.

He'd gone to the bathroom where he knew she'd taken her life. He'd stared at the stained flooring.

Harper had no one. Her once-perfect life was gone. Even as it was selfish of him to keep her, he knew he wouldn't change his mind. He held her hand a little tighter.

"I don't want to go in there," Harper said, as they came to the driveway of her home.

"I'll be in your room," he said. "Waiting for you. Remember you're one of us right now. Be fearless. Be a fighter. You've got no room for fear or backing down."

She nodded. "I thought you didn't have a group name."

"We don't, but it kind of fits."

She laughed. "See you in a minute."

He watched her go, and smiled. She really was something else.

Chapter Eleven

The days passed, and they turned into weeks. People at school gave them a wide berth, and Harper barely had two minutes to call her own where she could think. Behind closed doors, or at the very least, locked away in either Draven's home or Axel's, they trained her, all four of them.

She had the bruises to prove it.

Stepping out of the shower after three weeks of nothing but training, Harper was ready to crawl into bed and sleep for weeks.

She felt stronger than ever before though. With every single hit she took and gave, she felt stronger, ready to take on the world. She no longer felt like she was losing the will to live. It had given her a focus, a drive to be better. To prove to them she could stand by their side.

Harper stopped as she saw Draven on her bed, waiting for her. He'd been sneaking into her room every single night. She couldn't recall the last time she'd slept alone.

Ian never checked on her. She hadn't spoken to him since the morning he'd lashed out at her. She came home late or avoided him, or went out.

"Hello, beautiful."

"I don't feel it."

She went to brush past him, but he caught her wrist.

"And why don't we feel this way?" he asked.

"Oh, you know, fighting. Getting hit, pushed, and shoved will do that to you."

She gasped as he removed the towel. She was completely naked underneath. The towel dropped to the floor, and now she stood naked in front of him.

"Why is it you're the one that is always here?" she asked.

"You missing the others?"

She shook her head.

He stood up. "I'm the one that picked you. I started this, and seeing as I'm normally here, the others don't see a reason to be here." He kissed her cheek, and she felt her heart pounding as he knelt on the floor, his face next to her stomach.

Her ribs were bruised. In time, she'd heal. She looked forward to the healing.

Learning how to fight was fun. She liked being able to defend herself. Whenever she thought about giving up, she'd think of that guy in the woods. She could have defended herself. Not only that, she loved being with all four of her guys. They were hers just as she was theirs.

It was still surreal to think about, especially as less than a year ago, she would have been going home to her mom.

"I think I need to kiss this all better."

"You picked me?"

"Yes."

"Why?" she asked.

"I told you before, Harper. I saw you. I still see you. You've always been a good girl."

She chuckled. "You want to turn me bad?"

"No. I saw you were trapped. I saw you were always doing what others wanted of you and never what you wanted. That's no way to live, no matter what you think."

He touched a delicate spot on her body, and she winced.

"I feel like a giant baby."

"You did good. You're a fast learner."

"I like being a good learner." She stared down into his eyes. The green looked so much darker than she remembered.

She cried out as he cupped her pussy.

"Are you a learner in all things?"

He spread her lips open, and she closed her eyes, embracing his touch.

"You're always so wet for me."

"Yes."

Suddenly, he pulled his fingers away from her pussy, and she whimpered.

"I'm not here to sneakily give you an orgasm. Get dressed. We're heading out. Wear something nice."

"Nice? How nice?"

He got up and went to her closet. She picked up the towel and quickly covered her body.

He returned seconds later with a white dress covered in red roses. "Wear this."

"This is weird."

"Don't argue. Come on."

Harper rolled her eyes, but took it. Draven refused to leave her alone. She dressed with her back to him, even though she didn't know what the point of modesty was. He'd seen everything.

He helped with the zipper in the back of the dress, and she blew out a breath as she turned to him.

She lifted her hair up, about to put it in a clip.

"Don't. Leave your hair down," he said.

"You're very bossy tonight."

"I'm the one in charge tonight, and all you have to worry about is pleasing me."

"That's all I've got to worry about?"

"Yes." He took her hand, and she pulled him to a stop as he went to her bedroom door.

"Ian's down there with Hannah."

"I know, and I don't care. Remember, Harper, you're the one in control."

"He's still my dad." She didn't think of him like that though.

"You want to climb out of the window? Hide away?"

She shook her head.

"Then don't behave as if you're doing anything wrong. He's probably heard by now that you're part of us. Besides, he gave up his right to you, remember that."

Draven led the way out of her bedroom, and she followed him downstairs. Ian was there, as was Hannah. They both looked shocked to see them together.

Ian's glare was clear to see. He wasn't happy. Hannah turned on her heel and left the room.

"No. Go back to your room," he said.

She didn't stop. Thinking about his disrespect about her mother's suicide and also how he treated her, she'd had enough.

No more.

She was the one in control of her own destiny.

"Harper, I mean it."

"Why don't you go and fuck your wife, Ian? It's what you're good at," she said, brushing past him and following Draven outside.

She expected to find Axel and the others waiting, but they weren't there.

Draven helped her into the car, and she looked back at the house to see Ian standing in the doorway.

For the first time in weeks, he looked like a concerned father. She'd give him a ten for effort.

"Are you going to tell me where we're going tonight?" she asked.

"It's a surprise."

"It is."

"Yeah."

"I feel like I'm being spoiled."

"You are."

She didn't ask any more questions as he drove out of town. The sign that read "Welcome to Stonewall" always fascinated her, especially as she grew up and came to realize just how deadly the town was where she lived. Not once did it say run at your own risk. Danger always around.

On the surface, Stonewall looked perfect, like a sweet little neighborhood, but the truth was far deadlier and scarier than anyone could ever imagine.

"What are you thinking?"

"About the town. Is that why your parents picked this place?" she asked. "Because it was so unsuspecting?"

"They still get investigated from time to time. The only difference, the cops here are paid to not see a thing or to get rid of the evidence."

"Doesn't that bother you?"

"I grew up with cops coming to my house all the time. They sleep with the women my father offers them, and take the money. I'm not the one responsible for them and their ethics. That's up to them."

"It just seems like something should be done about it, you know."

"Harper, nothing can be done. That's the point. They're in charge. They tell everyone what to do. Your father fell in line as soon as they dangled a piece of willing pussy in front of him."

She winced. Rubbing her arms, she stared out of the window.

"What would you do if they told you to kill me?" she asked.

It was a risk. She was an outsider. No matter her

training, there were some things she doubted she could ever do.

"Don't ever think about that. Don't even say that."

"You'd kill me?"

"No. I wouldn't kill you."

"What if you didn't have a choice?"

"Harper, this is supposed to be a date."

"It is?"

"Yeah, I'm attempting to date you right now, and you're talking about me killing you. Don't. Let's not go there. Killing you is only a risk if you do something that can't be redeemed. Something can always be redeemed in some way. I have no doubt about that."

"What about betrayal?"

He jerked the car to a stop. Her heart started to pound. The grip he had on the steering wheel was quite alarming.

"Are you going to betray us?"

"No." She didn't sound so sure even to her own ears.

"You've got to understand, Harper. There are a lot of things I can protect you from. I'd even go up against my dad for you. But there are some things I can't."

"Like betrayal?"

He'd turned to look at her. She stared into his green eyes. For a long time, she'd ignored this guy.

He'd been part of her life in some way or another, admittedly on the outside. She never in her wildest dreams imagined herself sitting in his car, wearing a pretty dress, heading out on a date with him. Nor did she anticipate her own changes in joining with him. Becoming part of the group.

Her life since the death of her mother had taken a

complete turn, and he was the only one to understand her.

"Harper, betrayal is the only thing I can't help you with."

"It's not?"

"No, if you betray us, this, it's over. I can't protect you from that. You have to understand."

"I'm not going to betray you."

"You're not?"

"I won't."

"You're going to see a lot of shit you're not comfortable with."

She shrugged. "I know this sounds crazy, but I'm ready. Whatever it is you're going to throw at me, I'm ready. I just, I'm only getting used to this, but I'd never betray you, or the others."

"I'm not going to throw anything at you. I only hope you're truly ready when the time is right." He pulled away from the curb, and they were driving once again.

"Are you going to tell me who wrote all that nasty stuff on my locker?"

"No."

"Why not?"

"Consider it a test for when the time comes."

"Okay."

She sat back and stared out of the window at the passing scenery. It was getting dark, and there was a time when being alone with Draven would have made her really uncomfortable. In the past couple of months, he'd been sleeping in her bed, and now her life was bound to his.

She found more comfort in his presence than she did in her own father's. Running fingers through her hair, she expelled a breath.

"What are the guys doing tonight?"

"Some work. Nothing you need to worry yourself about."

"And you decided to take me on a date."

"Yes. I thought you'd been such a good girl, you deserved to be rewarded."

The pain hit her head. "Please, don't call me that."

"What?"

"A good girl."

"You don't like being a good girl?"

"It's not that. It's complicated."

"I'm here. I'm the king of complicated."

He was the only person she could trust and the others, Axel, Buck, and Jett. They were her strength.

"Okay, fine. My mom always told me that no one likes a bad girl. I always had to be good. Always had to do as I was told. I was never to make waves. No one likes a woman that made waves, or a girl. I was always to do the right thing. To make her proud."

"Wow," he said.

"That's what I had to be. When Ian did what he did, it was like he shattered her, only she didn't show it. I felt that because he'd been bad and so had Hannah, I needed to continue being good. So even though I wanted to do other things, I didn't."

"You were always good."

"Yes. Then one day, I went to school. I thought everything was fine. I got good grades. I always answered the teachers' questions. Putting my hand up, getting the answers either right or wrong. Giving it a go. Being a good girl so when parent-teacher night happened, they were happy with me. I was a bright student. Then I came home one day, and there was silence." She rubbed her hands down her palms. "Even

189

when there was only two of us, there was always noise in the house. Mom loved to clean. She loved to have a well-kept house. I guess that was her thing, you know, a well-kept house makes for a happy husband."

"He left anyway."

"Bingo. It didn't matter what my mom did. He'd have never been happy. Anyway, the house was so silent. No television. No music. Mom used to love watching the cooking channel. She'd watch the shows and try to replicate the meals on offer. It was a thing with her. I knew something was wrong. I could feel it. I remember calling to her. You know, 'Mom, I'm home.' Nothing."

Draven grabbed her hand, and she thanked him for the support.

"I went upstairs to my bedroom. My room was so tidy. So neat. I went to her room. It was all so pristine. Nothing out of place. I started to get freaked. Mom was always home. Then I needed to pee really bad. I went to her bathroom. We shared a bathroom in my old place. I opened the door, and there she was. When I saw her, it didn't register in my head exactly what I was seeing. It was my mom. My beautiful mom, and then I saw the water. I saw how pale she was. How her eyes were still open, staring at the ceiling. Lifeless."

She squeezed his hand a little tighter.

"I'm here."

"I panicked. I rushed to that bath, and I tried to pull her out of the water. There was no more blood coming from her. It had already filled the tub. There was nothing more to her. She was gone. I stayed at the hospital until Ian finally decided to come to me," she said. "This is a really morbid conversation."

"Your dad never deserved her or you. He wasn't worth the time or the effort. He's a fucking loser for leaving the two of you."

"I'm biased. My mom though, she loved him with every single fiber of her being. She lived and breathed for him." She covered his hand with her own. "Let's talk about something else."

"I don't mind if you want to keep talking."

"I really don't. The last memories I have of her, they're not good. I loved my mom. She was everything to me. I thought she was like a princess at times. So nice to everyone. Never a bad word to say. When Dad left, he ruined her."

"We'll never leave you."

"It's crazy to think what I've agreed to. My mom would hate me for it."

"Then don't think about it. Just think about us. About what you want, and you find happiness for you."

"I do enjoy being around you guys. Buck's the funniest," she said, smiling.

"Don't have Axel tell you that. He's sure he's the funniest."

"Nah, he's not. He's way too serious to be funny. Jett is the quietest of you all."

"And me?" he asked. "What am I?"

"The most mysterious."

"I sound awesome."

She laughed. Resting her head against his arm, she knew he'd once again brought her out of the darkness. Whenever she thought of her mom, it was always full of so much pain, so much anger. She hated delving into those memories.

Living under Ian and Hannah's roof, it was hard not to relive them. Not to see her mother's body in a pool full of water and blood.

She was an amazing mom, no doubt about it, but she hadn't been prepared to be rejected.

Knowing she wasn't strong enough to deal with

that kind of rejection, hurt Harper. Her mother, for all of her strength, had tried to hide a real weakness. Being a good girl didn't make you stronger, didn't make you more powerful. Her mother had been the epitome of a good girl.

No, Harper knew the key to her strength and to being happy was to be herself. Not to let anyone tear her down, and certainly not to rely solely on a man for her happiness.

She'd never rely on Draven, Axel, Buck, or Jett to make her happy. She'd find her happiness and in return be strong for them as well.

****

The guys knew Draven wanted to bring Harper to a fancy restaurant and to have the night with her. They didn't make waves, or make fun of. They gave him this night. In return, he'd make sure they got their own night in time.

Harper rested against his arm. The scent of lemons filled the car. It was the smell he always associated with her.

In the past couple of her weeks, her training had gone amazingly well, even better than any of them could have ever hoped for. She was strong and like she said earlier, a fast learner.

After his father had sent that guy to rape and kill her, they all knew her training had to be intense. They still held back for the most part.

None of them wanted to really hurt their girl, but she had to be strong to stand and fight. What he recognized was her pent-up anger. She held a lot of pain within her that needed a reason to come out and play.

For the most part, she tried to keep it all locked up inside, and that just wouldn't do. They needed her pain, her anger, her fear. It would help her drive forward and to do any kind of battle they needed.

With Ben and his gang lurking and watching, he knew it was only a matter of time before they got their revenge. Even though it had been months since that run-in at the diner, no one allowed that shit to slide. Not in their world.

There would be punishment coming their way.

He only hoped Harper was ready or that they were all together. There were a lot of classes they were separated for, and he couldn't get himself into all of them. It pissed him off, but as Axel told him, they needed to trust her to handle herself, otherwise what was the point in doing all of this.

When they pulled up outside the Italian restaurant, she lifted her head.

"Are we staying here?" she asked.

"I'm taking you to dinner." He climbed out of the car, and he shook his head, telling the valet to leave her door.

He opened it himself. Her brow rose, and she had a smile on her face.

"Our evening awaits us, Miss."

She laughed, taking his hand as she got out of the car.

Closing the door, he made his way to the maître d', said his name, and was shown in to the table.

He hated his father. Alan Barries was an asshole, but right now, Draven was more than happy to use his name to get what he wanted.

"This is really fancy."

"I'll have to thank my dad. He has a booth here all the time."

"I've never met your dad," she said.

"You're not missing much. Not even a little, believe me."

"You hate your dad?"

"He doesn't deserve the title." He wouldn't tell her about all the things he'd witnessed and been forced to do. Those kinds of nightmares were for him and him only.

Axel got it, understood it as he went through the same. They didn't need to share who had the worst childhood.

Pulling out her seat, she sat down, and he loved her smile.

"This is all amazing," she said.

"And it's all for you."

"All for me." She batted her eyes at him. Her hands clasped together, and he saw she was nervous.

"Are you okay?"

"I'm fine. It's all just a little new. I don't know if I really belong here."

He covered her hands with his. "It doesn't matter if you belong or not. You're here with me. That's all that matters. Own it. You're you, Harper. Don't let anyone ever tell you differently."

"You're always so nice to me."

"You're mine remember. Ours."

Her cheeks flamed. "Right. Of course. It's not like I forget that, ever."

This made him laugh. "I adore you."

"Really? I kind of adore you too."

He opened the drinks menu. "You want wine?"

She shook her head. "Water would be more than fine for me."

He nodded to the waiter. He ordered them both some water. He asked for ice for himself, and Harper wanted hers plain.

When he finished, he put down the drinks menu and picked up the food one. Glancing over the top, he saw her looking at him. "What?"

"I don't know. You seem really in charge. It is … I don't know. Ignore me."

"I'm not ignoring you. Come on, what is it?"

"You don't seem eighteen. You look and sound a lot older."

With all the things he'd seen, he didn't feel like a teenage kid.

"I'm sorry."

"Don't keep apologizing," he said.

She went to say it again, only she pressed her lips together.

"That's a start. Now, tell me what you want for dinner." He watched her as he looked down at her menu. For the first time in weeks, she looked like a real woman. Between her training and being at school, she'd blended in as one of the guys.

She was far from one of the guys right now. Her tits pressed against the tight bodice of the dress. He'd picked it for that reason alone. Her tits were so big, and the cleavage it gave her, it made his dick hard just watching her.

She hadn't opted for heels, so against him, it made her incredibly small. Her head came to his chest. She couldn't even walk in heels.

They'd both ended up in a fit of giggles one night when he asked her to try them on. She'd collapsed against him, and it had turned into a make-out session. He loved her lips. They were so plump, kissable and fuckable at the same time.

He needed to focus on the menu and not on taking her to the nearest room and ridding her of her virginity.

There was no doubt in any of their minds that he'd be the one to claim her cherry. None of the guys wanted to have it, even though they found themselves becoming more and more attracted to her with every passing day.

"You're staring," she said.

"You look incredibly beautiful tonight."

"You picked the dress. You're complimenting yourself." She giggled.

"Then I have excellent dress sense."

"I'd say." She winked at him. "I'd love the steak and potatoes if that's okay."

"More than okay." He signaled the waiter, gave his order, and they were alone again.

She glanced around the restaurant, and he watched her.

"Have you ever thought about what would happen if you went to college?" she asked.

"I'm not going to college."

"I know. I'm just curious if you even want to?" She tilted her head to the side and smiled at him. "I'm making conversation, Draven."

"Are you wanting to go to college?"

She shrugged. "It was a dream I had, but with everything going on, that's not going to happen."

"Why?"

"I'm not going to ask Ian for help with funding. The moment I can, I want out of there."

"What if I can set that up?"

"What do you mean?" she asked.

"I could get you your own place or you could come and live with me." It was a risk, but maybe with her being right in his father's house, he'd see how serious they all were.

"I don't know." She shook her head. "Let's not talk about that, and you answer my question about college."

"No, I wouldn't want to go. Everything I know and need to know doesn't involve a college education but a street one."

"You're not even tempted or a little curious?"

"No."

"I like that. I like that you know who you are."

"You know who you are as well, Harper." He picked her hand up and placed a kiss to the inside of her wrist. "You're a strong, beautiful woman. You've got a mean kick and throw a decent punch."

"Draven, they're not great skills."

"To a fighter, they're the best kind of skills. You're a fighter now, and you've got to look to your strengths, not your weakness. You're strong. Say it with me."

"I'm strong."

This made her smile, and seeing it light up her face, took his breath away.

You're falling for her.

He hadn't fallen for her recently. No, he'd fallen for her a long time ago.

Their meal came out. All talk about colleges and a change of life ceased. They talked about everything else. The training, Axel's need to always be number one, Buck's constant joking, and of course, Jett's mad skills with a knife.

He liked that even when they weren't with them, she was more than happy to talk about them. They were part of her life too.

She didn't want dessert, and he saw a bunch of couples together on the dance floor. He'd already paid the check, and before heading out, he took her hand, leading her onto the floor. Putting an arm around her waist, he drew her close. With the other, he captured her hand.

"This is nice," she said.

"I wanted this to be perfect."

She chuckled. "It really is."

She tilted her head back, and he brushed her lips with his own. She moaned his name, and he gripped her waist harder, not wanting to let her go. He loved the sweet sounds she made as he deepened the kiss. She opened her lips for him, and he plundered inside.

The sound of throats clearing had him pulling away. He nodded at the smiles and cheers.

"Come on," he said.

He gave them a little wave and left the restaurant. He had to show a great deal of restraint. He didn't want the kiss to end.

When it came to Harper, there were a lot of things he didn't want to end.

They waited for the valet to bring his car around. He kept Harper at his side. She cupped his cheek, and he stared down into her eyes, so captured by the color. *So expressive.*

"I'm ready, Draven."

"Ready?"

"Yes. I want this … tonight. You and me. Just you and me."

He cupped her cheek, knowing what she was saying. "Are you sure?"

"I've never been more sure of anything in my life. I want you tonight. Before we go back to town. Back to everything."

The car pulled up in front of him, and he tipped them. Opening the door for her, he closed it once she was inside. Placing a hand on the car, he took a few deep breaths. His cock was unbearably hard.

This was another turning point for the two of them. He wanted her, and she was a virgin. It wouldn't be easy, and he knew there would be pain as well.

Running a hand down his face, he walked to the driver's side. Climbing behind the wheel, he started up the engine and turned to her.

"You're sure?"

"Yes. I'm sure. I mean, if you want to. I don't want you to do something you don't want to do."

He laughed. "I want this. I just, I wasn't expecting you to want it tonight."

"Then we don't have to."

"You're ready. I'm going to shut up now before I spoil everything." He took her hand, kissing the inside of her wrist. She let out a breathy sigh.

He wasn't going to wait for this.

Harper was his, and he was going to claim her virginity. The first part of her belonging to all of them just how they wanted it.

Get a grip, Draven.
Don't fuck this up.

Chapter Twelve

The hotel was nice.

Harper stood in the center, staring at the bed as Draven closed the door, drawing the curtain and giving them some privacy.

She didn't want to go home, nor did she want this night to end. Her heart pounded, and even though she was ready, nerves flooded her. Turning to Draven, she forced a smile to her lips.

"We can call it a night right now. I can take you home."

"You got the room for the night." She slipped out of her shoes.

"I'm not going to force you to do this, Harper."

She laughed. "There's not going to be any force." She stepped up to him.

"Really? You look like you're going to throw up."

She shook her head. "I'm not. I want this. Can't I be a little nervous with everything?"

"You're nervous." He held her shoulders.

"Yes. I'm nervous. Everything I've done has been with you. I don't even know if you're my boyfriend, my friend, lover, I don't know what to call you."

"I'm everything. I'm your boyfriend, lover, friend, enemy, all of it."

She laughed. "You're not my enemy."

"Until you're ready, I'm everything you need me to be."

She tilted her head back. "Then kiss me, lover."

He slammed his lips down on hers, and she moaned as his tongue slid across her lips. His fingers sank into her hair, holding onto the locks, making her gasp as he gave them a tug. "I love your lips," he said.

"So fucking much."

She wrapped her arms around him, loving the feel of his body against hers.

The hard ridge of his cock teased her stomach, and the length seemed to pulse as if it had a mind of its own.

Gripping his shoulders, she'd gladly kiss him forever, the two of them locked within this embrace. The hand at her head moved, sliding down her body. He grabbed the zipper and started to ease it down her back, opening her dress.

She liked that he knew what he was doing. At least it made one of them. For so long now, she didn't have a clue what she was doing, nor did she now.

He pulled the dress from her body. It fell to the floor, exposing her lingeried self. A white lace bra and panties, no socks.

She tugged the shirt he wore out of his pants and worked on the buttons. She didn't tear at his shirt, even though she wanted to. One button at a time, she revealed his hard, muscular chest. Running her hands up to his shoulders, she pushed it off his body, and the shirt fell to the floor.

It always amazed her how much ink covered him. She traced a design across his chest, a rose over his heart, leading down his side. The thorns looked dark and threatening.

He took her hand, kissing the inside of her wrist.

With his other hand, he cupped her pussy, making her gasp. He pressed a finger against the material, and it grazed her clit.

She moaned as each touch sent the pleasure within her higher.

He let go of her pussy, and next, he removed her bra. He flicked the catch at the back, and her tits spilled free. He pressed a kiss to her shoulder, the touch so delicate that she leaned against him, wanting more. He knelt down in front of her, his fingers on her panties.

She nodded her head, letting him know she wanted this, reassuring him that she was more than fine with what was about to happen.

The panties found their space on the floor as she stepped out of them.

She was now naked while Draven still wore his pants. Gripping the belt buckle, she tugged him close. He pulled on her hair, giving her no choice but to look up. He claimed her lips.

His tongue slid across her mouth, and she opened up to him. She loved it when he kissed her. It made her forget all of her troubles. The only person she focused on or could care about was him.

They were in this moment together, and she wouldn't give this up for the world. He was everything to her.

His grip on her hair loosened, and he trailed his lips down to her neck, sucking on the pulse. His touch was soft at first but grew hard. He bit her, and she cried out. The pleasure and pain flooded her body, making her melt for more.

Draven moved her back. She collapsed to the bed, and he followed her down, moving her up, as he followed her.

"You're still dressed," she said, complaining. She'd not even been able to remove the belt.

"I'll be naked, all in good time."

He kissed her again and then moved down her body, each kiss making her moan. He took each of her nipples, in turn, into his mouth.

The pleasure intensified. Her nerves were building as he kept on kissing down her body. A virgin she may be, but she wasn't immune or completely oblivious to what was about to happen.

He spread her legs, and as his tongue danced over her clit, she screamed. The first lick of his tongue shocked her with the intensity. She wasn't expecting the instant hit of pleasure as he did so.

Draven didn't stop. He took her clit into his mouth, sucking on the bud. The man was an expert. She didn't want to think about how much pussy he'd enjoyed in his life. All she cared about was how good it felt.

He spread the lips of her pussy open, and she screamed his name as with a few strokes, she felt like she was going to explode. Should she be this close so soon? Was it natural to find release quickly?

So many questions and at the same time, she didn't have time to answer them all.

Her orgasm washed over her. The pleasure was unlike anything in her life, even that first time with Draven. This was better, way better.

She gave herself up to the sweet heaven that he gave and hoped there would be more to come. He laid another kiss to her pussy, and she watched as he stood up, removing his belt, sliding the zipper down.

When he pushed his boxers down and was completely naked, she was a little taken aback.

This was the first cock she'd ever seen. He already had a condom in his hands and was sliding it over his length. Even as fear crawled down her back, she didn't move.

He settled between her spread thighs. "Do you want me to stop?"

She found it so incredibly tender that at every turn, he kept making sure she was happy, that she was okay.

"No, I don't want you to."

More than anything else in the world, she wanted this. There's no way she'd want this to ever stop.

Cupping his cheek, she leaned up and kissed him. "Please, Draven, I want you." She tugged him down and loved hearing his groan.

"You're going to be the death of me one day, Harper."

She felt him reach between them, grab his cock, and slide it through her folds. It was poised at her entrance. She took a deep breath, and he thrust in deep, tearing through the wall of her virginity.

Harper cried out, the sudden grip of pain shocking her with its intensity.

He took possession of her lips as the pain continued to burst within her even as his cock stilled.

"Shh, it's okay. I've got you."

Time stood still. Draven didn't pressure her. His kisses were sweet release against the onslaught of pain.

She knew there would be some pain as there always was with a woman's first time.

"I've got you, Harper. I've got you. Do you want me to stop?"

"No. Please don't stop." She held him still.

He groaned. "There's only so much control I've got."

"Then don't show control. Take me, Draven. I'm here."

Slowly, he began to pull out of her. The pressure took her by surprise, the sudden bite of pain forcing her to grit her teeth. He took his time though, working his cock in and out of her until the pain started to ebb away.

One moment it hurt, and the next, it was gone as if it was imaginary.

In and out.

All the time.

The pleasure drove her up, fucking up against him as he worked inside her, over and over.

"Please, Draven."

"Fuck, you feel so incredible." He grabbed her hands, pushing them to the bed, holding her in place as he thrust in deep.

She wrapped her legs around him, feeling that crest once again, that point of bliss that made her ache.

Just a little more.

He rubbed her clit with each thrust, and as she came apart, she felt him do so as well. His release pulsed inside her, filling the condom. His groan echoed in the small hotel room.

When it was over, he collapsed over her, and she took his body weight, more than happy to. Running her fingers up and down his back, she smiled against his chest. Even though there had been some pain, it had been one of the best experiences in the world.

Draven pulled away from her.

"How are you?" he asked.

"I'm good. Honestly. I loved that."

He smiled, and then he kissed her, making it the perfect moment again.

****

"You can't take my mac and cheese," Harper said, swatting his hands away.

Draven laughed as he used his fork to try to steal some of her food.

Axel, Jett, and Buck were each doing the same. Their pizza tasted like a horse's ass, it was so bad. Her mac and cheese looked pretty damn good.

After a couple of weeks of Harper sitting with them, they'd stopped becoming the focal point of all the pointing and whispers. Not that it bothered him at all. He was used to having people talk shit about him behind his back.

For Harper though, it was all new.

It had been two weeks since he'd taken her out to dinner. Two weeks in which he'd claimed her as his. Every single night since then, he either snuck in her room, or they found some quiet time in his car.

He'd not taken her home yet. He was avoiding his father. The meeting with Alan and Harper could wait for as long as possible.

She giggled as he pulled her onto his lap and then stole her mac and cheese.

"See, where there's a will there's a way."

She rolled her eyes. "You just know how to cheat."

"Still winning." He held his fork up to her lips, and she took it. "And I always share."

Running his hand down her back, he gripped her ass, his eyes going from cold to hot in a second.

It was on the tip of his tongue to ask her to skip school when Ben and three of his little pals approached their table. He got to his feet, as did Axel, Jett, and Buck. With Harper at his side, he faced off with Ben, who held up his hands.

"We want to make a peace offering," Ben said.

"Not going to happen."

"Look, we know the ring is coming up any day now. We're all waiting, and we know it's going to be a bloodbath."

"The ring?" Harper asked.

"I'll tell you about it in a minute."

Buck chuckled. "He's trying to save his ass from a beating."

"Look, I meant no disrespect," Ben said, his gaze landing on Harper.

"You look at me, fuckhead. Not her."

"If I'd known she belonged to you guys, I wouldn't have touched her."

"I didn't even invite you to touch me. You need to learn to keep your hands to yourself," Harper said.

Ben's jaw clenched.

Draven saw it. Ben's anger was clear. He wasn't over what happened at the diner. There would come a point when he took revenge. It was only a matter of time.

The ring though, that wasn't the place to do it.

Ben couldn't take them on. With his little band of girls behind him, possibly, but not one on one. He was too scared about his precious arms and legs.

"Truce?" Ben asked, holding his hand out.

"No," Draven said. "No truce. Not going to happen. I've got no reason to trust you. Now get the fuck gone."

He sat down, moving Harper to the seat beside him. With his arm wrapped around her, he didn't let her go.

Axel, Buck, and Jett each took a seat, all of them ignoring the jocks.

Ben didn't linger as the insult was clear.

Draven would need to make sure Harper was taken care of.

"What's the ring?" Harper asked. "It sounds like some kind of cult."

Buck laughed. "It's not."

"It's a place a bunch of punk-ass kids go and fight it out," Axel said. "They like to be tough."

Harper looked at Axel before turning to Draven.

"You guys go, don't you?"

"Yes, we go," Jett said. "Draven's actually one of the best fighters there, and he likes to win big."

"Win. There's money involved?"

"My dad likes to put money on the fights,"

Draven said.

"Someone catches the entire thing, and he watches it," Axel said. "It's like they're auditioning for the next round of soldiers. It's pretty tough. Fucking fierce."

"When does it happen?" she asked.

"Any day now." Draven took another bite of his pizza. It still tasted nasty.

"Why am I only hearing about this now?"

"You thinking of entering?" Axel asked.

"Wait, you're going to go without me?"

No one answered.

"Wow, okay, fine. If you want to be that way." She pulled out of his hold and stormed out of the cafeteria.

"She's pissed," Jett said.

"No shit." Draven got to his feet.

"She's going to want to go," Axel said.

"Yeah, and everyone who goes there has to fight." Draven ran fingers through his hair. This was not how he wanted her to find out. He'd hoped the ring would come and go. He glanced over at Ben, wanting to kill the bastard.

"There are chicks there," Axel said.

"If she loses it looks bad on all of us," Draven said, reminding him this was about reputation.

"Yeah, and if she wins, we look fucking hot," Buck said. "I think she could hold her own."

"And if she can't, she'll be killed. I'm going to follow her."

He left the cafeteria and went in search of her. After finding her locker abandoned, he found her on the football bleachers. She sat at the top, and he walked up the steps to join her.

"That seat is taken," she said.

"Right." He didn't move. "You're upset."

"Yes."

"The ring has been around a lot longer than you've been one of us, Harper. It's dangerous."

"When I signed up for this with you, I didn't agree to only be half there. I'm in, one hundred percent. I mean it, Draven. If you guys fight, I want to be there."

"You've got to fight as well," he said. "It's not pretty."

She took his hand. "I don't need you to always protect me. There's no way I'm going to be able to handle that night if you're gone. I'll worry. Please, let me go with you. If I have to fight, I'll fight."

"It's not easy."

"I don't doubt it for a second." She laughed. "You guys are always making everything so complicated."

"It's what we do. Our lives are all complicated."

"That is so very true." She sighed. "I'm all in. Fighting or not." She rested her head against his shoulder. "Trust me."

He did trust her.

Everyone else they had to fight; he didn't.

"So, what's the verdict?" Axel asked, walking up the bleachers.

"Where's Buck and Jett?" Draven asked.

"They started a food fight in the cafeteria. They're on their own." Axel took a seat in front of them.

"She's coming with us," Draven said.

Axel's gaze landed on Harper. "It's pretty intense, and I'm not just saying that. There's a lot of bad shit going down."

"I know. I know. I get it. It's going to be hard for me, but I'm not going to let you guys go alone."

"You're willing to fight?" Axel looked worried,

and Draven was pleased he wasn't the only one with concerns.

"Yes. I'm either with you guys or I'm not. What is it going to be?" she asked.

"You're with us," Axel said. "It's going to be hot seeing you."

They heard the bell ring. Climbing off the bleachers, Draven wrapped his arm across Harper's shoulders, and they walked her to class.

"I'll see you guys after school." She kissed his lips and Axel's cheek.

Draven knew the guys hadn't been with another chick since he declared Harper as theirs. Where he was getting her at night, they were not getting anything.

Soon, they'd have her, and there would be no backing down.

They didn't go to class. None of the teachers forced them.

He sat on the hood of his car, staring up at the large building. It was a prison in its own way.

"She's not ready."

"We don't know that. She's strong, and she holds her own."

"We're talking fighters here, Axel. Not just some kids pretending to know what they're doing. They're after the prize. Some of the women, they're going to know who she is, and they're going to fight to hurt her, to scar her."

"Scars or not, Harper's ours. If you're not willing to go all the way with her, how is your dad ever going to believe her loyalty? This way, we get to see how much she can handle and how she works within the club."

Draven sighed. "I don't like this. I don't like it one bit."

"There's not a lot you can do. You know your

father's going to be watching. He's waiting to see her fall."

He nodded. "It pisses me off." He ran a hand down his face.

"Ben's going to go after her. He's pissed off and angry. That's not good for us."

"It's not going to be good for him either. He needs to leave well enough alone," Draven said.

"There's another auction happening," Axel said.

"There is, so soon?"

"A new shipment of girls arrived this week. I swear some of them are not even ten." Axel shook his head. "That's what I'd stop."

Draven knew it was hard for Axel when it came to the auctions. They had their own plans for what they'd do when the business finally came to them. "It'll be fine."

"Whatever you say, Draven. Whatever you say."

Chapter Thirteen

The Ring
Two weeks later

Harper stood in the open court. It looked more like an old football field. Large floodlights shone down, and music filled the air.

The tensions mounted, and as she walked between her guys, she sensed a caution inside them with every single step they took. The ring wasn't a joke.

Men and women stood around in groups or on their own. A couple of guys were collecting bets and giving tabs to people.

"Is all this arranged in advance or something?" Harper asked.

"No, not even close. Ticket numbers are read out, and the opponents are picked at random. Girls face off with girls and guys do guys. It's what they consider fair," Axel said.

"When does the fighting start?" she asked.

"When you hear the gunshot," Draven said.

He held her tightly as they moved through the crowds. They were stopped, and the man handed them each a ticket.

"No, she doesn't get a ticket," Draven said.

"You know the rules, Barries. Everyone here gets a ticket. No exceptions. This is not a place to bring your girlfriend, and without a ticket, you're not getting out, and you're not getting out without fighting. Rules are rules."

A ticket was placed in her hand. She looked down at her ticket. Number two-three-one. She took a deep breath.

"You have to be a good girl."

"Good girls don't get into fights. They don't go to

parties. They're good for a reason."

This was anything but good.

The gunshot went off, and everyone just stopped.

The lights turned to the center of what looked like a stage. It was a fighting ring that was built for the crowd to look at.

"That's right. Welcome to the new year of the ring, people. I can see some badasses out there tonight, and I'm only talking about the women here. Damn, girls, you've come for some serious dough. Let's get this started. We've got a lot of fights to get through tonight. Let's make this easy. Number three-one-nine, against two-three-seven. Up you come. Winner goes to the next round, loser goes home."

"Now you get to watch," Draven said. He pulled her in front of him so his arms were wrapped around her.

Her heart raced and not out of excitement either. There was no way any of this could be described as thrilling or exciting. More like scary. Yes, she was petrified.

The first fighters were two guys, and they appeared in their early twenties. She watched as they removed their jackets, and that was it, fists up at the ready.

"No protection?" she asked.

"Protection is for sports and wimps," Axel said.

She winced as the first hit was struck. Over and over, they hit, punched, kicked, and just fucked each other up. She didn't know who was who, but finally, one guy went down and he held his hand up in surrender.

"Loser," Axel said.

"There's no way this is a good thing. You do this every single year?" she asked.

"It's not that bad."

"This is awful. You can't do this. It's wrong."

"Harper," Draven said, spinning her around so that she could look at him. She didn't want to see him hurting. "This is what we do. We're not hiding this, and you've got to do this as well. You've got your ticket. I tried to warn you."

"I had no idea."

"Now you do. There's no getting out of this. No backing down." He pressed a kiss to her lips.

She turned back to look at the stage as someone else entered the ring. It was two new people, two new fighters.

With each fight, she found herself flinching less and less, even as her stomach turned from seeing the blood.

When two women entered the ring, Harper couldn't believe the violence they displayed. They tugged and pulled at their hair, one woman tearing out a huge chunk.

Pulling a band from her jacket, she did no more than pull her hair up on top of her head, ready in case her number went up.

"You look hot," Draven said.

"This isn't funny."

"I'm not laughing, babe. I tried to warn you. No backing down now."

She nodded. When Draven's number was read out, she watched him go. He released her hand, and Axel pulled her into his arms. He held her hands, and his body pressed against her back. She liked his heat and took comfort in his touch.

"He'll be fine," Axel said.

"How do you know that? I can't believe I'm about to watch this."

"Draven's a monster," Buck said. "He's one of the best fighters here. No one can best him."

Biting her lip, she watched as another guy entered the ring. He was huge. He had to way close to a hundred pounds more than Draven, and his muscles were twice the size of Draven.

"He's going to get killed," Harper said.

"Have faith." Axel wrapped his arms around her.

"Are you even his friend at all?"

"You've seen him during training. Draven is one of the hardest, fiercest bastards here. He could kill them all. It's why he's so deadly. Why his father keeps him so fucking close. Draven could take over now because he can make the hard decisions, and above all else, he can fight. He commands respect. Trust him, Harper, watch him."

So she did.

She watched as he shook his opponent's hand, and they stepped away from each other.

Silence rang out. No one spoke. Once the fighting started, she realized he'd been holding back. He hadn't been joking about testing her.

Draven unleashed a monster she had never seen before. Blow after blow he landed. He took a couple, but he shook them off as if they meant nothing to him. Each movement was carefully calculated.

He was a machine. No one stood a chance against him. He didn't need to strike every single time. He landed blows to the face and body, and when the guy went down, Draven didn't pursue him. He waited.

Once again, the guy was up, not ready to call the fight quits.

Draven got hit in the face, and then he twisted the guy's arm, backhanding him, and kicking him down.

He got up again, only to be pummeled in the face and shoved hard. That one shove and the guy lifted his hand up in surrender. Blood poured from his nose and mouth.

Draven was the victor.

He grabbed his ticket and jacket, and walked back over to them. She saw there was a little bruising on one cheek.

"Did you let him hit you?" Axel asked.

"I had to make it look good."

"Wait, you let him hit you?" This was insane. Crazy. She couldn't even believe they were having this discussion.

"It is what it is, baby," Draven said, kissing her.

They stood together again. Axel had to fight, followed by Buck. Both of the guys were fearless. Buck lost his joker face, and she'd never seen how deadly he was. The change in him scared her, and the same for Axel, even though he was more serious to start. There was something off about him. Like he'd been putting on a mask for others to see, and now she saw the real him.

Four more fights and then her number rang out. She held her ticket, and Draven gripped her arm.

"You've got to let me go."

"Get angry," he said. "Don't lose control. But feel that anger spread."

Her number was called again.

"Don't turn your back."

"I won't." She pulled out of his arms and headed to the ring.

Draven, Axel, Buck, and Jett followed her. They were close to the stage for her first official fight. Removing her jacket, she did what she'd seen others do and dropped it to the ground.

Climbing into the ring, she presented her ticket and glanced at the woman opposite her.

"So, you're the Stonewall whore," the woman sneered.

Harper didn't even recognize her. She didn't say anything.

"I'm going to pound your face into the fucking dirt. They're never going to want to fuck you again."

"Well, well, well, ladies, we've got a newbie here, and let's see what she's got," the man said.

Stepping away from the woman, Harper waited for the bell, and when it happened, the woman charged. Harper moved quickly, but the woman expected it. She didn't even have a clue who she was.

The brunette clearly hated her.

Harper was grabbed and thrown to the ground. A blow landed against her stomach, and as she gasped, another went to her face. The woman was too fast.

Trying to wriggle away, she couldn't.

Draven, Axel, Buck, and Jett are counting on me.

Fuck!

It hurts.

Feed the pain.

Drawing her hand back, she punched the woman square in the nose with all of her might. It was enough to stop the blows, and she shoved her off.

Getting to her feet, she placed her fingers against her own nose and came away with blood. Her cheek was smarting as well, not to mention her stomach had taken a beating.

Note to self, never, fucking ever, come to the ring again.

Staring at her opponent, she saw the damage she'd done. Blood dripped down her shirt, and guilt flooded her.

It didn't last for long as the woman charged at her.

Lifting her foot up, Harper kicked, hard. Channeling her anger, she got knocked off her feet as the woman twisted her foot out, and Harper didn't get away in time.

Just as the woman tried to straddle her, Harper used her weight and remembered her training of attacking Draven to get on top.

She straddled the woman. Even as she didn't want to, she kept on hitting. She had to keep hitting until the woman quit.

When her hair was pulled and more vile words spilled out of her mouth, Harper lost it.

"You're nothing but a disgusting whore. Nothing more than a cunt."

She had joined with Draven, Axel, Buck, and Jett. They were her friends. They were there when she needed them most. At the diner when Ben touched her. In the woodlands when she was attacked. They were her friends. Her people, and there was no one in this world that was going to talk shit about her.

Drawing her hand back, she slammed it against the woman's face, over and over again. The image before her became blurred. Her father. Her mother. Hannah. Her attacker. Ben. They all rolled into one, and it pissed her off.

Suddenly, she was being pulled away.

"Get the fuck off me," Harper said.

"Enough, Harper, enough," Draven said.

Axel was there as well. "She's done. She's finished."

Harper stared at the woman. She'd been hitting her, and her arm was up in surrender.

Her stomach twisted. Rushing to the edge of the pitch, away from everyone, she threw up.

Her hands were covered in blood. Her thoughts were so fucking dark she couldn't see straight. Every part of her body ached.

Someone was there, rubbing her back. Another held her hair, and hands soothed her. It was all of them, all four of them.

"It's fine. We've got you," Draven said. "Don't worry."

"Did I kill her?" Harper asked.

"No, but she's going to need some surgery, and I doubt she's going to call you a whore anytime soon."

"Huh, what?"

"That's what you screamed at her," he said. "You yelled that you were not a whore. That you were never a whore."

"Oh." She didn't even have a clue what she'd been saying. It was all a blur.

****

"I've never been inside your room before," Harper said.

"After tonight, you deserve it."

Draven held the first aid kit open. They had already had a shower, but now he wanted to check over her wounds.

The fighting had continued for three more hours. Harper was called up twice more, but the women had held their hands up and surrendered.

She didn't have skills, but her rage had done all the talking for her.

His heart had broken for her as she screamed at the first one. He'd seen the woman's hand go up, and Axel had been the one to see that Harper was no longer in a fight. She was hurting whatever she saw in her head.

They had no choice but to pull her off. No one else could stop her. People were now afraid of her.

Ben and his boys had been there to witness it. He hoped it would keep whatever revenge they planned at bay.

There was only so long that Ben and his boys could wait, but Harper had proven she was a force to be reckoned with.

"Do you hate me?" she asked. Her voice was so small.

"No. Why would I hate you?"

"I saw how the others fighters looked at me. They thought I was crazy."

"You're not crazy. You got into the zone." He pulled out some alcohol wipes and pressed them on her knuckles.

She let out a wince. "I wasn't in anything."

"Where were you?"

"I got so angry, and then I couldn't stop. It was like I was fighting everyone. Ian, Mom, Hannah, Ben, that guy out in the woods. I completely lost it."

He cupped her face. "I know it freaks you out, but you did us all proud."

"How?"

"You showed them that you're a fighter. You have a right to be part of us."

"You do that every single year?" she asked.

"Yes."

"I don't know if I can do another year."

He laughed. "I don't know if anyone would want to fight you. You're being trained by me, and I'm one of the best."

"How do you know how to fight so well?" she asked.

"I'm a Barries. My dad demands the best from me. I had to learn to fight. I've been training since I was a kid."

"Instead of doing normal stuff that kids do."

"Exactly."

"Have you ever missed doing stuff that other kids

do?" she asked.

"Like what?"

"I don't know. Playing, having fun, hanging out, fixing cars. I don't know what normal guys do."

He sighed. Wrapping a bandage around her split knuckles, he smiled. "Those kids don't grow up in this kind of house or this town. You know the rumors and what I've told you. The evil Stonewall hides is very much present within this room. It's never going to go away. I'm stuck here."

She touched his cheek, and he turned his head, kissing her wrist.

"I think we should play a board game."

"That sounds all great, but I don't own any."

"None at all?"

"None."

"Then one day I'm going to pick one up, and you're going to play with me."

He lifted her up and pressed her against the bed. As he kissed her head, she wrapped her legs around his waist. "There is one game I love."

"Yeah, what is it called?"

"Hide the sausage."

She burst out laughing. "Really?"

"Yes, also known as sex."

"You want to have sex?"

He pressed his cock against her. "Don't you feel how much I do?"

She moaned. "Yes."

"Do you think you can handle me?"

"There's no reason why I can't handle you."

He thrust against her. The small shorts she wore did nothing to hide her from him. Kissing her neck, he eased the strap of her shirt down, exposing her tit.

Sucking on her nipple, he did the same to the

second strap until both tits were exposed for him to suck on. Pressing her breasts together, he flicked his tongue back and forth, loving each hard peak.

Letting them go, he slid a hand down her body, working beneath her shorts to find her wet clit.

Like all the times before, she was wet, and he was hard. They were a perfect match.

Sliding a finger inside her tight heat, he added a second one. She thrust up against him and he kept on licking and sucking at her sweet tits.

So sweet. So sexy. All his.

Until I have to share.

He pushed those thoughts to the back of his mind.

Sharing wasn't a problem. He loved his friends. Axel, Jett, and Buck, they were his brothers. In fact, they were closer than any brother he could imagine ever having. He'd die for them, and there was no way he'd ever let anyone come between them. Not even Harper.

No matter what he felt for her, he knew his friends would take care of her. They were going to share her to cement their bond, to guarantee nothing and no one came between them. They were happy to wait now, but once they were together, there would be no more waiting. No more holding back. Harper would belong to all four of them.

Harper belonged to all three of them too, even if she shared his bed most nights. Well, the other way around. He shared her bed.

Biting down on her nipple, he heard her cry out. In his home, he didn't have to keep her silent. She could scream all she wanted.

No one would come running in his room. His father was busy over at Axel's father's place. With a new shipment of girls, he'd be too tempted to take one for himself.

Again, he pushed that out of his mind. All he wanted to focus on was his woman. Harper. She was his, his fierce woman.

"I love it when you do that," she said, sounding breathless.

"Doing what?"

"That, with your mouth."

"You love it when I bite your tits?"

"Yes, yes, it feels so good. Don't stop."

He smiled and kept on licking and sucking at her tits. They were big, just how he liked them.

Teasing a third finger inside her wet cunt, he stretched her. Drawing his fingers up, he began to stroke her clit, and she rubbed herself against him. His cock pressed to the front of his boxers, wanting inside her. He always wanted to feel her come around his dick.

Pulling his hand away, he moved off her but helped her onto her knees.

"What is it?" she asked.

"On your knees." He stroked across her ass, tugging her shorts down and cupping her cheeks. He spread her open, staring at her pussy and asshole.

Reaching behind him into the drawer for a condom, he tore into it, sliding the latex over his length, and pressing the tip of his dick at her entrance.

He watched, which was way better than any porno, as he slid, inch by glorious inch within her.

She opened up around him, her sweet pussy pulsing as he filled her.

Gripping her hips, he thrust in deep, and closed his eyes. He slid his fingers between her slit, stroking over her clit. The first touch to her nub had him groaning as her cunt tightened around him.

Each touch and stroke set her off, squeezing him even tighter.

He stayed perfectly still within her, wanting to feel her come first. Kissing her shoulder, he stroked her clit and saw her hands clenching the blanket as he drew her closer and closer to orgasm.

The moment she came apart, he had to control his own release as it nearly set him off. *So tight. So wet. So fucking sweet.*

He couldn't concentrate.

She strangled his cock, and finally, when he couldn't take it anymore, he stopped playing with her and started to work his dick inside her.

Pushing in and out.

Over and over.

The condom wasn't a pretty sight, but he couldn't do anything about that. So he fucked her, seeing her cum over the condom.

One day, he'd take her without it, and he'd get to live out his own porno when it came to her. He'd have her every single day, full to the brim with their cum. There was so much he wanted to do to her. In time, he hoped to share every single memory with her.

Pulling out of her, he disposed of the condom, and walked back to the bed, cuddling up to her. Her curvy ass nestled against his pelvis. He wrapped his arms around her, cupping her tit.

"I need to wrap your hands," she said. She grabbed his hand, and her thumb ran around the wounds that hurt.

"I'm good."

"You don't have to play the tough guy to me."

"They don't hurt. I don't feel them." Hitting things was something he was good at. No matter how many times he did it, it no longer caused him pain.

"I'll never get used to this."

"You're going to have to." He kissed her

shoulder.

"Draven?"

"Yes."

"One day it's not just going to be you and me, is it?"

He gripped her hip tighter. "No."

"Will you be able to share me?"

"Yes." The lie fell easily from his tongue.

"Will I have to share you?"

"Never."

She rolled over, and he cupped her cheek.

He watched as she opened her mouth, then closed it. "What is it?"

"Nothing. It's fine." She leaned up, kissing his lip. "Good night, Draven."

She rolled back over.

He wouldn't let her go. Not ever. Staring across his bedroom, he held her in his arms, waiting for her to fall asleep.

Time passed, and it took her a long time to finally relax and go to sleep. Lifting up, he stroked a curl away from her face.

"If I didn't have to share you, I wouldn't. I'll do anything for my friends, even get them to fall for the girl I've been wanting all my life. You've been mine from the first moment I saw you, Harper. I'll never let you go, and I wouldn't change that. They're my brothers, and I would die for them."

He laid a kiss to her head and settled in behind her. Breathing in her lemony scent, he found peace as he slept also.

Chapter Fourteen

The following morning, Harper stared down at a sleeping Draven. He looked so content in his sleep. She didn't have it in her to wake him up.

She climbed back into her shorts and crop top. Instead of waking him with kisses, she'd make him some food.

Pulling on a pair of socks, she left his room and headed toward the kitchen that he'd showed her last night. She didn't pass anyone in the hallway or on the stairs. His parents hadn't been home last night, and as she entered the kitchen, she went straight to the fridge.

He loved bacon and eggs. It was the one thing she'd always cooked with her mother on the weekends. Opening drawers and cupboards, she found everything she needed to make a delicious breakfast.

The bandage on her hand was a reminder of what happened last night.

She placed a hand to her stomach, counted to ten, and got to work making breakfast. Turning on the coffee machine, she hummed to herself, just enjoying the freedom.

"Well, well, well," a very masculine voice said.

She gasped, spinning around with the carton of eggs in her hand. She bumped into the corner of the island and ended up dropping the six eggs onto the floor.

"Shoot, I'm so sorry."

"Who are you?" he asked.

She tucked some hair behind her ears and stared at the older man. Draven looked similar to this man. He had to be his father.

"Erm, I'm Harper."

"Ah, Miller's girl."

"You're Draven's dad?" she asked.

He looked her up and down, assessing her.

She didn't like that. No man should be looking at her as if she had some kind of price tag.

"Yes. Where is Draven?"

"He's in bed." Her cheeks were on fire as she stared at his dad, who smiled.

"Interesting."

"I was just making him breakfast."

"I've been meaning to meet you."

"You have?" Her voice squeaked, and she tried to clear it.

He smiled. "Do I make you nervous?"

"No, no. It's fine." She nibbled her lip. This couldn't have been any more awkward.

"Does your dad know you're here?" Draven's father moved across the kitchen toward her.

The urge to step back was so strong, but she stayed perfectly still even as he brushed past her.

Run.

This man was a monster, a truly evil person.

She sensed it in the way he stared at her. She didn't know why her father worked for him or why he'd even want to. Pushing those thoughts aside, she kept him in her sight as he grabbed a bottle of water out of the fridge.

"Is it okay to … cook?"

"Of course. I'd love some bacon and eggs. You're going to need to clean up that mess though."

She stared down at the oozing raw eggs. The shells had cracked.

"Yes."

She wished she hadn't come downstairs in such skimpy clothes.

Grabbing a small bowl, she lifted up the carton and placed it inside. She'd have to find the trashcan.

Every step she took, she was aware of him watching her, observing her. Her skin crawled from it.

She tried to ignore it, but every glance back at him, she saw him smirking as if he knew he was making her uncomfortable.

After everything was clean, she washed her hands and focused on making Draven some breakfast.

"How are you liking school, Harper?" he asked.

"It's good." Her hands shook as she cracked the eggs into a bowl.

Come on, Harper. You're stronger than this.

"I saw your fight last night."

The egg she'd pressed on the counter top cracked under the pressure.

"You did? You watched?"

"I find it an interesting sport that my son takes part in. He makes me proud."

Staring at his dad, she felt a little sick to her stomach. She was under no illusions about this man, and she wondered how Draven had grown up somewhat normal.

He's not normal.

Killing people comes easy to him.

Fighting is a game to him.

This is the family you need to be loyal to.

"Your face is so easy to read, just like Hannah's."

This made her freeze. She didn't know why he'd brought up Hannah and didn't care for him to talk about her father's new wife. "Why Hannah's?"

"Hannah is an associate of mine. A good one. She's a woman that knows her place in the world." He smiled. "Do you know yours?"

For some inexplicable reason, she thought of her mother. She remembered the blood.

So much blood.

The pain.

"Did you know about my mother? About my dad?" she asked.

"Girl, who do you think introduced Ian to Hannah? As for your mother, why should I give a fuck about her?"

"Morning," Draven said. He walked into the kitchen as if he owned the place, and in a way, he did.

His father had introduced her father to Hannah. He'd set about the spiral that ended her mother's life.

Alan was staring at her with this huge smile. She hated him even more.

Turning away from him so he couldn't read her face, she stared at the counter. Right in front of her were a set of kitchen knives.

It would be so much fun to kill him, to make him realize the pain he'd caused her, caused all of them. Tears filled her eyes, and she wanted to hurt him so bad.

He'd helped in some way to take her mother away. It wasn't fair. None of this was even close to being fair.

You can't do anything.

Draven moved up behind her. "I've got you," he said, whispering the words against her ear.

The moment his hands wrapped around her, she felt herself stop falling. He magically waved a wand that kept her focused.

Opening her eyes, she turned in his arms to see him smiling down at her. It was forced, but his father was still in the room.

A quick glance over his shoulder and she saw his father wasn't impressed by this.

"Morning, beautiful," Draven said.

"Morning. I thought I'd make you breakfast."

He took her hands, kissing each bandaged one

after the other.

"You really don't have to do that."

"It's so very domesticated of your girlfriend, Draven, to cook you breakfast. Make sure she knows her place before you take it any further."

She heard a chair scrape across the floor and waited for him to leave before collapsing against the counter. She pressed a hand to her chest.

"It was him, wasn't it?"

"He forced Hannah onto Ian. It was your father who took the bait. In his defense, he took a little longer than my dad anticipated, and he was even drunk the first time."

Tears filled her eyes as the pain flooded her. "I can't think right now."

"You don't need to think. I'll finish breakfast."

She shook her head. "No, I can still do that." She chuckled. "I meant what I said. I want to feed you a good, hearty breakfast."

She grabbed his arms and moved him into a chair. Her hands shook a little from the conversation she had with his father, but she wasn't going to allow it to affect the rest of her day. She walked back to the stove and finished making them both breakfast.

"I didn't think he'd be back home until later," Draven said. "I didn't want your first meeting to be unprepared and not without me."

"You've had to put up with him your entire life."

"Yes."

"How do you do that? How do you put up with that?"

"It's easy if you know what to do," he said.

"What do you mean?"

"He wants a strong, powerful, capable son to take over his line. To be ready for anything."

"And you're ready for anything?" she asked.

"Not everything, but I'm ready for most things," he said.

She looked back at him after flipping the bacon to crisp on the other side. "What are you not prepared for?"

"You. I wasn't prepared for you."

"Oh."

"It's not a bad thing, Harper. You blow my mind."

"You didn't think I was boring before? I was the original good girl. The kind of girl to have her hand up for the teacher, never get into a fight. Never, ever to *train* to fight. My life has completely changed in the last few months."

"What I want to know is if you're happier?" he asked.

She had to think about it.

"Is it really that bad?" he asked.

"It's not bad, I guess. Compared to where I was when I first moved in with Ian, I'm a lot happier."

"But not compared to when you lived with your mom."

She removed the bacon, and finished stirring the eggs to scramble them up. "I'm not explaining this well. Mom was like … full of happiness. She was a beacon for it, and every time I was near her, I felt the world was a good place, a great one. Without her, it has been darker. Sometimes more than I could handle and it does still scare me. I'm never going to have her be there at any wedding or any event. I don't even know if I'll ever have a wedding. If I'll ever want babies of my own. I mean, we're eighteen, and in the future, this may not be what you guys want. It's so much to take in."

"If you wanted a wedding, you'd get a wedding."

"Draven, you can't marry four guys."

"It's simple. You'd marry me."

"I don't know if any of this makes any sense to me. How can I just marry one?"

"I'm the one that made the selection. I'm the one that is guiding you, waiting for you to be ready. It'll be me who'll marry you."

"And kids?" she asked, chuckling.

"We can have as many as you like. I'd happily give you them. Just say the word and we can start now." She stared at him a little shocked. He'd not mentioned the other three.

"You know this is all crazy right? You get that?"

He laughed. "Live like we have for eighteen years, it'll age you faster than life itself, Harper. We all know what we want, and what we want is you."

She put his plate in front of him and moved behind him, wrapping her arms around him, kissing his cheek.

"Thank you."

"Never forget, Harper, you'll always have us. Every single one of us."

Whenever she got nervous about what was to come, what they expected of her, she thought about this, about their connection and how she was now bound to them. Her nerves disappeared, and she found she could finally breathe again.

They were enjoying their breakfast when Axel suddenly appeared.

Before she knew what was happening, he'd moved to her side, cupped her face and was kissing her.

His lips were hard against hers at first, giving her no choice but to open her mouth and to yield to him.

Seconds passed, and finally that hardness disappeared to make way for his gentleness, taking her by surprise with the force of it.

"You okay, man?" Draven asked.

Axel pulled away, and she saw the pain in his gaze. He nodded.

She watched as the two shared a look. They were clearly talking without the use of words. Whatever had happened to Axel, it had clearly messed with his head, and she hated seeing him so confused, almost broken.

"I'm going to go and get changed," she said.

"I'll show you up. I don't want my dad stealing any more of your time."

"You met his dad?" Axel asked.

"Yep. He's pretty intense." It was the best word she could think of that was polite enough not to offend Draven.

"He's been called many things, never intense. That's an upgrade to him," Axel said.

"Come on, Axel," Draven said. "I'm not leaving you behind either."

"Where's Jett and Buck?" she asked.

She was used to seeing them all together, especially in the morning. It was strange not having all of them around her.

"I haven't gotten the call yet to pick them up," Axel said. "After every single party, they always stay for the after-party, which always ends up out of town somewhere."

Draven laughed. "We'll pick them up, and one of them will complain about how they're never partying again."

"They always go back out and party?" she asked.

"They never miss a party," Axel said. "Even when they should."

They entered Draven's bedroom, and she grabbed her clothes.

She was about to head to the bathroom when

Draven pulled her close. "He needs you."

Axel wasn't even looking at her, but she saw he was … broken somehow. She didn't have a clue what had happened to make him like this.

Her heart broke, and pulling away from Draven, she walked up to Axel. His eyes were almost vacant.

Taking his hand, she pulled him toward the large, soft chair. Sitting him down on the chair, she moved to straddle his waist. Cupping his face, she kissed him, and she wanted to make him feel so much better. She hated seeing the darkness that clouded his eyes.

Knowing Draven was there, watching her, it thrilled her. She didn't care in that moment if anyone called her a slut. Axel was one hell of a kisser, and he ran his hands down her back to cup her ass.

Harper gasped as pleasure rushed through her body at that single touch.

"Do you have any idea how long I've been wanting to touch you?" Axel said.

"No."

"Too fucking long." His hands moved from her ass to the straps of her shirt.

Within seconds, he had them down her arms and his mouth on one nipple as he cupped the other.

She felt Draven's gaze on her, and as he opened her eyes and stared in the mirror across the room, it showed Draven. He sat on the bed, hand wrapped around his cock as he watched them.

The heat within his gaze drove her wild as Axel touched her.

He wasn't as expert as Draven, but she enjoyed his touch, his desperation firing her own blood.

"I want you, Harper. Fuck, I want you."

She looked toward Draven.

Only if he gave permission.

She belonged to him, and he'd been the one to bring her in, so only on his say so, would she commit right now.

****

Draven stood in his father's study, staring at all the books that were mainly for show. He'd never seen a book open in his father's hands, ever.

"What do you want, Draven?" Alan asked, entering the room.

"Nothing."

"Is your bitch still in my house?"

He smirked. "No. I took her home." Axel was now keeping her company.

"Good. I don't want her here."

"She's mine."

"Do I look like I give a fuck? I don't want her here. This is my house, and until you've got your own place, you'll do as I say."

"I've been doing as you say for years. I'm not giving her up."

"You're making a mistake with her," Alan said, sitting back. "Girls like her are huge pains in the ass for men like me."

Draven took a seat, staring across the desk at his father. He thought about Harper. How her gaze had looked toward him when Axel said he wanted her. He loved that she instantly went to him for guidance, as it should be. "You can't do the takeover."

He watched as his father sat up. "Do you think you can presume to tell me this shit, boy?"

He smiled. "I haven't been a boy for a long time, and you can keep pretending you have some power here. You attempt to do that takeover, to kill Cook, it will be your downfall. This isn't the way you agreed to work. You're Cook's right-hand man. Taking the reins from

235

him right now, you don't have the right people for the takeover."

"Draven, clearly all that pussy has gone to your head. Get the fuck out of my office before I beat some sense into you."

There was a time he'd have taken the punishment, stood beneath his father's fist and taken the pounded that he *deserved*, but no more. Getting to his feet, he left his father's office slowly. Grabbing his keys, he got in his car, and drove out of town to where Buck and Jett were waiting to be picked up.

They'd gone to a party straight after the fight last night, and Axel had left them there as he got called home.

He didn't know what Axel had to do, but the one look at his friend this morning, and he knew he needed some time with Harper, and not just a heavy makeout session. He'd not given his permission to Axel. After they kissed some more, he'd explained that Harper needed to leave. One look at Axel, and his friend knew he didn't want his dad near her.

They were very much aware of the monster that lurked within the man.

Besides, Axel needed some alone time with Harper and not just sex either. One day soon, he'd have to share her.

That wasn't today.

For now, Axel would have to be content to just kiss and hold her. It was enough.

They weren't just there for Harper, to help ground her and bring her protection and safety. She was there for them for this very reason. She gave them peace.

In their world, they were used to the pain, fear, and chaos that was their lives. She gave them the power to be better. So they didn't have to think about all the women and girls they'd ignored over the years. Just because they were used to working in the trade of human flesh didn't mean they were happy about it. He knew for a fact Axel was fucked in the head because of it. They all were. They had no choice though. Until they were in charge, they all had to fall in line and learn the business. He knew Axel didn't want to deal with the trade of human flesh. Neither of them did, and that would be one element they cut loose. Draven was also determined to have some businesses that were legal.

An hour later, he pulled up into a rundown, old-looking diner. Buck and Jett looked hideous. They'd clearly been partying into the early hours of the morning.

Climbing out of the car, he leaned against it and smiled.

"You two look fucking awful," he said.

"Fuck off, Draven." Buck spoke first, rubbing at his temples. "Why didn't you stop me, huh? Why did you have to make me go and party?"

"In case you didn't know, you're the one that is always begging for a party, not the other way around. I had to deal with Harper last night," Draven said.

"How is she?" Jett asked.

He didn't have his knife in his hand. Draven had noticed more and more that Jett rarely used the knife on himself anymore. It was always part of him, but he didn't hurt himself with it, and he didn't seem to constantly rely on it either.

"She's doing much better."

"She went so fucking crazy on that chick. I heard she had to have her nose reset or some shit," Buck said.

"It should keep Ben off her back as well," Jett said.

They all knew Ben would retaliate one day.

Draven hadn't watched Ben last night at the fight.

His overall focus had been on the woman fighting her first fight. He had no doubt she got lucky. Not all fights ended that well. He'd known Harper was harboring some serious pent-up aggression, but he just didn't know exactly how much lingered within her.

He got behind the wheel as Buck and Jett stumbled into the car, both of them groaning.

"So, we deal with Ben before he attacks us," Buck said.

"That's not thinking right," Draven said.

"Why not? We've got a beef with him, he's got issue with us. We take care of him now before he goes and hurts someone we care about. We don't want anything to happen to Harper. I sure as hell know I don't want nothing to happen to her."

He glanced back at Buck.

"If it was that simple, we'd not have all the problems we have, Buck."

"I think you fucks overthink everything. Wake me up when you get your heads out of your asses."

Buck slumped down, and within a matter of seconds, snores filled the car.

"World fucking record with that one," Draven said.

"We could kill him."

"Ben is connected to a politician in town. Something happens to the son, we get the heat. You know how it works. If he was just anyone, I'd say let's go."

"The diner," Jett said. "You were happy to throw him out of a window."

Draven gripped the steering wheel tighter. He'd been more than happy to do that, but he'd also not been thinking.

Ben shouldn't have touched Harper, so anything

that happened to him, was brought on himself. He wouldn't apologize for that.

"That's not my problem."

"You like Harper a lot. She's not like a lot of other girls."

"She's not. It's why I know she'll be a good fit for all of us."

"I thought you were crazy bringing her into the fold. Still do."

"You like her?"

"She makes my dick hard, and I also happen to like her. You picked well."

"But?" Draven asked.

"Where do you see this going?" Jett asked. "I know when we all planned this, we all thought it was the fucking dream."

"You don't think it is?"

"Your dad, Axel's old man, all of us, this life, I don't know." Jett rubbed a hand across his face. "I just got a bad feeling is all. Ignore me."

"I can listen."

"I don't think it's going to work out the way you think it is. You're Alan Barries's son. Axel's a Cook. You don't get that high up in this world by sharing a woman with your friends. I'm sorry, you don't. I doubt this will last all that long, and I'm going to be there for the ride, but it's not going to happen." Jett leaned back against the door.

Draven glanced back at Buck, who was still sound asleep. Jett had his eyes closed.

"It'll work," Draven said.

"Fine. Fine, Draven. You're the boss."

And that's how it had always been. He'd been the one to take charge, to make the decisions. They all fell to him, and he'd watched so many men and women fall through jealousy and greed.

He refused to lose any of his friends.

They were his only rocks in this world, and yet, he knew it was only a matter of time before his plans fell all around him. He couldn't keep it together, not for much longer.

His father wasn't going to allow him to take this path, so he only hoped he had the strength to keep what he wanted and to fight his father and win.

Chapter Fifteen

Fall turned to winter, and with the change in season, the snow hit. A cold dusting landed all over Stonewall. The roads were too dangerous to use, and the school closed for a week. During that time, Harper spent much of that week with Draven, hanging out at his place with Axel, Buck, and Jett. Draven's father got caught in the city out of town, so he wasn't due back until the snow either melted or conditions improved.

Harper didn't care though.

Even as her father glared at her, he didn't make any move to stop her. She didn't talk to him or to Hannah and hadn't done for weeks. She often avoided them.

Her time with Draven and the guys was the best of her life. Most of her nights in bed were with Draven, but during the day, they were all together. One solid unit, united, and ready to take on the world.

The five of them together were a team, a force to reckon with. They'd trained her to fight by their side. She didn't for a second think she was up to their standard, but she didn't shy away from all the hard work.

She relished the fights. Each time she stood, facing any of them, she allowed herself to let go. To no longer fight that anger as she stared back at them, but to give it an avenue to expel. They knew how to handle her, and no matter how hard she hit, they could defend themselves.

After each workout session, she'd stare at her reflection in the mirror, and for a short time, she'd be a little afraid of who she saw staring right back at her.

The woman she saw scared her.

The good girl was long gone, and now she stared at a woman who didn't hide her anger, didn't pretend to not care anymore.

The woman staring back at her was no pushover, no good girl. She gave a shit, and if anyone stepped in her way, she'd push them right back out of it.

"You know it's minus five outside," Harper said, staring at the pool.

Draven had given her a long shirt to wear over her underwear to go swimming in. He had an indoor pool, and he fancied a swim.

Jett and Buck were already throwing water at each other while Draven stood right in front of her, his hands on her knees.

"I know. The pool is nice and warm."

She sighed. He stroked up and down her thighs. She had a couple of bruises from his kisses alone. He liked to nip at her during sex. She loved it when he got a bit rough with her.

"Come on, Harper. Stop being a scaredy cat," Axel said.

She rolled her eyes. "I'm not scaredy cat."

"Then how about you get that ink?" Buck asked, winking at her.

They'd been talking about her getting some ink. She noticed that on all of the guys, they each had a separate tattoo that said all of their last names. Draven's was on the inside of his wrist. Barries, Cook, Perry, Henry. They were in a scroll, and right underneath Henry's name, was hers, Miller.

Each of them had it in a different place. For instance, Jett had his inked up his side. Axel's was along the back, all within a scroll of some kind. Buck's was on his thigh.

"You're one of us, aren't you?"

"Yes," she said. "Isn't that supposed to be the initiation? I thought you guys organized that."

Silence met her question.

All of the guys were staring at one another, and she chuckled. "Seriously, what is it I'm missing?"

"The initiation isn't the ink," Draven said.

"It's the fucking," Buck said. "Where we all have sex. We all take you. Make you ours. Think of it like a cum fest. Once that happens, no bitch will get another look in."

Jett hit Buck around the back of the head.

"What the fuck! Seriously, dude, she asked."

"And there's a lot more tact to be had, dude," Axel said.

"Oh," Harper said. "I've been meaning to ask you about that." She wasn't going to show them it made her nervous. Draven continued to stroke her thighs, and she took comfort in his touch. "How does that work?"

"Cock in pussy," Buck said.

Axel threw the ball he held, and it hit Buck's head.

"Dude, enough already. She's asking the questions. I'm simply answering them. We've got to talk about it eventually, and you know, no one is. We've been letting Draven handle everything, which we're all cool with."

Draven gripped her thighs, and she stared down into his eyes.

"What do you want to know?"

"Do you expect it to be one after the other? Are you all going to be there? Is it going to involve something more than I can handle? I'm just a little nervous about it."

"I bet. I wouldn't have to have four cocks either," Buck said.

"Will you shut the fuck up?" Draven said.

Harper froze at the aggression within his voice. She'd never known him to be so … firm. He made her worried, and the shock on the other guys' faces as well, let her know she wasn't the only one a little taken aback by it.

"Dude, I'm just messing around," Buck said.

"Well, don't. This isn't a fucking game. It's not a joke. This is serious, and if you can just sit there and laugh about it, then we can change it. She's part of us no matter what. Sex or not, she's with us."

"Draven, it's all good," Axel said.

"No. It's not all good. Every single day we're getting closer to taking over. You think what we want from all of this is going to be easy. We can't walk away. We don't get that luxury. It's why we've agreed to this." Draven's touch was almost bruising now.

"Are we to never have sex again?" Jett asked.

"What?" Draven asked.

"If you want us to change this, then do we have sex with other people? Isn't that against what we all agreed to? You get some, but we don't?"

"I don't mean that," Draven said. "I just … I don't want this to be something we laugh about. It's serious. This is all of our lives. Our future together, and it can't be joked about."

Silence fell on the group. Harper hated to see them conflicting right now.

"Don't argue because of me," she said.

"We're not arguing over you," Draven said. "This needs to be addressed."

"There's no rush," Buck said.

"We all need to be ready." This came from Jett. "Draven's right. This is our future, and we have to be ready for everything. It's not a joke."

"This is not something we can force, Draven." Axel surprised her with his comment.

"I joke," Buck said. "It's what I do. We all

planned this, but if I'm truthful, I never expected us to find a girl like Harper. You're different. You're special. I can see that. I know you'll complete us. Have our backs. You're strong. I want this to work out. I do."

"I shouldn't have yelled at you guys," Draven said, rubbing his eyes. "Shit, this is fucking messed up."

"What are you thinking, Draven?" Axel asked. "It's up to you. We're all here. You want to change it, we change it. You don't, then we stay on this course, but you change your mind and you don't want us to be solid, I'm getting pussy elsewhere. I'm not living like some kind of fucking monk."

Draven chuckled. "No, we stick to the plan. All four of us. It's what we agreed to. I don't want to turn out like my dad."

"Agreed," Axel said, really fast, without a single hesitation.

Jett and Buck agreed as well.

Seeing all four friends together, she saw the concern. They all came from different parents, and their lives were all separate and yet, they were brothers. All of her life, they had been together. In the past few months, she'd spent more time with Draven, but that was only at night, when it was time for bed. Most of the time, they were all together. She'd seen how they all worked together, as one, as a team.

"I want the ink," she said.

The scroll ink was really pretty, but she wanted something different.

They all turned toward her.

"You do?"

"Yes. It's really important to you guys, so as soon as you can arrange it, I'll be there."

"I know a guy. If you're ready we can have it done tonight," Axel said. "Do you have any idea what you want?"

"Yes, I do."

"Okay, bitches, let's get this party moving. I'm ready to get me some pain!"

So, three hours later, Harper sat in the basement of a rather grungy-looking home. She straddled a chair, very much aware of the five guys in the room.

Axel, Buck, Jett, and the artist were behind her while Draven offered to distract her up on top.

She didn't catch the guy's name. He didn't have any shop, but this was where all the guys come to for their work. They had amazing work, and for the right cash, he'd do anything. She didn't have money, but Draven threw a bunch of hundreds down. Again, she wasn't going to ask where he got the money. For her, it was always better to not know.

The first touch of the needle, and she tensed up, shocked.

"You okay in there?" Draven asked.

"Yeah." She didn't like it. The pain took her a little by surprise. Gripping the chair, she closed her eyes and quickly remembered, Draven saw her.

He burst out laughing as she tried to pretend she wasn't entirely in pain. Nothing helped.

Breathing in and out.

Nope.

Draven suddenly sat in front of her on one of the spare chairs and took her hands. She tried to pull away, but he wouldn't let her go.

"Stop," he said. "Don't pretend. Squeeze my hands."

"You're insane." She gasped, and the man behind her paused.

"You okay?"

"Fine, fine, fine."

The buzzing started again, and she closed her eyes.

"Are you wishing you said no?" Draven asked.

Opening her eyes, she rolled them. "No."

"You're hurting."

"So? It's no different than being hit down at that ring. I can handle this."

"You were on fire in that ring," he said.

"I hate thinking about it."

"Then don't. You need to learn to let shit go."

"Like you do?" she asked.

"I let stuff go."

"What was that in the pool?"

"Nothing. It's serious what we're doing."

She shook her head. "No. There's more to it than that. You can't pretend with me."

"Harper, not now."

She stared at him, waiting, but he clearly wasn't in the mood to talk. "Fine. Not now but you're going to tell me."

"What makes you think I will?"

"We've all got to share our concerns with someone, Draven, even you."

"And you think you know all about my worries?" he asked.

"I have an idea. Your dad doesn't exactly scream out fatherly love."

Draven squeezed her hand as if he was asking her without words to not bring up his father again. She had no problem with that. After all, he was a monster, and Draven would know that more than anyone else.

****

One week later

"You got a tattoo?"

Harper turned around to see Ian entering the

kitchen. She thought she was home alone and had taken the opportunity to just make her breakfast without rushing out of the house. Normally, she took a snack in order to avoid any kind of confrontation that she couldn't stand.

Her shirt had ridden up.

The tattoo that had all four guys' names swirled within thorns had come out amazingly well. She loved it. All dark ink, no color anywhere. She loved it where she'd gotten it down at the base of her back.

One look at Ian though, he looked ready to explode.

"You like?"

"What the fuck, Harper?" he asked. "You didn't even consult me about this. You're a child."

She rolled her eyes. "How could I consult you? You're never around anymore."

"Harper?"

She shrugged. "I'm not wanting to argue with you about this." She went back to her cereal.

He sat down beside her, and she knew he wasn't going to let it go.

"I want you to get it removed."

"No."

"Harper, that's four boys' last names. You're getting it removed."

"I'm eighteen. You don't get to tell me what to do. Not anymore." She stood up, throwing her cereal in the trash and washing out the bowl.

"What the hell happened to you?"

She gripped the edge of the sink, trying to find the strength to deal with him.

"You were always such a nice girl. Your mother, she raised you right."

Harper spun around, glaring at him. "That's right,

my mother raised me right. She raised me to be a good girl. You know what? I am."

"Hanging around the likes of Draven and Axel, they'll ruin you."

"Like you ruined Mom?"

"Harper!" The warning was there.

She smiled. "Don't talk about Mom. Don't talk about how she killed herself. Don't talk about anything that could make me feel because I don't want it to be my fault when the truth is, it is because I decided to fuck a woman far younger than me and I couldn't handle being a responsible parent." She spoke calmly, hands clasped together. "Don't forget, Harper, be a good girl. Don't make waves for your dad. He doesn't like it when you do. Don't worry, Ian, I'll be out of your life for good soon. I'd go now, but you won't let me leave."

"No matter what, you're still my daughter."

She snorted. "You called the cops on me."

"I didn't."

She rolled her eyes.

"Hannah did, and as I explained to the cop and to your fucking boyfriend, I would never call the cops on you because I never wanted to hit you. I shouldn't have hit you in the first place. You think I don't know that? I told Hannah she shouldn't have done that. You're my fucking daughter, and believe it or not, I do love you."

Harper gritted her teeth, hating the sudden sweep of emotion that rushed through her. "Are you done?"

"I've not even started. You shouldn't be around guys like Draven."

"You work for his dad. How bad can he be?"

"It's because I work for him that I know just how bad he is, Harper. They're dangerous. They're not boys. They've never had a day of playing around in their lives. They're not allowed to play. It has always been training, work, preparing them. They're men, plain and simple. I don't … it's dangerous for you." He went to move toward her, but she took a step back.

"I've got to go," she said.

"Harper, please listen to me."

The doorbell rang, and she glanced behind her.

"That's him, isn't it?" Ian said.

"I've got to go." She repeated the same words.

"I know I've not been a good parent, but I want to. It has been hard, losing … *her*."

This made Harper stop and stare at her father for a long time. He thought it was hard now?

"You don't get to say that."

"I mean it."

"No. I couldn't even talk about her."

"You think it's easy for me?"

"You left her. You left her for a woman who is not even a match to her. You've had a baby with her."

"Harper."

"No." She shook her head. "You don't get to pretend after all this time. You don't get to make me feel like crap just because you can't handle the fact I've grown up or that I'm dating a guy you don't like."

"She always wanted you to be the good girl. Why have you changed so much?"

"Look in the mirror and maybe you'll see." With that, she turned on her heel, grabbed her bag, and left. Draven was waiting on the doorstep.

"What's up?" he asked, the moment he looked at her.

"Nothing, I just really need to get out of here, like, right now." She had to leave to get as far away from Ian as physically possible.

"Skipping school?" Draven asked.

"Yes, please yes." She climbed into his car, and

he took off. They didn't speak, and she watched the school as they drove right on past it.

There would be time to catch up on all of her classes soon, just not right now.

Rubbing a hand across her face, she tried to clear the confusion, the chaos, the mess. Nothing worked. She pressed a hand to her chest, trying to not think of all of the things her father said.

"You okay?" he asked.

"Yes."

"Are you going to tell me what's up?"

"I will. I just need a few minutes."

He drove to a diner that was out of town. He parked and, throwing her bag into the back of the car, she climbed out and joined him. Draven cupped her hip, drawing her in close, and she loved the comfort of his body surrounding her.

They entered the diner, found a small booth, and the waitress came to pour them some coffee. She wasn't really hungry, but she looked over the menu anyway to see if there was anything she wanted.

Draven didn't even pretend to look. He sipped at his coffee.

The taste was bitter.

"Have you told me the whole truth about everything?" she asked.

"No."

"Why not?"

"Some stuff you don't need to know. It won't help you to know."

"And you're the judge of that?"

"I'm going to protect you. Axel, Buck, and Jett will always be there to protect you, Harper. You're never going to be alone or afraid again."

"I'm not afraid right now."

"This is your dad, isn't it? He's gotten to you?"

"He's not gotten to me. He freaked out when he saw my ink."

"How is it looking now?" Draven asked.

She stood up and showed him the ink.

"It's healing well."

"I'm a good girl, remember? I follow instructions and do as I'm told."

"That's not always a bad thing."

"It's not?"

"No, what's gotten into you?"

"I don't know. I'm just … freaking out. He messed with my head, and now I need to put everything back together again. He told me how hard it was losing her, and I can't deal with that right now. It was that hard? He didn't cry at her funeral. He's not shown any feeling at all, and it kills me. I couldn't even talk about her."

"Okay, I don't want you to think I'm taking his side because I'm not, but have you ever thought that it maybe is hard for him?"

"You're taking his side."

He laughed. "I'm not taking his side. Not even close. You've not been able to talk about her and that could be that he's not being a total asshole for jerk's sake. Maybe it is too hard. Crying in front of Hannah, he might feel bad about it."

She shook her head. "I don't know. I don't have a clue. Ugh, this would all just be easier if I didn't have to deal with him. He doesn't want me seeing you anymore."

"And what do you think?"

She pointed at her back. "A little late to be playing the concerned parent."

"That's not really an answer?"

"A few months ago, I may have listened to him. You know, been kind of excited that he's paying some kind of interest in me. Now, I'm not interested. I know that makes me sound like a super bitch, and I don't want to be that, but I can't be what he expects. Not now." She grabbed his hand. "I have you guys, and getting this ink, joining with you, fighting, I didn't do this all lightly, and I'm not going to turn my back on any of you. Not now, not ever."

****

Later that day Draven knocked on Ian Miller's office door. He'd sat in this office a couple of times. More often than not, Ian would turn up at his father's house, complete with paperwork that they always had to sign. Always so much paperwork, it pissed him off.

Ian looked up from his desk, and Draven couldn't help but smile at the instant anger that flashed in the older man's eyes. "I guess I don't need a rocket science degree to know that you're pissed?"

"What do you want, Draven? I was unaware of you stopping by."

"No one knows that I'm here if that will make you feel any better. I figured you and I were destined to have a little chat."

Ian dropped his pen to the desk and leaned back in his chair. The money his father paid this man had bought all of this. The fancy office, Hannah, all of it. In a way, his father's meddling and jealousy had also helped Draven get Harper. Kind of a win-win for him.

He walked toward one side of the room where there were lots of boring law books.

"You read all of these?" Draven asked.

"Most of them. I use them for reference as and when required."

"Always the lawyer."

"Why are you here in my office?"

"I'm sure you're aware right now that I'm seeing

your daughter."

"I'd like you to leave Harper alone," Ian said.

Draven smiled. "I'm sure you would. It makes me wonder if you've even taken the time to talk to her, to look at her, to see the truth of what she's been going through."

"I know my daughter, Draven. I don't need you or anyone else to know what I'm going through."

"So you understand the pain and anger. How moving in with you and Hannah, the main cause for her mother killing herself, hurt. You understand that at night, Harper wakes up from nightmares of being covered in blood. Her mother begging for help and she not being there to save her."

"How do you know this?"

"I don't need to tell you how it is that I know about Harper's dreams. You were an eighteen-year-old, you think about it."

"Harper's a good girl."

"Harper will always be a good girl," Draven said. "There's no doubt about that. The thing is, that day, and maybe even before that, there's been a little bad inside her as well. Anger and rage from being ignored, from watching her family crumble before her very eyes, and all this time, you've ignored it."

"You haven't?"

"I've not tried to get Harper to be the good girl. I've got her to be the person she wants to be without fear of the door being flung shut in her face."

"I know what you're capable of, Draven. I'm not a fool."

"So you know exactly what I'll do to you if you think for even a second of interfering with what is going on with Harper, me, and my guys."

Ian sat up ramrod straight. "The rumors are true."

"She belongs to all of us."

"And you think in five years' time, ten years, that's going to be good enough. You're all going to use her until you've had your fill and spit her back out again."

"We're not like you. We value what's ours."

Ian flinched. "It's not happening."

"The time for fighting it was months ago. When you first moved your daughter into your home. You should have recognized the signs. I did. You chose to ignore her. The pain and the memories were too hard for you to cope with. In turn, you lost her. She's ours now, and if you even try to force her to stop seeing us, or in any way affect our relationship with her, I will come for you. I will make you wish you'd never set eyes on me, or that you hadn't gone and gotten Harper."

"You don't scare me."

"Then why are you pissing your pants right now? You know what I'm capable of. What my father is capable of. I don't fall far from the fucking tree. Right now, Harper keeps me ... sane, shall we say? Take her away and I will make sure that you feel everything I do to you. I won't numb your body. You'll feel every single bit of sting."

With that, he turned on his heel and left.

Chapter Sixteen

Christmas came and went within the Miller house. Harper spent most of it with Draven and the guys. They either stayed at Axel's or Draven's. She preferred Axel's place, but she'd never met the guy's dad yet. He always seemed to be out or on business, whereas Draven's was there all the time.

Watching.

Waiting.

She got the sense he was anticipating another one-on-one with her, and each time she glanced Alan's way, his gaze was on her. It creeped her out, so she did everything she could to avoid him.

By the New Year, she was feeling pretty good, and she knew it wouldn't be long before the initiation. She had the ink, and she had feelings for all of them. When it came to Draven though, her feelings were the most intense. They spent the most time together, whereas Axel, Buck, and Jett tended to spend time with her but also keep her at arm's length. She didn't mind at all. They were good friends, and she was loyal to all of them. That was the difference. They were all friends, but with Draven, it was something more. There was no denying that. It hadn't come between the guys though. She watched them all, making sure she didn't create a problem. They were united as one.

Of course, it meant a lot of girls at school hated her guts; nothing wrong with that. No one had defaced her locker though. She heard the usual whispers and gibes as she'd pass people either in class or the hallway. They tried to keep it quiet.

One time, someone wasn't so quiet in their whisper, and the moment he called her a whore, Axel had slammed him up against the locker, arm across his neck, and asked him to repeat for the entire school to hear.

It had ended up with the kid getting a broken nose, and now they often avoided her and of course her guys.

The violence still shocked her. There was no getting away from how uncomfortable it made her feel, especially as she recalled her time in the ring. That scared her, how she'd lost control and in doing so, had hurt someone.

She didn't know how the other woman was doing. When she asked Draven about it, he told her the key to dealing with the ring was not to think about it, to just ignore what had happened and to move on as if she didn't have a care in the world.

Harper did care.

She moved on though. There was no other choice as he wouldn't allow her to find out how the other woman was doing.

Stretching her arms above her head, she made her way back toward the locker rooms. She'd just finished physical education, and it was the last lesson of the day. Running laps irritated her. She hated doing it, and she was sure the only reason the teacher made them do that was to amuse himself.

He'd called time as she was the furthest away from the room, so as she entered, most of the girls were already leaving.

Draven would be by to pick her up with the guys. They were heading out of town for the weekend. Ian was pissed at her and had tried to make her stay home. Since their confrontation, he tried to talk to her more often, but she just couldn't bring herself to make it easy for him, not after everything.

Standing at her locker, she opened up the door and yawned. She was so tired. Glancing down at her workout clothes, she shrugged. There was no need to change out of anything. She wasn't exactly going to the ball, or doing anything of any use.

Grabbing her clothes, she started to fold them up, before placing them neatly into her bag. She already had all the necessary books and homework ready. Even though the guys rarely did homework, she still found the time to do it. Her grades were fine, so far. If they were affected by everything, she'd consider taking extra time, but for now, she was happy.

"Well, well, well, look what we have here?"

Harper looked up as she spotted Ben and several of his buddies entering the girls' locker room.

She finished putting the last item in her bag and did it up. "What do you want?"

"I think you owe me a little something."

She raised her brow. "Seriously, what the hell for?"

He stepped toward her, and she saw the intention in his eyes. Before she could stop him, he had her slammed up against the locker door. The sudden action startled her.

"You think we were going to let this go? We were going to let you walk on out of here? The first time the Stonewall slut has been alone. You think I was going to miss the opportunity?"

"Fuck off, Ben. You really don't want to go there."

"You think I'm afraid of your men?"

She chuckled. "Of course, you are, otherwise you wouldn't be here with me now. When I'm alone. When my men are not here. Of course you're afraid." She snorted.

Lifting her head, she glared at him.

Don't show any fear.

"You've really got a lot of spunk inside that body of yours, haven't you?" Ben said. "Don't worry, you'll have jock spunk by the end of this. Then you'll get to feel like a real whore."

She drew her knee up and slammed it against his nuts.

He groaned, and as she tried to brush past him, he tripped her up. She landed hard on her knees.

His guys were there, holding her down. She screamed, and it was cut off as one of them covered her mouth.

"I should have known you were a slut. You weren't the good girl everyone pretended you to be. You're nothing but a fucking cum dump."

His nails scored her flesh, digging into her skin as he started to pull down her shorts.

This couldn't be happening, not now. She moved her mouth and bit down hard into the man's hand.

He growled, and as he drew his hand back, she used the seconds to scream for help. She didn't get long as he slapped her across the face, hard, shocking her. The pain stilled her fight, but only for a second.

Ben tore her shorts down and spread her legs wide. He cupped her pussy, and she bucked, trying to get away. They all laughed.

"She's got a lot of fire inside her. I can't wait to fuck it right out of her."

Just as he was about to pull her panties down, Ben was suddenly gone, and she heard him slamming against the locker.

She was released, and she lay on the floor and watched as one by one her guys beat the shit out of Ben and the ones that were there.

They were not a match for Draven, Axel, Buck, or Jett.

Her hands shook as she grabbed her shorts, pulling them back up.

Time seemed to pass, and the sound of grunting, cursing, and pain filled the air. She watched them, not really sure what to do. When Ben was out cold, and the others were on the floor, Draven turned.

She got to her feet, and he rushed toward her, holding her close.

Before she even realized what was happening, she collapsed against him sobbing, needing his strength, his everything, to surround her.

One by one, Buck, Jett, and Axel placed a hand on her shoulder, and she felt their protection. She was safe.

She didn't want to stay in that room, so Draven lifted her up.

Without even looking, she knew one of the others would grab her bag for her. They were the only ones in her life she could rely on.

Draven put her in his car, and she didn't ask where they were going. Staring out of the window, she closed her eyes, and all she saw were Ben's hands as they grabbed at her, trying to tear her clothes off.

"That could have gone really bad today," she said.

"It didn't, so don't think."

"I can't stop thinking, Draven. It's like I can feel him." She rubbed at her thighs.

He took her hand, placing hers on his thigh as he gripped hers. "I'm right here. We didn't let anything happen to you. We wouldn't let anything happen to you."

"They were disgusting."

"I know. They won't touch you again."

"Will you get in trouble?" she asked.

"No. He attacked you. Tried to rape you. They'll

want to keep this under wraps. Not with you being able to testify against him."

"Draven, in case you haven't noticed, my reputation is shit."

"Don't."

"Everyone in town thinks I'm fucking all four of you. Ben called me a whore. Nearly everyone thinks I am. Even Ian thinks I am."

"We don't care what people think. We know the truth right now."

"Not for much longer. When you initiate me, we all know what's going to happen." She noticed he gripped the steering wheel tightly, his knuckles white from the sheer force of it.

"Either way, Ben deserved it, and I'll deal with whatever the consequences are."

He pulled up at the abandoned parking lot that led into the woods. She didn't wait for him to open her door or urge her out. Harper needed the fresh air. Rounding the car, she took Draven's hand without any complaint. They were already heading into the woods when she heard Axel's car pull up.

Draven wouldn't let her go, and when he came to a spot near a tree, he removed his jacket, placing it on the ground and pulling her down to sit between his thighs.

His hands were on her body, his warmth seeping through her clothes, and she leaned back, sighing a little as she relished his touch, craving it.

"I can get used to this," she said.

She let out a little squeal as Axel dropped a bunch of wood.

"There is something about being out in the open, right? Any bears could attack us," Axel said, letting out a growl.

"Dude, there's no bears around. I'm sure Harper

can see right through your shit, right?"

She nodded at Buck. Jett came back, and she sat in silence as they built a fire.

"You know we should totally tell ghost stories," Buck said. "Get some marshmallows, have a blast."

"You'd be asking me every ten minutes to come with you to take a piss. Everyone knows you hate the dark, Buck," Axel said.

"I do not."

"You do."

"Do not."

"Do."

"Fuck you, Axel."

"Look at me, I'm afraid of the dark," Axel said, mocking him.

"I hate the dark," Harper said. "I've always been afraid of it."

Draven's arms tightened around her. "Why?"

"I don't know. I guess since I was a kid. I always had a wild imagination, and I could turn a shadow into something scary. Something that wasn't actually there but I'd think it was. I used to drive my mom crazy with it. She'd put me to bed, and I'd make her check under my bed and in all the scary corners."

"Bad things lurk in the dark," Draven said. "Everyone knows that."

"See, Axel, it's cool to be afraid of the dark," Buck said, taking a seat as Jett got the fire lit.

They all gathered around the heat. Harper knew they should probably head home, but right now she didn't want to face Ian.

"You're all a bunch of pussies. What you need to learn is this, be the worst motherfucker around and no one will ever scare you again."

She chuckled. "I doubt I'll ever be so bad."

"That's why you've got us to protect you. You're our queen, Harper." Axel winked at her. "When you're the top of the food chain, you've got nothing to worry about."

She rested her head back against Draven's chest. Staring into the fire, she watched the flames as they burned.

"You okay?" he asked.

"Right now, I'm not okay. I'm not nearly close to being okay, but I will be." She wouldn't let what Ben tried to do hurt her.

She was a fighter, and she wouldn't let him hurt her.

Tomorrow she'd fight.

For now, she'd curl up in Draven's arms and let him take away all of her fears.

****

"You wanted to see me," Draven said, entering his father's study. He noticed his old man was in fact alone.

Odd, considering he spent most of his life trying to stick his dick into pussy.

"I got a call today from a certain politician. His son is naming mine as having attacked him and half of the football team."

"So?"

"Care to tell me why I'm throwing money at this asshole to keep your ass out of jail?"

"He attacked what's mine and he had to pay."

Alan sat back, fingers pressed together.

Draven waited. He didn't look away, nor did he back down. He knew it would be pointless to do either.

"The Miller girl, again."

"She's ours. We don't allow anyone or anything to touch her, besides us."

"You do know she's nothing more than a whore."

Draven clenched his hands into fists. He had to stay in constant control, especially around his father. Reacting now would not work, not even for a short time. It's what he wanted, and Draven wasn't prepared to act stupidly.

"Are you done?"

"One day, son, you will realize that all women are just a means to an end. Somewhere for you to have a little fun and then dump at the first opportunity. Harper Miller is no better. She's a whore."

Draven chuckled. "What exactly did you have against Catherine Miller? What did she do to piss you off?"

"Who the fuck is Catherine Miller?"

Draven glared at his father. "Ian's ex-wife. Harper's mother."

Alan burst out laughing. "Oh, fuck, the one that committed suicide. She did nothing to me. Ian's important, and I wanted to make sure he stayed in line. Hannah's a good fuck. Figured an old bastard like that wouldn't mind some young pussy, even if it's used a bit."

"You really don't care?"

"About what?"

Draven shook his head. "Fuck this shit. You're a piece of work."

Now his father looked pissed. "You be careful, boy."

"I'm just like you, Dad, I'm exactly how you raised me, don't forget about that."

"Then don't forget, son or not, I will end you."

"Oh, come on," Draven said. "You and I both know that's not going to happen. One, you do not want to have to deal with another screaming brat running around.

Second, I'm your only heir. The only person that you can pass all this on to, and seeing as Axel's my best friend and you know I'm the leader, I'm your best shot of even getting on top."

Axel was no leader. Neither were Buck and Jett. They were followers. None of them could make the big decisions or the ones that could cost lives.

As much as Draven cared about his friends and Harper, he knew he'd be able to make the sacrifices that not many could. To put people in the line of fire that meant risking lives. His father had told him and taught him that you have to lose a few to save the many.

"I'm as safe as your precious cook," Draven said. "I don't see you killing her any time soon. You like her. She's the only one that can deal with you." He stepped up to the desk, put his hands flat on the surface, and smiled at his old man. "Or should I go and kill her now? She's a weakness, Dad. A weakness you cannot afford."

"Enough, Draven."

"You'll leave Harper alone, and in return, I'll leave your precious cook alone. Deal?"

"Get the fuck out of my office."

Draven smirked. He'd made a deal.

Leaving his home, he found Harper leaning against his car, looking every bit as sexy as he remembered. Not that it was hard to remember really. He'd been balls deep inside her just last night.

She pushed her hair off her face and smiled at him.

The memory of Ben still lingered in her troubled gaze. He walked up beside her, pulling her close.

"Is everything okay?" she asked.

"It's fine, more than fine. It's not something you ever need to worry about."

"When it comes to your dad, I'll always worry."

Draven glanced over his shoulder and tensed as he saw his father standing right there at the window of his office, staring at him.

He didn't have a doubt in his mind that soon, there would be payback. His father would find some way for him to regret what he'd said, but for now, he'd wait. He'd deal with the consequences when they arose.

"Come on," he said, kissing Harper's head. "Let's get out of here."

Chapter Seventeen

Present day

No more waiting.

Harper grabbed her jacket, and to avoid her suddenly caring father, she took the window to make her escape.

It had been a couple of months since Ben's attack.

Rumors were rife around school, but no one had even thought to say another word to her. It was a good thing because it would mean standing up to her, to Draven, Jett, Buck, and Axel.

All four of them would stand by her. They were her best friends, her soul mates in more ways than one.

Draven, though, he was the head of the pack.

She was drawn to him more than the others, and if it wasn't for what they both had, she wouldn't be making her escape to the initiation.

She was ready, even as her hands shook a little.

Climbing down and nearly to the ground, she felt Draven's hands at her waist, helping her. He pulled her to the ground, and she snuggled against his side as they made their way over to the guys.

None of them looked back as they left. Harper climbed into Draven's car.

No noise.

Nothing.

Just pure silence.

She stared out of the window, and she couldn't be afraid. This was what she wanted, all of them together.

They were her protectors, and she bound them together.

It was sex.

In a lot of ways, it was going to be weird, but she

could handle it. She could handle whatever they threw at her.

Pushing fingers through her hair, she let out a breath. Glancing over at Draven, she saw he was focused on the road.

They were not going to his place, or Axel's, or even the condemned building they seemed to love. She hated it when they hung out around the condemned building. It was like they were trying to test fate, to see how far they could push before something bad happened. She had no interest in that. Still, she always got a kick out of it when they ran out of the building.

Draven drove for an hour straight until they arrived at a country house.

"Where are we?" she asked.

"Axel's country home."

"He owns the house?"

"Technically, yes. His father bought it, but it is in Axel's name."

Seconds later, Axel arrived.

"Are you ready for this?"

"I doubt it, but you guys know what you're doing, right?"

"There's no backing out. You'll belong to us. Your future will be with us. There's no getting out of Stonewall. No going to college. Everything will be with us from here on out."

"I thought that's what I was doing?" she asked.

"This is the final commitment, Harper. No running away. No leaving. You'll be bound to us."

She stared up into his green eyes and smiled. "This means you can't get rid of me either."

"I wouldn't want to ever get rid of you."

"You don't know. You've only seen the good stuff so far." She tried to crack a joke.

"I see everything, Harper. I see you. You're it for me. My everything. I don't care about anything else. All I've ever wanted is you, and I'm going to keep you, no matter what." He gripped the back of her neck, tilted her head back, and claimed her lips.

She moaned against his mouth, grasping his jacket as he consumed her.

"Draven's already getting the party started." Axel whistled.

"Don't listen. They're just jealous." He took her hand, and they all made their way into the country house.

"I called ahead and had the butler arrange everything so we have food, warmth, and comfort."

She entered the house and was shocked to see that it was actually bigger than his home back at Stonewall.

"Why do you live there when you can be here?" she asked.

"Dad likes his things a certain way, and well, Stonewall means he can keep an eye on things."

She looked at Axel and saw him staring at Draven. Something was going on there, but she didn't know what.

"I'm going to grab a beer," Buck said.

"Beers all around." Draven took charge as he always did.

She watched him as he entered the sitting room. All the curtains were drawn, and there was a large area made up in the center of the room. Pillows were all around the floor, blankets. A small fire was dancing in the small earth, with logs stacked beside it.

It reminded her a little of festive movies. Rubbing at her arms, she stepped into the room, kicking off her shoes and socks as she did.

Buck returned, holding out a beer for all of them. She took hers and sipped at it. She didn't want this night to end up in intoxication, but it was certainly going to help with the nerves she couldn't budge.

Tilting the bottle back, she drank deeply. After only a couple of swallows, she put the beer down as Draven moved up behind her.

He helped her out of her jacket. His lips brushed across her neck, kissing her. She let out a gasp as he nipped at her flesh. Her nipples hardened beneath the onslaught of his touch.

"You have any idea what you do to us?" Draven asked.

"No."

"Open your eyes."

She did, and it was to see them standing close, hands on their dicks, rubbing. Her heart picked up speed, and as Draven removed her shirt and flicked open her bra, she saw the hunger in their eyes.

According to Draven, they had denied themselves the pleasure of using anyone else, of being with another person. All waiting for her. For this very moment. Draven had told her it wasn't his choice to wait this long. The guys wanted to make that choice themselves, but they also wanted her to be ready and prepared for all of them.

"They want it to mean something the first time we're all together."

She was petrified and yet thrilled at the same time.

Her life hadn't taken the course she wanted it. In the back of her mind, she heard her mother's disapproval, but it faded away as everything did, especially when she thought about how much the guys had helped her over the past few months. They'd been there for her grief, for the pain, for everything. They helped her to heal in her own way, and in return they asked for this.

To some it was too high of a price to pay. For her, she was more than happy to pay it. They were hers, and she belonged to them. Their names were inked into her flesh, and soon, all of them would be forever imprinted on her soul.

She spun in Draven's arms, tugging his head down to kiss as she worked his jacket off. It fell to the floor.

Harper heard the others getting naked, their clothes hitting the floor and the unmistakable clink of belts as they were opened and dropped.

Draven finished with her clothes, and before long, they were all naked, all exposed, all prepared for what was to come.

She didn't know if she was ready, but one look at Draven, and she'd happily drown in his gaze for the rest of her life.

"We will always protect you, Harper. You belong to us now. There's no backing out. No disappearing. What is ours, is yours, and what is yours, is now ours."

She felt the first touch of fingers down her back. Another was on her hip, followed by another on her thigh.

Keeping Draven's gaze, she saw the fire in his eyes. There was a hint of jealousy there. She loved seeing it, knowing that this was what he wanted even as much as he hated it. He didn't want to share her, but to be together, he would.

Lips touched her skin, and Draven ran his hand down her body, cupping her tits together, leaning forward, sucking on the hard buds before using the flat of his tongue to soothe out any pain after he bit them.

She cried out his name, and as someone grasped her ass tightly, giving her a little slap, she moaned. The pain and pleasure were all around her. All the hands touching her body sent her higher.

When Draven opened her thighs and cupped her pussy, she whimpered.

"You're wet, Harper, wet for us."

It was moments like this, she knew she was out of her depth and these guys knew exactly what they were doing. Their touch wasn't hesitant or nervous. They were sure, experienced. They knew what to do to make her moan and gasp.

Draven kissed his way down her body, and as he did, Buck cupped the back of her head, turning her so that she kissed him. His tongue traced across her lips, sliding inside, owning her.

Breaking from the kiss, she looked down to see Axel and Jett both touching her nipples, and Buck, he squeezed her ass.

All of them, their thick cocks stood at attention, waiting, hoping, and she gripped them, hating her own inexperience when it came to this.

She wrapped her fingers around their lengths, working their flesh up and down. Their moans filled the air, echoing off the walls and helping her as she learned their bodies, learned what they liked.

Axel and Jett thrust against her hands as Draven licked her pussy. His tongue stroked over her clit, his fingers working in and out. Buck stood at the back of her, kissing her neck and sucking on her pulse, making her moan even more.

The pleasure was so intense that she nearly crumpled as Draven pushed her into a surprise orgasm.

They helped her to the floor, all of them descending together. Draven was between her thighs first, his cock already covered in a condom. He was always safe, always prepared, always ready.

As he slid his cock between her folds and pushed

deep within her, she cried out.

Buck, Jett, and Axel, they took over their cocks, working the length up and down, watching as Draven fucked her.

His cock slid in and out of her. His hand rested on her stomach before traveling up, touching her, cupping her, holding her. The pounding of his cock, and seeing them all watch, it was a heady experience, one she didn't want to give up.

He held her captive, keeping her in place as he fucked her.

She was so close, and Draven touched her clit, stroking her to completion. She cried out, no name spilling from her lips as she gave herself over the pleasure of their touch. They all started to groan, and she opened her eyes, watching mesmerized as they came. Buck first, his cum spilling from the tip of his cock, as it coated her stomach. Then Jett, followed by Axel, and last, Draven, who pulled out of her, tearing off the condom and spilling onto her stomach.

All of their combined releases pooled on her stomach, their pants filling the air. Draven moved to her side, kissing her lips as someone else wiped the mess from her stomach.

So long as she had Draven, she was happy.

****

Draven woke up to find the spot where Harper had fallen asleep empty. Last night had been a long, intense, and thoroughly satisfying night. One glance around the room and he saw Axel, Buck, and Jett all passed out on either a sofa or chair.

After they had taken a turn with Harper, Draven had made love to her and now she was gone, and he saw her clothes had also gone.

Getting to his feet, he pulled on his clothes and

went in search of her. He didn't have to go far in order to find her.

She sat out on the wall in the garden. It was a cold morning as many of them were in Stonewall until you got to the height of the summer. She looked deep in thought.

Last night couldn't have been easy for her.

It had been hard for him to see her with his friends, but the initiation was complete. She was never leaving them, never backing down, and to do so, well, it would be the biggest betrayal. What happened tonight would stay among all of them. No one would ever really know what the initiation meant, what it would mean to be part of them.

Harper would always be the only one to ever know.

She held a cup in her hand, the steam rising up.

"Morning," he said.

She gave a little jerk and turned toward him. He'd startled her.

"Morning," she said.

"What are you doing out here?" he asked. He walked toward her, resting next to her. Placing a hand on her knee, he stared into her beautiful blue eyes.

"Thinking."

"That's always bad. You're tense."

"Just thinking about last night."

"Then don't."

"It's really hard not to when, you know, what happened. Wow, everyone is going to call me a slut for sure now."

"They won't. Not if they know what is good for them."

She laughed. "They call me that anyway, and now they're right."

"Harper, don't. This is between us. You're ours, and we won't let anyone hurt you."

"Draven, you're not going to be around all the time to make sure people are nice to me."

"You're aware of the kind of power our family has. Give it time and you'll see them all bowing down for respect." He took her hand, kissing her wrist. "Are you sore?"

"A little but it's fine."

He saw it wasn't fine.

"I don't think any differently of you," he said. "None of us do. We all care about you."

"You don't think they're going to see me as easy?"

He laughed. "No. You're anything but easy."

She rolled her eyes, and he thought it was cute.

"We're a team. Me and the guys. We've had chicks begging to suck our cocks. Begging to be part of us. Only ever thinking they know the truth of the initiation when they don't. We're a family, Harper. For better or for worse."

"You're quoting wedding scripture."

"Maybe, but we're all married to each other. We all know that the only way to survive in this world is to be together. We trust only each other. You're safe, and you bind us all together. Other women, they would work to tear us apart, and none of us want that. We're a unit, a team, a club, whatever you want to call us." He glanced toward the kitchen and saw the guys were already up. "If you're nervous because you think they're going to treat you differently, come with me. I'll prove that they won't."

He took her hand, and before she could protest, they were inside the kitchen.

Axel was at the stove, murdering some eggs,

while Buck and Jett were drinking coffee.

"Harp, I'm trying here, but I'm running out of eggs and they're burned on the bottom." Axel lifted an egg and dodged the fat spitting up. The underside of the egg was black. There was also a lot of smoke.

"You've got it all too hot."

"Help me make breakfast and remember I'm the considerate one," Axel said. He gave her a wink, and she sighed.

No one mentioned last night. Buck was drinking his coffee, and Jett was watching as always.

"Okay, yes, fine."

"You like the gardens?" Axel asked.

"They're beautiful."

"I'll take you for a walk around them. They're really something."

"I'd like that." She opened up the carton of eggs. "Do you have anything else? You've used three already."

"Told you, you should wait," Buck said. "He cannot cook to save his life."

"Shut up."

Axel grabbed more ingredients out of the fridge, and they got to work cooking breakfast.

Draven left them to it. He went into the sitting room and started to put it back to how it was, lifting up the pillows, plumping them up.

"Is she okay?" Jett asked, coming to join him.

"Yeah, why wouldn't she be?"

"Last night couldn't have been easy. It's why we waited so long so she could adjust."

"She's worried. I think she expected you guys to go talking about it, but I told her not to worry."

"Last night was private. No one gets to know what happened."

Draven ran a hand down his face, thinking about

his father. It seemed that no matter what he did, his father knew.

"You're in love with her," Jett said.

He turned to Jett, who held his hands up.

"It's fine. I get it."

"No, you don't," Draven said.

"I do. I mean, what's not to love? We all care about her, but I've seen you with her. You're careful around her. You don't let her see the ugly you have to deal with."

"Are you really going to try and analyze me right now?"

"I'm not trying to do anything, Draven. We're all a team, but if you wanted her to yourself, all you had to do was say."

"I want her to be protected. You're the only guys I trust more than anyone else." Even before his father. He knew Alan wouldn't kill him. What he said to Alan in his office was very much true, but that didn't mean he wouldn't try to hurt Draven in some way, to come between all of them to see his goals through. It was always a risk.

"Does she know?"

"No, and you're not going to say anything either."

"I'm sure she'd love to know. There's something between the two of you. I don't know if the others can see it, but I can. She looks to you for reassurance. You're always there for her."

"I'm not going to take her away from you guys."

Jett snorted. "This isn't about that. It's about the two of you. If your father has seen what I have, be careful."

Draven tensed. "What do you mean?"

"One look at her and I see your weakness. She's

the key to breaking you, Draven. If your father ever finds that out, then I'd worry for Harper even more. You're going to have to keep her in your sight."

They finished putting the pillows and blankets together. Harper called breakfast, and Jett didn't linger to finish off. Draven didn't mind the few minutes he got to himself. Once he finished, he found them all sitting around the dining table. Harper was near the head of the table. Buck, Axel, and Jett took seats along the sides. Axel sat next to Harper while Buck and Jett were on the other side.

These guys, they were his family. They were his home.

One look at Harper, and he knew it was different for him.

For so long, he'd been watching her. He wanted to see every single dark part of her. To show her she didn't have to be afraid of the dark.

Harper thought she knew darkness, but she hadn't even come close to the dark yet. She had a long way to go before she even touched him.

She looked up, and that smile, it undid him every single time. "Breakfast," she said.

He smiled at her, aware of his guys watching him, so he stayed on guard. He'd never tell Harper how he felt, or anyone else. Never would he openly admit his feelings. They were for him and him alone.

"So, I'm thinking we should party today," Axel said. "You know, celebrate."

"Let's stay here. Rent a couple of movies. Hang out," Buck said. "I've got nothing better to do."

"You, Harper?" Axel asked.

She looked over at the clock on the wall and shrugged. "Ian's probably hunting for me and is freaking out, but in all fairness, he left me without even a note so whatever. I'm good to hang out."

Draven stared at her.

She was no longer blushing, and in time this would just be a memory for all of them. Their first time together. Their own secret as to what bound them together that all others only tried to guess the truth at.

He would keep them together at all costs. Even if it meant killing his father, he'd do it.

Chapter Eighteen

After the initiation, everything was normal.

For Harper, she felt like everyone was whispering about her and the guys. The rumors were there, but no one came out pointing. No one dared go against her guys even for a second. For the most part, Axel, Buck, Jett, and Draven didn't change. Draven was the one who still kissed her in public, and claimed her as if she were his. Behind closed doors, the others would touch and kiss her.

Only when Draven gave them permission though, never any other time. It was always him. She truly believed all the guys got off on him being in charge, even though when his back was turned, they'd sneak in a kiss, and it would make her laugh at how they behaved. Draven knew though. He'd often wink back at her, and it always filled her with so much joy. All four of the guys gave her so much, and she only hoped that in return, she could give them everything their hearts desired.

Ian was a problem. The weekend she spent with the guys after the initiation, he did indeed call the cops, and he was the one to drive to the country house late Saturday night. No one else was around to see, but she saw the look in his eyes, the shock.

Above all else, she saw the fear.

They hadn't talked about it, and for that, she was thankful. He always demanded that she stay home, and for the most part, she did. Draven would sneak into her bedroom window, or she'd sneak out of it.

She didn't know why Ian tried to control her movements when he never said anything the following morning or evening when she finally returned.

"You're staring long and hard into that window, and I'm not going to freak out because it's a baby one," Draven said.

Harper pulled out of her thoughts and stared into the baby shop window.

"You want to tell me something?" he asked, pulling her close and kissing her neck.

"No. Of course not. A baby would be crazy, right? Totally, insanely crazy. Besides, we're careful."

"We can never be too careful," he said. "Protection doesn't always work."

"Sometimes, but for the most part, it does. I'm going to see the good in it."

He chuckled. "The guys are causing a line at the burger stand."

She glanced back to see that the line had gone from three to twenty people. "What are they doing?"

"Trying to decide what burger it is they want," he said. "I never said I had normal friends."

"No, you really don't. You have crazy friends, the weirdest of the weird."

He tugged her close and kissed her. "Then you've got to make us sane and normal."

"Wow, I doubt I'm all that normal."

"You'll do for us." He pulled her in close and kissed her lips.

"I've got to use the bathroom," she said.

"I'll come with you."

She rolled her eyes. "Seriously, to the bathroom. I'm starving. Grab the guys and make them, I don't know, stop being weird. I'll go to the bathroom and then join you."

"Be careful."

"I'm always careful." She kissed him again, stepping away.

She left Draven to deal with the order and went in search of the toilet. Entering the room, she saw two women at the sink, washing their hands and starting to reapply makeup.

She went into a cubicle. The women suddenly stopped talking, and she heard them leave.

Finished on the toilet, she left the bathroom and went to the sink. Staring down into the water, she washed her hands.

She looked up just as she was grabbed.

Before she could do anything, one of them had put a gag in her mouth to keep her silent and she was being pulled out of the toilet. A blow to the head, and she was lifted over his shoulder.

The blow startled her for a few seconds, the gag in her mouth making it impossible for her to do anything.

The men who had her didn't go back near the food court. They took her to the parking lot and passed no one as they dumped her into the back of the van. The door closed, and they were pulling out of the parking lot. She tried to scream, but it was no good.

"The boss did say she had to be unharmed," one of them said.

Her hands were tied behind her back, and she was on the truck floor.

Who was the boss? What the hell was going on? Nothing made any sense.

She tried to pull her hands away from the rope.

"Look, I don't give a shit. She's in one piece, but I'm not going to listen to her scream until we're closer to him."

They made no move to touch her, and she tried to fight. She could breathe, but she could barely move except for rolling around. She stopped trying to scream as it was useless. She'd need her voice for when they took off the gag.

Was this an enemy of Draven's?

Was it someone close to him?

This made no sense.

Why take her?

Silence fell in the truck. No one made a sound. She groaned as they went over certain speed bumps in the road and she hit her head a couple of times.

Harper only knew they were getting close as the guy lifted her up off the floor and turned her so that he could remove the gag.

"What is going on?" she asked.

Her arms were bound, and she couldn't remove the spittle from her chin. Staring out of the window, she was confused. They were on the street where she and Draven lived. Only, they were heading to his home.

They pulled up onto the drive, and she was grabbed again.

"Let me go!"

The men did no more than drag her inside the house. Their grip on her was terrifying as they led her into Draven's house.

Was he here?

Why were they taking her to his home?

Nothing made sense.

When they forced her into Alan's office, she saw him there, looking smug as he stared at her.

"What is going on?" she asked.

"Did they see?" Alan ignored her question, talking instead to the man at her right.

"No. She was alone, and we made sure. We don't know how much time you've got before he figures it out."

"We've got plenty of time," Alan said. His gaze fell to her, and fear ran down her spine.

This was bad. The longer she stayed here, the worse it was going to be.

"So, my son and his friends have turned you into

a whore." Alan tutted as he poured himself a drink.

Harper's heart raced, and she fought against the hold of his goons who'd taken her from the mall. She didn't like this, not one bit.

Draven would be pissed. Axel, Buck, and Jett would be willing to start a war. They were her guys, just as she was theirs. Together they would fight, but against their own parents, or at least one of them, she didn't know.

"You're making a mistake."

He nodded at the goons, who pushed her forward, slamming her against the desk. It didn't matter how many times she'd been hit, she would never get used to the pain, even as she forced herself to stay in focus, to not lose herself.

"Let me go."

Her shirt was pushed up, and his hand touched her back. She closed her eyes as his fingers traced across the ink at the base of her back. A hand held her neck, keeping her face flat to the surface of the desk.

"Stop it."

"You know a pussy is nothing more than a hole, and yet it causes so much fucking trouble. You, girl, are a fucking thorn in my side. There is always pussy that is willing to take cock without needing to know every detail of their lives. You all need to learn to keep your heads down and your legs spread."

The insult had her attacking even harder. The sudden force took the goons by surprise as she slipped from the grip. Grabbing the letter opener on his desk, she stabbed the blade through the first goon's shoulder, and grabbed the gun she'd also seen, and pointed it at the two men.

Alan burst out laughing, clapping his hands. "They sure have trained you well."

She wasn't fast enough to dodge the hand that struck her around the face.

He kicked her in the stomach twice, and she tried to get away.

Alan grabbed her hair, pulling her back up against him. She tried to fight, but a grip around her neck held her still as he started to choke her. With nowhere else to go, she was at his mercy, and it terrified her.

"Hear me properly, I can kill you. I can make the next few years of your life unbearable, but I have a feeling I've got a way of getting what I want, by removing you from the picture and you keeping your life."

"What?" she asked as he let go of her throat.

"I want you gone."

"Not going to happen."

Alan smiled. "I want you gone. Your bags packed, no trace of you ever. As far as my son and his boys are concerned you skipped town because you couldn't handle being known as his whore."

"He'll know differently," she said.

"You've run away. Gone. You've run at the first opportunity."

"And if I don't do this?" she asked. "What then? You're going to kill me? Draven wouldn't allow that. He'd be your problem."

"If you don't go in the next twenty minutes and be out of Stonewall, I'm going to kill Draven and his boys. First though, I'll make sure that Draven knows you did this. You caused this, and I will make them all beg for mercy before I do it."

She shook her head. "You're bluffing."

"I figured you'd say that."

She watched as he lifted his cell phone up while also turning on a computer screen. One look at it and she saw it was the security feed inside the mall. Draven was there with her guys. They were all there, talking, and across from them, she saw the guy holding a gun.

"So my little guest here knows it's you turn in a circle."

The guy did.

"Good, I want you to kill all of them," Alan said.

She watched as he raised the gun. Draven and the guys didn't even see them, didn't even know danger was right there.

The man raised his gun, and she watched as it went off. The bullets were lightning quick as he fired into the crowd.

Draven ducked, and she hoped the others did as well. Did any bullets touch them? What the hell happened?

"No! Stop!" She screamed, and the screen went blank. Panic rushed through her as did tears.

"Wait," Alan said.

"I'll do it. I'll go. I'll do anything, just please don't hurt them."

Alan smiled. "Keep them in your sight. Don't let them leave."

He hung up his cell phone, and she watched as he grabbed an envelope from across the desk.

"My guy here, Laser, will take you to the bus stop. He'll make sure you leave."

"Why are you doing this?" she asked, tears in her eyes. "I love your son."

"Aw, that is sweet. The thing is, I've got plans, lots of good plans, for Draven, and you are standing in my way of accomplishing them. I'm being nice, Harper. You're a distraction I can't afford. Not only am I letting you live, I'm not going to keep you here." He reached out stroking a finger down her breast. She pulled away.

He laughed. "Well, I'd be careful who you go showing your pussy to. You come back here, and your life is mine."

"There's nothing else you can do to me."

"Oh, yes, I can. I can use you day and night. I've got a huge appetite, and seeing as you're fresh pussy and ass, I could work you until you bleed. I'm not squeamish. I'd love to fuck you raw."

She stumbled back, and Alan laughed.

"I'll be keeping this." He held up her cell phone as if it was some kind of trophy. "Harper, if you think for a single fucking second this is over, think again. I'm going to need some … leverage. If you don't do exactly as I say, I'll make sure Draven says his goodbyes."

"What the hell does that mean?"

Alan smirked as he stepped up to her. "Let's just say I've got evidence of you running off with my enemy. With Draven's enemy. He's never going to want to see you again, and if you want him to live, whenever I need you to do little jobs for me, no matter where you go or what you do, you will do them. If not, I'll make sure to torture every single one of them. Contact Draven, and I will find out. Anything you do, everything you do, is mine and mine alone. Now, get out of my fucking house. Go."

As she turned on her heel, Laser was there, leading her back out in the van. She couldn't believe what she was doing to Draven.

Tears filled her eyes as Laser pulled out of the driveway. The money in her hand made her feel sick to her stomach. This couldn't be happening.

She couldn't think of a single thing to do to stop it. Calling Draven wasn't an option, not anymore, and the manic look in Alan's eyes, she didn't have a doubt that he would go through with his threat. He would kill

Draven.

Just the thought of never seeing him again, of going through this life alone, filled her with regret, with anger, with rage.

One day, she'd find a way to get back to Draven. She only hoped when that time came, he would forgive her.

****

"I told you she was not worth it," Alan said.

Draven stared into the fire. Buck had gotten hit today by a madman in the mall. Harper was nowhere to be found, and Ian had said she hadn't returned home.

He stared at his father and knew something had happened, but she'd not contacted him.

She'd not come to him like he asked.

He'd begged her not to run away.

She'd come here and begged his father to give her some money. She'd said she would even go to the cops with information she had about Ben, about everything.

Running a hand down his face, he couldn't believe he'd been so wrong about her.

"You're sure this was her?" Draven asked. The photograph still in his hand confirmed his worst fears.

"I'm sure."

"How can I believe you?"

"You can't. You can try and find her, son. I'll help you locate her. She was the one that told me she'd made a huge mistake being with you. That she couldn't handle being here, being known as your whore. The whispers, the rumors, all of it, she was done. She had enough. But she knew she couldn't convince you, and when one of my enemies found out about her, found out how weak she was, they used her to exploit you. It's how they knew you were at the mall today."

With every word his father spoke, anger flooded

Draven as well as betrayal.

Harper wasn't who he thought she was.

He'd thought she was better than that, better than all of them.

"Fine! She's gone. She is nothing to me, to us." He looked up at his father. He was completely dead inside. Any hope, any ray of light was gone, wiped out, destroyed by knowing Harper betrayed him. There was only one way to go now, and that was with his father. "Now tell me what you need me to do."

Alan smiled.

It was time to go to war.

To be Continued...

www.samcrescent.com

SAM CRESCENT

Printed in Great Britain
by Amazon